KAT AND THE RING

Published under licence by Brown Dog Books and
The Self-Publishing Partnership Ltd, 10b Greenway Farm, Bath Rd,
Wick, nr. Bath BS30 5RL

www.selfpublishingpartnership.co.uk

ISBN printed book: 978-1-83952-302-1
ISBN e-book: 978-1-83952-303-8

Cover design by Patrick Knowles
Internal design by Andrew Easton

Printed and bound in the UK

This book is printed on FSC certified paper

Lisa Stewart

BROWN
DOG
BOOKS

Chapter 1

It was no use, *Jane Eyre* was stuck firmly on to *The Man With The Golden Gun*. Kat eased them apart with a butter knife as the pink bubble gum stretched into stringy blobs.

'Excuse me.' She heard an awkward coughing noise.

Kat glanced up from where she'd been kneeling on the floor, wrestling with the returns.

'Yes?'

'I wonder if I might get some help locating these books?' The young man waved a piece of foolscap paper in the air. She frowned at him, sweeping the fringe out of her eyes. He wore the same monogrammed top as last week; his hair was a mess of untamed curls, his legs exposed below baggy shorts.

'Isn't anyone else around?'

He shuffled in the unlaced trainers and mumbled something along the lines of 'Not really.'

Kat sighed, stood up and wiped her hands on her skinny jeans. She replaced the unlikely matched pair on the trolley. Her dark eyes flashed with irritation. 'Fine. What are you looking for?'

The student gave a grateful smile and read from his list. 'Okay, so the first one is called *Partial Differential Equations* and it's by Fitz John.'

'Right, well I'm guessing it'll be in our mathematics section. Have you tried looking there?'

'I, er, I … well, I wasn't sure.' He trotted along behind Kat as she zipped between the tall wooden racks of books. She took a sharp left and stopped abruptly. 'All the maths stuff is here.' She indicated two shelves with a slender hand.

'Great.' He gave a sheepish thumbs up.

'Next?' She checked her watch. It must be nearly lunchtime.

'Righty. So the next one is historical. *Mary, Queen Of Scots and the Murder of Lord Darnley*. It's by Alison Weir.'

Kat tutted. 'That's right over at the other side.' She set off down another aisle, past the children's section where a toddler had his nose pressed against a glass cabinet displaying local nature finds.

Kat strode over to the shelves under the high windows. She could lay her hand on any section in her sleep. 'This is where all the Scottish history is kept. Is that everything?' She noted with anxiety that the toddler was now licking the glass.

'Just one last book – a novel this time. *Winning the Cowboy's Heart* by Karen Rock.'

Kat raised her eyebrows. 'I wouldn't have you down as a Mills and Boon fan.'

'It's for my gran.' He blushed. 'I'm definitely more a *Scandi Noir* reader.'

'If you say so.' She double backed down the aisle, crossed the library and ran her fingers along a shelf of plastic-covered books. 'Here's our romance section. If we have it, it'll be here.'

'Thank you so much … *Katharine*,' he said, squinting at her name badge.

'It's Kat.'

'And I'm Angus.' He held out his hand but she'd already turned to walk away. 'If you feel like grabbing a coffee?' he called after her. 'I work next door at the Coffee Shack. If you ever have a break and want …'

Kat ducked under the wooden counter and began searching the cupboards underneath.

'You might at least have thrown him a bone,' Morag said, smiling as she unpacked a delivery of recycling bags.

'What?' said Kat. 'What do you mean? A bone?'

'I mean, you might have given the lad a chance. He comes in every week and follows you about like a devoted mongrel. I'm sure he just makes up obscure titles to get your attention. I bet those books lay unopened all week.'

'Don't be daft,' Kat muttered. She gave a sly glance at Angus, who had his head twisted sideways as he read the spines.

'What are you after?'

'Who's moved my antibacterial spray? Oh, there it is.'

Kat scooshed some on to the glass case, rubbing at it with a cloth.

'Anyway, you go for first break, Kat. I'm keeping my eye on Mr McAuley over there. Last week he tried to make off with *The Complete Fishing Manual*.'

Kat replaced her overworked spray. 'Fine.'

'And if Angus needs any more help shall I come and fetch you?'

'Please, no!' Kat hurried off towards the staff room, conscious of being observed from the romance section.

'What you got today?' Janice asked with her mouth full.

Kat peered into her plastic container. 'It's supposed to be beetroot, feta and rocket salad but it looks like a hamster's been bludgeoned in a field.'

'Nice. I can't be doing with a salad when it's so bloody cold outside.'

Kat shrugged. 'But it's warm in here. Why would it matter

what the weather's like outside?'

'S'pose,' Janice nodded, biting into a sausage roll. Flakes of pastry stuck to her lips, which she brushed on to the floor. Kat examined a fork on the draining board before washing it and picking up her lunch. She sank into the armchair across from Janice, her phone in one hand.

'Did you hear I'm getting moved back to Gilmerton?' Janice asked. She gulped from a can of Irn Bru, burping out loud. Kat remained focused on her phone.

'Cos Sarah's coming back in a couple of weeks and I was only meant to be covering for her op. It's not my fault she had complications.'

'Mmm,' Kat mumbled.

'This is way over the wrong side of Edinburgh for me. I only offered as a favour but it's been nearly three months. Did you hear they left something inside her?'

'Sorry?' Kat looked up.

'Yes!' Janice announced with wide eyes. 'Apparently the surgeon left something behind.'

'Not his Rolex, I'm guessing?'

'Ha! No. I think it was a swabby-thing. Anyway, they had to open her up again and get it out. She won't be back at work yet but I can't keep getting two buses here. It takes me nearly an hour. Jaffa cake?' She held out a packet, waving it under Kat's nose.

'No, thanks.'

'Not on a diet, are you? Scrawny little thing like you. You ought to eat more pies. Men like to get a grip of something in bed.'

'Janice!'

'S'true! You'd be like a slippery eel. Of course, I've got plenty for Dave to get a hold of but it's like he's just got a new sofa deal.'

'How do you mean?'

'No interest for two years,' Janice sighed.

'Isn't that your break nearly finished?'

'Morag said she'd come and swap when time's up. Oh, aye – that's her now. Here, take the rest of the packet.' Janice winked before heaving herself out of the chair.

Chapter 2

'I'm home!' Kat called as she threw her jacket over the newel post. Getting no response she jogged up the stairs, pushed open her bedroom door and flopped on to her bed. The luminous stars she'd stuck on the ceiling as a young teenager remained above her head. She'd painted the ceiling black and the walls purple and had chosen the only black carpet on offer – apparently usually reserved for exhibition areas. She gazed out of her window, which, during the summer, overlooked her neighbour's lush silver birch trees. As they headed into September the leaves began to crisp and drop.

'Kat!' her mother, Dell, shouted from the bottom of the stairs. '*Kat!*'

She heard impatient footsteps pounding up the stairs.

'There's a kettle on the pavement,' Dell announced, barging into the bedroom. 'I think it must be Dusty's. Can you go and ask her?'

Kat sat up, swinging her legs round. 'What?'

'Didn't you see it when you came home? There's a kettle appeared on the pavement. It looks like it might belong to Dusty but we'd better check.'

'Why don't *you* ask her?'

'Don't be like that.'

'Like what?' Kat frowned.

'All belligerent. Anyway, I've got my hot yoga tonight and

I'm already late.' Dell removed her cardigan and unfastened her straining skirt with a *pop!*

'What about Dad?'

'He won't be home until it's dark and we can't leave it on the pavement. Someone might take it.' Dell stepped out of her skirt, the tan tights wrinkling at her feet.

'Maybe that's the whole point? Maybe it's getting collected?'

'It's not rubbish day. Just go.' Her mother tugged at Kat's hoodie. 'Come on – now!' She turned to leave the bedroom, tripping over a stack of library books. 'Flip's sake, Kat! I just about broke my neck. What're these doing here? Isn't it enough that you're surrounded by books all day?'

'They're decommissioned. We get first pick. Some of them have got pages missing but they're still good books.'

'Honestly, Kat, I despair.' She bundled Kat down the stairs and pushed her out the front door.

Kat picked up the cream-coloured kettle and rang the doorbell of the house next door. An elderly lady, dressed in a baby-pink tracksuit and white plimsolls, opened the door. Her choppy white hair was held in place by a sweatband, her face flushed scarlet. She puffed as she leant on the door frame.

'Hi, Dusty,' said Kat.

'Oh, hello ...'

'Kat.'

'Yes, I knew it was Kat! I was just getting my bearings. I've been working out with Davina McCall. She's quite a taskmaster, isn't she?'

'I suppose she is pretty fit.'

'Absolutely! She swam right across a lake once for one of those charity efforts but I won't be doing that. I don't like getting my hair wet. Are you coming in?'

Kat held up the kettle.

'Oh, you didn't need to bring a kettle, I've already got one.' Dusty opened the door wider. 'In fact, it's just like that. Come in, dear.'

Kat followed Dusty into the house, which smelt like a mixture of polish and soup.

'It's lucky I was in, you know. Thursday's my usual day for having coffee over the road with Betty but this week her daughter from Tighnabruaich is visiting and – much as I'm quite fond of her Aoife – I can never be bothered with her endless stories about her latest ailment. Like none of *us* has ever had a persistent itch.' Dusty stopped in her tracks. 'What the …? Where's it gone?' She spun in a circle, scanning every work surface in the kitchen. 'But?'

'Are you looking for this?' Kat held up the kettle.

'Yes, but … I mean. Did you take it?'

'No, of course not!' Kat replaced it on the worktop. 'What do I want with your kettle?'

'Yes, you're quite right.' Dusty wrung her hands. 'Are you sure that's mine?'

'Well, it was sitting on the pavement outside your front gate.'

'What was it doing there?'

Kat rolled her eyes. 'Maybe you took it outside to do something with it?'

'Like what? To give the birdies a cup of coffee? I'm not mental, you know.'

'Of course not – I just meant … Anyway, maybe we better check it still works alright?' Kat filled the kettle from the tap and plugged it in. She waited for the reassuring rumble.

'My son-in-law thinks I'm dementing.'

'Who, Arthur? I'm sure he doesn't.'

Dusty lifted two mugs down from a cupboard. 'Will you join me?'

'I guess I could have some tea.'

'Yes, Arthur! He says I'm getting all confused and shouldn't be living on my own.'

Kat was about to protest when her eye caught the calendar hanging on the kitchen wall. She noticed September's page had been torn off, leaving a photo of October's Urquhart Castle on display. The kitchen clock ticked above the window – an hour later than it should have been.

'We-ell, maybe some things are just a bit off?'

'What do you mean? Are you saying I'm nuts too?'

'No! Not at all. I'm sure you're just imagining it.'

'I'm not imagining it – he says it every time he visits. They want me to go and live with them in Fife. Did you say tea or coffee?'

'Tea, thanks.'

'Milk?'

'It depends.'

'You mean depends if it's got lumps in it or not?' Dusty snorted. 'I remember the days when you wouldn't be seen without your wee fleece blanket!'

'What's that got to do with the price of cheese?'

'I'm just saying! It wasn't so long ago when you were the one who couldn't tell the time or know the day of the week!' Dusty sloshed milk from a carton into the two mugs and slammed the fridge door shut.

'It would have been about seventeen years ago since I wouldn't give up my blanket. Not unless you count my double duvet.' Kat peered into the mug and took a reluctant sip.

'Seventeen years? What are you talking about? Aren't you still at the High School?'

'Dusty, I left school last year. I work at the Red Brick library now.'

'Oh yes, so you do.' Dusty slumped on to a kitchen chair. She removed her sweatband, throwing it on to the table between them. 'I don't know who I'm kidding with all this keep-fit nonsense. I'm old just like everyone else.'

'You're not *old*! Just older than me.'

'*Everyone's* older than you.'

'Anyway, I better be getting back. Dad'll be home soon and I can't risk one of his fridge stir-fries. He gets a bit carried away with the veg drawer. I keep telling him – no one likes stir-fried turnip.'

'Oh well. Thanks for coming by.'

The next morning Kat was huddled over her Honey Loops when the doorbell sounded. '*Door!*' she yelled to no one in particular.

A muffled squawk came down from the bathroom. 'In the shower.' Kat sighed as she sloped down the hall, cereal bowl in hand. She opened the door to Dusty, who wore a knee-high quilted dressing gown and sheepskin slippers. Kat poked her head out, checking for other neighbours.

'Oh, thank goodness you're in!' Dusty wailed.

'What's up?' Kat enquired with her mouth full. 'House on fire?'

'It's my toaster!' Dusty cried, wiping her nose with a tissue. 'Someone's taken my toaster.'

'Whoa – who are you accusing of thievery?' Kat asked. 'I'm the one who's been *replacing* your kitchen appliances, not nicking them.'

'I don't mean you, Kat. Someone else,' she added, with a furtive look over her shoulder.

'Who would possibly want to steal your toaster? You can get them in Tesco for a tenner.'

'It's not about the money. I want toast for my breakfast and now it's gone.'

'Sorry, but it's not here.'

Kat's father appeared in the hall, straining to button a shirt over his stomach.

'Morning, Dusty! Oh, I say, a bit informal today, aren't we?'

Dusty clutched at the neck of her dressing gown. 'Oh, Ron – someone's moved my toaster and I just thought that, since Kat was kind enough to find my kettle yesterday, that maybe she could—'

'Gotta get to work,' Kat said, turning to go.

Ron Carmichael ran a hand through his damp hair. 'Kat, I'm sure you can spare five minutes. Pop over and help Dusty. You'll be in and out like a flash.' He winked.

'Thank you so much!' said Dusty. She trotted off down their path and up her own. Kat handed the bowl to her dad with a scowl. 'Cheers, Dad.'

Kat followed Dusty into the kitchen where she was jabbing at a space on the worktop. 'It sits right here and now it's gone.' Dusty grasped the kettle as though it were about to fly off the counter. Kat looked around the kitchen with a sigh. She made a few cursory glances into cupboards, opening and closing the doors. Bending down to check the lower cupboards, something in the oven caught her eye. Pulling on the oven door, she discovered the toaster lying on the middle shelf. 'Ah ha! There you are.'

'Oh my!' Dusty collapsed on to a nearby chair. 'But what's it doing in there? I didn't put the toaster in the oven – I know that's not how you make toast!'

'We-ell, it didn't jump in itself.'

'But ... but!'

'Look, I have to get to work – I'm already late and there's a class coming in at nine.'

Dusty looked around the kitchen in bewilderment. 'What madness is this?'

Kat shook her head and left Dusty frowning at the roaming culprit. Returning home she hurriedly brushed her teeth and grabbed her jacket.

'Any luck?' her father called from the kitchen.

'It was in the oven.'

'Course it was!' he laughed.

Chapter 3

The remainder of Friday passed without incident. Not unless Janice having a nosebleed over *Notorious murders of the Twentieth Century* counted. Arriving home from work, Kat briefly checked Dusty's garden for electrical appliances before entering the house. 'I'm home!' she shouted before heading for the stairs.

'Good timing,' Ron replied from the kitchen. 'Dinner's ready.'

Kat dumped her jacket and bag on the floor.

'What is it?' she asked, sniffing the air.

'Duck surprise.'

'What's the surprise?'

'There's no duck.' Her father guffawed, lifting a casserole dish out of the oven. He was a stout man with salt and pepper hair and ruddy cheeks. This evening he wore a Heinz Ketchup apron over a police officer's uniform.

'What's with the apron?'

'Can't afford to spill anything over my uniform.' He picked out a large serving spoon and scooped vegetable curry on to a plate. 'Help yourself to rice.'

'And can I ask why you're dressed like that? Has there been a *murrrder*?'

'Aye, well there will be if I get anything over this costume. Mo and her hubby arranged a murder mystery for their silver wedding anniversary. Someone's let them down last minute so they asked me if I'd fill in, which is no problem. Mind you, these trousers keep falling down. Must have hired it for a right fat bastard.'

'After twenty-five years you'd think they'd have murdered each other.'

'True enough.'

Kat spooned rice on to two plates and sat at the table. 'Where's Mum?'

'Said she'd be late. There's some kind of cake do at the centre. What about you?'

'What *about* me?'

Ron stabbed a chunk of butternut. 'Oh – hot! Aren't you going out this evening?'

'Nah.'

'Really? But it's a Friday night? Aren't you going out with any of your pals?'

'What pals?'

Her dad shrugged. 'What about Shelley?'

'She's working this weekend. Anyway, I'm not bothered.'

'Come on, Kat. It's Friday night – live a little! You can't stay cooped up in your room all weekend.'

'Suits me.' Kat poured herself a glass of water.

'Look, why don't I give Mo a ring and ask if you can come along to this party tonight? Should be a laugh. You could always play the dead body.'

'I'm not *that* much of a loser.'

'When I was your age I was out *every* Friday and Saturday night – up town clubbing. Sometimes on a Thursday too. It's how I met your mother.'

'Bouncer was she?'

'I mean, how are you going to meet anyone if you don't leave your room? I doubt there's much talent hanging around the landing.'

Kat shrugged. 'I'm not interested. Anyway, it's all different now. Everyone meets online.'

'Oh, you mean those dating sites?' Ron wiped his mouth on a tea towel. 'They're full of psychos and weirdos.'

'Like you'd know, Dad.'

'A guy I work with said his daughter met someone through one of those dating thingies. Thought he was lovely – an accountant or something. Anyway, she went round to his house for dinner and apparently he held her hostage for hours. Wouldn't let her leave the house. In the end she climbed out the bathroom window and broke her ankle in two places.'

Kat rolled her eyes. 'Yeah, Dad. That's what happens to everyone.' She grunted, pushing her chair back.

'You not finishing that?'

'Help yourself.'

'I'm not wasting good food,' Ron muttered, clearing her plate on to his.

Chapter 4

Arthur and Cherie Kerr sat facing each other over the small pine table. A pair of aluminium crutches leant against the back door.

'*What* did you say this was called?' Arthur asked, poking at the brown mush with a fork.

'It's goulash.'

'Is it? I thought goulash was full of cream.'

'You're thinking of stroganoff.'

'Am I?' Arthur frowned.

'Yes, dear – one's Hungarian and the other's Russian.'

'What's wrong with mince?' Arthur grumbled, removing a length of red pepper from his teeth.

'Mince is boring! We're international in our culinary influences these days.'

'But why does it smell of mulled wine?'

Cherie blushed. 'Oh, well, the recipe said to add paprika but we didn't have any so I just used cinnamon. It's not like I could run out to the shops!' Cherie chewed furiously, wondering why the beef chunks had the consistency of a hot water bottle. Arthur's phone vibrated on the table, the screen glowing. He snatched it up as he stepped outside on to the neatly trimmed lawn, toppling the crutches with a clatter. Cherie sighed, wishing her husband would stop treating every call as though he were in the CIA.

'Look, I told you *I* would get back to *you*!' Arthur said in a furious whisper. He paced the tiny lawn that Cherie had insisted was sculpted into the shape of a heart. 'I just need some more time.'

He gave Cherie a dismissive wave as she glared out of the kitchen window. 'I don't know!' he hissed, tugging at his moustache. 'A couple more months, maybe?' He winced, holding the phone away from his ear. 'Okay, a few weeks, then. And stop calling me!' Arthur disconnected but remained by the fading roses, staring up into the dull evening sky.

Chapter 5

Kat snuggled under the warm duvet as the wind rattled the bedroom window. She reached for her mobile, scrolling through the messages. '*Damn!*' she cursed, curling into a ball. She held off for as long as she could before dragging herself to the bathroom. Returning to her room, she flicked open the curtains. 'Great – wind *and* rain.' The trees over the fence shook as a swirl of leaves was thrown against the window. Kat rubbed her eyes, thinking she was seeing things. Arthur's lanky form appeared in Dusty's garden. He glanced over his shoulder before striding up to the nearest silver birch. From a plastic bag he removed a black evening dress, which he knotted round the trunk. He reached into the bag again, this time taking out a pair of gold-coloured slingbacks that he rammed on to a couple of low branches. Arthur suddenly looked up. Kat ducked down, unsure why she needed to hide. He scattered a few pairs of tights around the garden before heading back indoors.

Kat cut her toast into thin strips as she waited for her raspberry tea to brew. She stared into space, her chin resting on her hands. Dell bustled into the kitchen encased in a full-length crimson raincoat. She began opening and closing drawers at speed.

'Feeling the cold?' Kat asked mildly.

'Oh, Kat, you haven't seen my Spanish phrase book, have you?

I'm going to be late for the hairdresser and I said I'd lend it to wee Emma that washes my hair.'

'*No me preguntes.*'

'I'm sure I popped it in one of these drawers so I wouldn't lose it.'

'Why would you leave it in the cutlery drawer?'

'So I'd see it!' Dell replied tetchily.

'Have you tried the fridge?'

'Good call!' Dell opened the door, slamming it shut in despair. She slumped at the table with a rustle. 'Think … think, woman. Anyway, what are you doing moping about here?'

'Nothing.'

'No plans?'

'I just got a message from Shelley. We were meant to be going up to Dundee in a couple of weeks but she's had to cancel.'

'Oh, that's a pity, love. Why?'

'She's got chicken pox.'

'Bit old for that, isn't she?'

'Think she caught it off her nephew. All the kids at the nursery have it.'

'What will you do?'

Kat shrugged. 'It's the long September weekend so I'm off Friday and Monday anyway. I've got a few new books I want to read so I—'

'Toilet!' Dell cried. 'I left it on the cistern so I'd see it! Thanks, pet.' She kissed Kat on the head and scurried out of the kitchen.

Kat laced her boots and pulled on a waterproof jacket. Her slight frame buckled against the wind as she made her way to the bus stop at the foot of the road. Dark clouds hung over the city and rain streamed past in overflowing gutters. The bus shelter was crammed as Saturday shoppers hunched together in an effort to stay dry. Cars swept by sending fountains of muddy water over the pavement. Kat was jostled up against a vaping teenager and was treated to a blast of cherry menthol. The double-decker arrived like a steaming tank of anoraked cattle and the queue surged forward. Kat let the bus go but the next one wasn't much better.

Alighting from the bus at Ferry Road, Kat turned right and walked up the middle of a quiet tree-lined street. She bent to pick a handful of wild poppies that were trembling in the wind. The rain had eased and she lifted back her hood, walking between two pillars. She breathed in the smell of freshly cut flowers mixed with the earthy tang of heavy rain on grass. Footsteps crunched on the gravel path. Kat sloped under the tall beech trees, keeping her head down. The perimeter wall led to a tangle of ferns and thistles that grew unwatched. She plucked a leafy fern, using this to tie the poppies into a posy. Kneeling in front of the dark marble Kat used a tissue to dry off the stone, laying the flowers with care. In her pocket her fingers curled round the miniature Highland cow; feeling the tiny plastic horns and the soft wad of wool. Her thoughts fell into a jumble, disturbed by the murmurings of a growing huddle. The group shuffled towards the chapel. She sighed. As the drizzle turned to a steady patter Kat pulled up her hood and retraced her steps.

Kat returned to an empty house. She shrugged out of her coat and hung it on the rack, kicking off her boots in the hall. The kettle was boiling when Ron burst through the back door, a hammer in one hand. 'Ah, Kat! There you are. Thought for a moment you'd taken my advice and booked yourself into an all-day rave.' He grinned.

'Tea?' Kat ignored his jibe.

'No, thanks – just trying to turn a stable into a convent. I wish I'd never suggested *The Sound Of Music*. Forgot *I'd* be the one having to work my magic with a few yards of chipboard and a handful of nails. Then I need to get started on the Alps.'

'Don't let me keep you.' Kat dropped a teabag into a mug.

'It's just that Arthur's been on the phone. He's worried about Dusty.'

Kat peered into the almost-empty biscuit tin. 'Who ate all the caramel logs?'

'Not guilty,' said Ron, brushing coconut crumbs off his overalls. 'So do you mind popping round to check on her?'

'What? Why is it always me? Where's Mum?'

'She has the baby-massage class on a Saturday afternoon.'

Kat groaned. 'What's the hurry? Can't she go later?'

'Arthur was pretty anxious. Then Cherie came on the phone. Apparently Dusty is doing all sorts of weird things. And she completely missed her dentist appointment this week. I can't get on with all these interruptions. At this rate Mother Abbess will be *climbing ev'ry mountain* in a timber yard.'

'Fine,' Kat snapped. 'Can I at least have my tea?'

'Course you can, love. Take the key in case she doesn't open the door to you. She's not been letting anyone in since things have been moving about her house.'

'Maybe it's haunted?'

'Could very well be. Edwin was always a bit of a prankster.'

Chapter 6

Kat pressed the doorbell twice but with no response. She bent and squinted through the letterbox. There was no sound or light. *Crap*, she thought, *maybe she's had a fall?* Kat used the key, pushing the door open. 'Hello?' she called. 'Dusty?' Kat stepped round the Ramsay ladder that led to an open attic hatch. 'Dusty?' she shouted up to the square in the ceiling.

'Up here!' a reedy voice sounded.

Kat let out a groan. She climbed the ladder to find Dusty sitting on a square trunk amongst a clutter of boxes. A small, opaque window in the roof let in a little daylight but most of the light came from a head torch fastened to Dusty's forehead. A nylon housecoat, buttoned over her dress, was streaked with grime and cobwebs.

'Dusty!' Kat protested as she clambered into the attic space. It was tall enough for her to stand upright in the centre. She observed the usual attic stockpile: Christmas decorations, a rusty-runnered sledge and a couple of sagging deckchairs. She nervously looked around for spiders waiting to pounce. 'What are you doing up here?'

'Well, if I'm having to move I'll have to get rid of this lot.'

'Where are you going?'

Dusty was raking around in a plastic container balanced on her knees. She picked out a metal brooch. 'Look at this stuff that Edwin collected over the years. What a load of old rubbish!'

'Where did it come from?' Kat settled herself on to a nearby suitcase that sank rather alarmingly.

'Oh, he used to pan for gold.'

'Really? Like in America?'

'No – Scotland!'

'Eh? Surely not.' Kat replayed Ron's words in her head.

'Oh yes – Edwin had quite a lot of luck up in the Highlands. And some in the Borders too. Look.'

Dusty held out her hand to reveal a discoloured nugget the size of a pea.

'Is it worth anything?'

'It can be if you find quite a few pieces. Anyway, what are *you* doing up here?'

Kat blushed. 'Dad asked me to check if you were alright. Said Cherie was worried about you.'

'I told you – they think I'm going round the bend! Just because I missed the dentist this week. I was sure I left plenty of time but, by the time I got the bus there, I seemed to be an hour late.'

'So you're okay?'

Dusty grumbled under her breath. 'I'm fine but no one else thinks I am. They threatened to call Dr Millar.'

'What for?'

Dusty tapped the side of her head. 'To make sure my marbles are still there. They're putting the house up for sale and I'll be moving in with them.'

'In Dalgety Bay?'

'Yep. Edwin will be furious. He always hated visiting them in Fife and now we'll be there forever!'

'But isn't ...'

'Oh, I know what you think but I've kept Edwin's ashes on my mantelpiece since he died and he's been perfectly happy there.' She put the box to one side. 'Here, I must show you this, Kat!' Dusty stood up, lifting the lid of the metal trunk. From inside she retrieved a glittery waistcoat, which she slipped on. She lifted out a pair of shiny black patent tap shoes and, sitting back down on the trunk, kicked off her slippers and wriggled her feet in. With effort she reached down and fastened the buckles. Then Dusty stood up, placed one hand on a wooden beam and stepped on top of the trunk, her head a couple of inches from the roof. She adjusted her head torch, took a deep breath and tapped her toes against the metal lid. Her feet clicked back and forward.

'Go, Dusty!' Kat cried in surprise.

'Give me a beat, then,' Dusty urged.

Kat clapped her hands as Dusty made slow arcs in her shoes, tapping the front, then heel of each shoe.

'You never told me you could tap dance!'

'You call this dancing? A pair of snails could look more lively.' Dusty click-clacked her shoes in a small circle as her torch swung a beam around the attic. 'And jazz hands!' She grinned. 'Gosh, I'm so out of practice.'

'Where did you learn to dance?'

'Oh, I used to go every Monday night down at the church hall. You should have heard us – we made quite a racket on the wooden stage.'

'Did you put on any shows?'

'Oh yes!' Dusty panted, leaning against the beam for support. 'I was never a lead of course but we were always asked to perform in the Easter variety show. We were the *Twinkle Toes*. There were about ten of us. All women, except for Christopher – but we let him join because he was better than all of us put together. Here

– give me a hand.' Kat helped her off the trunk as Dusty flopped down, out of breath.

'But why did you stop if you enjoyed it so much?'

'Why? Why do you think? I'm too out of puff to go much past my knees so I wouldn't be much use if I needed someone to change my shoes, would I?'

'But …'

'Do you mind?' Dusty waved a hand at her feet.

'Seems a pity, though.' Kat turned the worn leather shoes in her hands, wondering how many times the taps had beaten a rhythm.

'It *is* a pity. But I can't turn back the clock. Unless of course I did and that's why I was late for the dentist!' Dusty chuckled as she threw her waistcoat and shoes back into the trunk. 'I'll need to clear out so much junk. And I could never face getting rid of Edwin's stuff so most of this belonged to him.' She picked up the plastic box again, running her fingers through the knobbly grains. Frowning, she held up a discoloured white envelope. 'What's this?'

'A letter?'

'No, it's got something inside.' Dusty read the outside of the envelope. '*Fished from Loch Assynt.*'

'Where's that?'

Dusty shook her head. 'It can't be. The only time we've been up to Loch Assynt was on our honeymoon and that was in 1966. Edwin was none too pleased that he missed the final as that's the day we travelled home.'

'What's inside?'

Dusty opened the envelope and tipped a gold ring into her hand. She held it up to the light from her head torch. 'It looks brand new.' She examined the ring, which had a large diamond and two smaller – one nestled either side. She passed it to Kat.

'Wow! Nice ring.'

'But why would Edwin hang on to it? He always sold anything of value – it's what he called his beer money.'

'You could buy quite a few pints with this!' Kat examined the ring closely. 'Here – pass me your torch.' Dusty removed the headband, leaving her hair sticking up in clumps.

'There's an inscription inside it,' Kat said, screwing up her eyes. She turned the ring under the light. '*Marry me, Jess? Love Hamish,*' she read out loud.

Dusty clapped a hand to her mouth. 'Oh my! It's an engagement ring! But why did Edwin hold on to it for all these years?'

Kat shook her head. 'How would he know who to return it to?'

'He could have sent it to the local police station,' said Dusty indignantly. 'This doesn't make any sense.'

'Do you think he knew them, maybe?' Kat asked. 'What if he was holding it for Hamish?'

'I wouldn't have thought so.' Dusty checked the envelope again. 'All it says is *Fished from Loch Assynt*. Surely he would have said, *This belongs to Hamish* if he knew him?'

'Maybe he didn't want to sell it because he didn't think anyone else should wear it?'

'Possibly. He could be quite sentimental that way. Maybe he thought that if Jess wouldn't or couldn't wear it then no one else should.'

'What if …' Kat breathed. 'What if she *was* wearing it and something happened to her? Like she drowned in the loch?'

'Don't say that!'

'Or …' Kat thought out loud. 'What if something happened to *him* before he could propose?'

'How awful,' Dusty replied. 'Imagine if some poor devoted

young man was about to propose and then he was murdered!'

'Dusty!' Kat protested. 'You've been watching too much *Silent Witness*. In any case, what's to say that *she* wasn't the one that was murdered?'

'But wouldn't they have stolen her ring? It looks like it's worth something.'

'Perhaps it wasn't about the money. It might have been a crime of passion!'

'Who's the one getting carried away now?'

'Well, I guess we'll never know, will we?' Kat handed the ring back. 'Come on, Dusty, let's get you back downstairs before one of us goes through the ceiling.'

They made their way down the ladder and Kat pushed the attic door closed with a wooden pole.

'Cup of tea?' Dusty offered.

'Sure,' said Kat, brushing down her jeans. She flicked a hand through her hair to remove any cobwebs. 'I need to wash my hands.'

While they waited for the kettle to boil Dusty removed the envelope from her pocket. 'Do you think we ought to return it?'

'Return it to whom? To where?'

'I don't know,' said Dusty, puzzled. 'I've no idea where I'd start – but it doesn't feel right keeping it.'

Kat shrugged. 'I could check at work if you like? We have a huge database in our newspaper library.'

'Oh, Kat, that would be lovely! What will you look for?'

Kat raised her eyebrows. 'I suppose I could search for announcements of engagements – or marriages?'

'Yes – look for Jess and Hamish.'

'It's difficult without surnames. And they could have got

together any time before nineteen sixty-six.'

'But the ring is so new-looking,' argued Dusty. 'I hate to say it but it doesn't look as if it's ever been worn.'

'Then maybe I need to check for crimes in that area? Look to see if anyone's reported a stolen ring?'

'Better check out deaths too.'

'Dusty!'

'Just saying ...'

'Anyway, it'll need to wait until Monday.'

'Fine. Milk?'

Chapter 7

'*Blue Lagoon* or *Striking Cyan*?'

'Sorry?'

'I wish you'd pay attention, Arthur. Which of these two colours do you prefer?'

'I honestly don't care.'

'That's not the attitude! It's your spare room as much as mine.'

'It's more of a laundry room,' Arthur muttered.

'And are you implying that laundry falls into my domain?' Cherie bristled. 'Push me further down the aisle – I'm worried these blues will dominate the space. Let's go for a creamier colour.'

Arthur sighed, negotiating the wheelchair past a stack of paintbrushes.

'You don't seem overly keen, dear.' Cherie waved towards the lighter colours.

'Yeah, well, the sooner we buy the paint the sooner you're going to expect me to get decorating.'

'So?'

'I don't exactly have a lot of capacity at the moment. You've got me running back and forth to check on your mother every week.'

'That's unfair! You know I'd go if I could.'

'Yes, well, it doesn't change the fact that I'm expected to manage the situation.'

'She's not *that* bad.'

'Oh really? Putting the toaster in the oven? Missing appointments? And yesterday I arrived to find she'd hung her ballgown and shoes from a tree in the garden. There were tights strewn all over the lawn. In the middle of a storm!'

'What are you on about?' Cherie fretted. 'Is she alright?'

'Of course she's not alright! Look!' Arthur shoved his mobile phone under Cherie's nose. 'How do you explain this?'

'Oh dear,' said Cherie, blowing her nose. 'My poor mother, all alone. The sooner she sells up and moves in with us the better.'

'Correct,' Arthur agreed with satisfaction. 'I think you better speak to her about it again.'

A wiry lady with plant pot in hand approached Arthur. 'Excuse me, young man – can you tell me where the plumbing section is? We've got a blocked toilet and my Brian has gone looking for a plunger.'

Arthur scowled. 'Do I *look* like I work here?'

'Of course you do!' the woman snapped. 'Do you think I'm in the habit of approaching total strangers and confiding my domestic scenarios?'

'Well, I don't,' he replied, resting his hands on the wheelchair.

'Then you shouldn't go around dressed as a B&Q employee, should you? It's very confusing!'

'I happen to be wearing a black fleece and black jeans,' Arthur protested. 'It's hardly a uniform.'

'Get out of my way, then, if you're not going to help me.'

'I think plumbing's down in that direction,' Cherie offered, pointing to the left.

'And I don't know why *you've* bothered to come here in a wheelchair,' the woman grumbled. 'It's hardly a day out. You'd be better going to the King's Mall – at least you'll get a coffee there.

Brian!' She set off down the aisle at speed. '*Brian!* Where are you?'

'I think this'll be better,' Cherie announced. 'Let's get a couple of tins of *Almost Oyster*.'

'Whatever.' Arthur scrolled through the football scores. *Damn!* He had twenty pounds on Tottenham to score by half time.

'Push me, then!'

Chapter 8

Kat opened the garage door, a mug of Bovril in hand. 'Mum said to bring this out to you.'

'Cheers, Kat! My hands are freezing. She's home, then?'

'Yeah. She's still raging over that Gracie girl.'

'Uh-oh. The one who keeps abandoning her baby?'

'This week she said she needed Mum to help out while she took an emergency call. When Mum went looking for her in the break the girl was outside having a fag. Mum got coriander oil all over her new blouse.'

Ron stretched his back with a groan. 'Well, I've been bent over this bloody pulpit all afternoon.'

'It looks like a Dalek.'

'You're kidding? Well, it'll have to do. I've got to move on to making a Mercedes next. Fancy giving me a hand?'

'Not particularly – why?'

'The Dalek needs to be varnished. And you're so arty, Kat.'

Kat grunted. 'Flattery, eh?'

'That's my girl!'

Kat lifted a spare pair of overalls off a peg and rolled up the sleeves. She reached for the tin of varnish and selected one of the brushes soaking in a jar of turps.

'How did you get on with Dusty?'

'I don't know what her daughter's on about. There's nothing

wrong with Dusty. They've got her all upset by making her move to Fife.'

'Well, maybe it's for the best,' Ron said. 'You might want to shove on a pair of goggles while I get the bandsaw going. It fairly churns out the sawdust.'

'Best for who?' Kat argued. 'Dusty doesn't *want* to move. She's fine where she is.'

Ron shrugged. 'Maybe we don't know all the ins and outs. For all we know she's crying her heart out every night on her own over there.'

Kat pictured Dusty tap-dancing on the metal trunk. 'I don't think so.' She prised off the lid of the varnish. 'Anyway – that Arthur is up to no good.'

'Hmm? What do you mean?'

'I mean – I saw him mucking around with Dusty's clothes yesterday. Hooking her dress onto the tree and stuff. He's weird'

'I don't think you can accuse him of weirdness for hanging out her washing.'

'He wasn't —'

'Kat! Be careful with that varnish, love. You're dripping it all over the floor.'

'I'm just saying,' she muttered.

'Watcha doing?' Janice breathed over Kat's head with the sweet smell of toffee cupcake.

'Searching.'

'*Searching – looking for love!*' Janice sang.

'What? No!'

'Too early for you? Hazell Dean? The nineties?'

'Janice, I wasn't born until nineteen ninety-nine.'

'*Gonna party like it's nineteen ninety-nine!* Prince? Seriously, though, what are you doing?'

Kat leant back in the chair, rubbing her eyes. 'My old neighbour was clearing out her attic and she found a ring.'

'Go on,' Janice urged. She pulled up a chair, peering over Kat's shoulder.

'The ring was found by her husband over fifty years ago but it looks brand new.'

'Found where? In the attic?'

'Loch Assynt.'

'And where's that when it's at home?'

'Up north. Towards Ullapool.'

Janice pulled a face. 'Don't talk to me about up north. My Dave's family is from up north. Which is why we go to the Lake District for our holidays every year. We only visited his folks once – just before we got married – and his father asked him whether he could afford to keep me in buns. Dave was so furious he never spoke to him again. Although he might admit now – that's why we've never been able to afford to move out of our wee flat. Coffee and walnut is my *absolute* favourite. Although I don't turn my nose up at anything.'

'Anyway. The ring ...'

'Oh yes – the ring!'

'Well, it has an engraving inside – *Marry me, Jess? Love Hamish.* We think we know where the ring came from but we've no idea who it belongs to. I thought maybe I could find out if there was anything in a local paper. I've checked the *Press and Journal*, the *Northern Times* and the *Ullapool News*. Not a thing.'

'How intriguing! Morag – listen to this!'

Morag trotted over, a book in each hand. 'What's up?'

'Kat's found a ring with an inscription – tell her, Kat.'

Kat repeated the story.

'*When* did you say this was?'

'Nineteen sixty-six.'

Morag tutted. 'Well, we all know what was in the papers *that* year. Have you read all the announcements? Births, deaths, marriages? Engagements?'

'Of course she has,' Janice interrupted. 'Kat's a smart cookie.'

'What timeframe are you looking at?'

'I've concentrated on nineteen sixty-four to nineteen sixty-six so far.'

'Any headlines about a burglary? You hear about women who take off their rings and leave them by the side of the bed. Or to do the washing-up.' Morag dragged another chair across.

'I couldn't possibly take off *my* engagement ring,' Janice said, waving her chubby hands. 'They'll have to cut mine off with wire cutters when I die. Not that it's worth anything of course. Dave saved everyone's Green Shield Stamps for a year. His mum needed a new iron but he bought me this ring instead. I don't suppose that helped her take a shine to me, either.'

'Problem is,' Morag said, her mouth in a thin line, 'just because that's where the ring was found, doesn't necessarily mean it's where it came from.'

'Oh, listen to you with your glass half-empty,' Janice mocked. 'Maybe if we *all* help we'll find something.'

'I need to stop now, anyway,' Kat said, glancing at her watch. 'I've got a P-Five class coming in at ten. I'll try again at lunchtime.'

'How exciting!' Janice clapped her hands together. 'I love a good mystery. Did you ever watch *Tales of the Unexpected*? I loved that as a kid.'

'Nineteen ninety-nine?' Kat said, standing up.

Morag took Kat's seat. 'Right, remind me – how far back have you gone?'

'What, nothing?' asked Dusty in despair.

'Not a sausage.'

'So what now?' Dusty placed two mugs on the table. 'Biscuit?'

'No, ta. Dad's got the dinner on.' Kat shrugged. 'It'll just have to remain one of life's great mysteries. Like the Loch Ness Monster.'

'How awfully unsatisfactory,' said Dusty, dunking a chocolate finger until it collapsed into her coffee. 'It feels like Edwin kept this ring for a reason. Like he meant for us to return it. You know, Kat,' she said, lowering her voice. 'I asked him last night.'

'Who?'

'Edwin. I asked him for a clue.'

'And …?'

'Just at the point when I said, "Edwin, what did you want me to do with this ring?" – well, the clock chimed and I just about had a heart attack!'

Kat laughed. 'I bet you did.'

'But it was a sure sign.'

'Of what? That it was nine o'clock?'

'That the *time* has come.'

'For what?'

'For us to return the ring.'

'Eh? There is no *us*. And in any case, perhaps you missed Tolkien's trilogy, but this one has already been written.'

'But, Kat, I feel it's my duty. Anyway, I never watch those soaps.'

'Look, if it makes you feel any better, why don't we send it to the police? They'll have a lost property department – they can sort it out.'

Dusty shook her head in defiance. 'No, Kat. We need to go back and find out who it belongs to.'

'I keep telling you – there is no *we*.' Kat was beginning to wonder if Dusty's daughter was right to be concerned. She really was going off the rails. Kat stood up to leave. 'Sorry, Dusty, but I honestly think we've done all we can. I better head off before Dad chucks a rat in the ratatouille.'

'But …' Dusty stood wringing her hands at the front door.

Chapter 9

The following evening Kat returned home from work later than usual. Morag had insisted they all stay behind to complete their mandatory online training. Morag led the way with fire safety and Kat contributed to the module on information governance. But then Janice denied having been asked to provide an update on equality and diversity, which meant they all had to plough through the assessment together. 'I don't understand where all this has come from,' Janice protested. 'In my day everyone got picked on for something, but we considered it a rite of passage. It's what made us who we are today: stronger and more resilient.'

'So you were bullied at school?' Morag asked with compassion.

'Course I was!' Janice retorted.

'Were you picked on for being overweight?' Kat asked.

'No – what makes you say that?' said Janice. 'Before I got braces everyone called me Bugs Bunny.'

Kat entered the house to hear voices coming from the kitchen. She was surprised to find Arthur perched on a chair, an empty mug in front of him. He was still wearing his work suit, the tie loosened off. She could never understand why he maintained such a ridiculous-looking moustache. Dell sat across the table, pouring from a large teapot. A plate of shortbread remained untouched.

'Dad not home?' said Kat.

'Kat! Where are your manners?' Dell asked, overfilling the mug. She wiped up the spillage, tutting loudly.

'Sorry. Hello, Arthur,' Kat mumbled.

'Good evening, Katharine. Gosh you haven't half grown since I last saw you – you must have been yea-high.' He indicated his chest.

Kat groaned inwardly. 'Hmm.'

'Your dad's nipped down to the centre with the Alps – he says it'll take him a few runs.'

'So what's for dinner? I'm starving.'

Dell flapped her hands. 'Oh well, Kat, I'll pop something on in a minute. Arthur has been telling me all about Dusty and how she's deteriorated so quickly.'

'Right.' Kat scowled. 'Call me when dinner's ready.' She turned to leave the kitchen.

'Hang on, love,' said Dell. 'Arthur came across to seek a favour.'

'What favour?' Kat asked grumpily.

Arthur cleared his throat. He tweaked at his oiled moustache with finger and thumb. 'Look, it's about this ring business.'

'Not the ring again!' Kat exclaimed.

'You know how obstinate Dusty can be when she gets something in her head,' said Arthur, shrugging his shoulders. 'She won't let it go. She's determined to take it back personally.'

'So?'

'So Arthur has asked whether you'll drive her up?' Dell asked in a bright voice.

'*What?*' Kat spluttered. 'No way! Are *you* mad?'

'Now, Kat, there's no need to be rude,' Dell chided. 'We're all just trying to do our best here for Dusty.'

'I know it's a big ask,' said Arthur, holding his hands up.

'Then why don't *you* take her?'

'I'd love to drive her up there,' Arthur replied, smoothing his hair. 'It's such a fabulous part of Scotland – wild, rugged mountains and beautiful, clear lochs. Forests as far as the eye can see. But I need to sort out the house sale and make the arrangements for moving her stuff. Goodness knows where we'll put it all.'

'And of course Cherie is pretty incapacitated at the moment, poor soul. You must send our love to her, Arthur. Anyway, it'll only take a few days,' said Dell. 'Dad says you can borrow the Volvo – it's a solid, safe car for that kind of journey.' Dell looked down at her hands. 'And I do know that your plans for the long weekend have fallen through …'

Kat narrowed her eyes. 'Oh, you've got it all worked out for me, haven't you?'

'Well,' Arthur continued with a smug smile. 'I did say to Dusty I'd be more than happy to take the ring from her and to sort it out myself.'

'Yes, he did offer,' Dell concurred.

'I'm sure he did.'

'I can get Cherie to book you somewhere comfy to stay from Friday for three nights – and of course we'll pay for all the petrol.'

'Three nights?' Kat frowned.

'It'll be a nice wee break for you,' said Dell. 'Now, I really must get the pasta on.'

'Of course,' said Arthur, standing up. 'Thanks, Kat – that's such a relief! I'll give Dusty the good news.'

Kat stomped up the stairs and slammed her bedroom door.

Chapter 10

'I've never been over the new bridge,' commented Dusty as they crossed the Firth of Forth. 'Ooh, it's very arty.' She craned her head to one side. 'Looks like white lolly sticks. Wonder what they'll do with the old one? Maybe they'll build houses on it – looks like houses are popping up everywhere. Mind you, it'd be a bit windy up there.'

Kat shook her head in silence, her hands gripping the steering wheel.

'*Where* did you say we were stopping?'

'Dusty, we've been on the road for exactly fifteen minutes. Is this really how it's going to be for the next five hours?'

'Oh, I didn't mean I wanted to stop now. It's just I hadn't heard of the place before.'

'The House of Bruar?'

'I don't really drink beer. Where is it?'

'It's near Blair Atholl.'

Dusty unfolded the unwieldy map, stretching her arms out in front of the windscreen.

'Dusty!' Kat protested.

'Sorry – just need to fold it back to the right part. I knew Edwin wouldn't have thrown away his old maps. I found a whole pile of them in a case. Now, where did you say?'

'Blair Atholl.'

'And where's that near? I just need to find it on the map.'

'It's on the A9 – just past Pitlochry.'

'Hmm.' Dusty peered at the map, rustling the paper. 'I can't see anything that looks like Pitlochry.'

'Well, it doesn't matter as I know where I'm going – it's a pretty straight road.'

'Oh, I've got it upside down! I was looking at the Borders!' She ran her index finger over the map. 'Ah- –ha! Found it. So it looks like you more or less stay on the A9.'

'Right.'

'Humbug?' Dusty offered, sticking the bag under Kat's nose.

'No, thanks.'

'Too chewy? They do get stuck in your dentures a bit. Still, at least you don't have to worry about that! Gosh, look at that big Amazon factory. Is that where everything comes from? Cherie's always ordering stuff from Amazon but I had a notion it all came from a jungle somewhere. No wonder it arrives so quickly. I couldn't understand how she could order something one day and it would arrive the next. But if it's only coming from *Fife.*'

Kat turned the radio up louder.

'I love this song! Don't tell me … is it Diana Ross?'

'No idea.'

'My two pals and I had a bit of an act we used to put on for parties – you know, like at Hogmanay and stuff. We called ourselves *Dusty* Ross and the Supremes. I think we even played what you call *gigs*. Not that we were ever paid. Paid in Babycham, maybe. I can't bear to touch the stuff now. What about you?'

'Sorry?'

'Do you like Babycham?'

Kat wrinkled up her nose.

'What about a boyfriend?'

'How do you mean?'

'I mean – are you courting? Got a special lad at the moment?'

'No.' Kat brushed away her fringe.

'You need to get back out there. I always had a boyfriend on the go when I was your age. You should be playing the field – getting as much action as you can.'

'Hardly!'

'Don't you ever meet anyone at the discos or clubs?'

'I hate those places.'

'Well, what about at work? Our staff canteen was a great place for talent.'

'Dusty, I work with two other women in a library.'

'Oh … look at that lovely house on the hill. Gorgeous! What about dating agencies?'

'Can we change the subject, please?'

'Suit yourself. Mind that blue van – it's weaving all over the place.'

Chapter 11

The bedroom was stuffy with the odour of stale perfume and dried lavender bags. Arthur approached the dressing table, his image reflected in three mirrors. He sat on the faux leather stool, his gangly legs bent double. From his jacket pocket he removed a leather barber set, which he unzipped. Selecting the comb, he placed it an inch above his left ear. Drawing it back he parted his hair and smoothed it to the right. Next he pulled out a miniature pair of scissors. Taking his time he trimmed the moustache, keeping close to his top lip. Shards of ginger floated over the polished surface, which he brushed on to the floor. Next he withdrew a bottle of moustache oil. He squeezed a few drops on to his fingers and massaged it into the coarse hair, teasing it up at either end. Replacing each item with diligence he tucked the kit back into his pocket, admiring the overall effect. *Much* better!

From his seat Arthur opened the top drawer, which was stuffed with an assortment of velvet-covered boxes. His hand reached to the back and felt a flat case. He held his breath as he prised the case open. The gold necklace, studded with diamonds, twinkled even in the dim light. 'Bingo!' he murmured, slipping the case into a rucksack. He rifled through the remaining drawers, carefully selecting his treasures. Next he pulled down the Ramsay ladder and made his way into the attic. He swept the torch in an arc, quickly assessing the contents. What a load of old junk! The first couple of boxes he tried contained fusty clothes and faded photo albums. It had to be here somewhere. Cherie had mentioned something about a brown leather attaché case. The wooden flooring came to an end and Arthur had to stoop uncomfortably as he inched his way along one of the beams. His foot slipped and he lurched on to the loft insulation, the fibreglass snagging his ankle. '*Shit!*' He reversed along the beam and tried the other side of the roof space. Rain pelted down against the small window, which let in a slow drip. In frustration he shoved cardboard boxes aside, knocking over a felt-covered card table. Behind it lay a walnut attaché case, its corners dented with age. Arthur snatched it up and stumbled back down the ladder in his haste. He placed the case on the kitchen table and eased open the rusty clasps. Cherie had remembered correctly. Her father *had* been an avid coin collector. Arthur ran a greedy finger over the precious coins and picked out what he thought looked an impressive silver piece. Whipping out his phone he scrolled through the images. 'Ha!' he cried in delight.

Arthur closed the front door behind him, hanging his jacket on a peg before finding Cherie sitting at their home computer in the spare room. She quickly shut down the site.

'How did you get on?' Cherie asked brightly, swivelling round in her chair.

'Fine,' Arthur replied, slumping on to the sofa. 'Got some of your mum's stuff sorted.'

'That's great, Arthur – thank you so much. I feel awful landing you with all this extra work.'

Arthur shrugged. 'You can't help it if your mother has steps up to her house – and I'm not carrying you up them.'

'I know! Anyway, you must be hungry.' Cherie reached for her crutches and hopped through to the kitchen. 'I found an online recipe for fish stew – should be nearly ready.'

'Can't wait,' Arthur mumbled, popping a can of beer.

Chapter 12

'What's that annoying bell noise coming from the back?' Dusty asked.

'I think it's probably one of Dad's cow bells,' Kat replied. 'He was in such a hurry this morning he didn't get a chance to empty the boot completely. I think there might even be a couple of nun outfits kicking around there too.'

'Well, I suppose that's the problem when you own an estate car – you get asked to do all the transporting.'

'Oh yes – he's had everything in the back – wardrobes, bikes, beds. I think he even once got asked if he could return a couple of goats that had escaped into someone's garden.'

'I expect it's lovely to drive?'

'If you're into driving tanks. Do you drive?'

'Oh no! I tried it once with Edwin. It was the closest we've ever come to getting a divorce. He didn't mind that I could never remember what all the levers and buttons do. He didn't even mind when I knocked the wing mirror off when we passed a number twenty-seven bus. No – it was the driving it through a ford that made him blow a gasket. Probably quite literally.'

'Oh dear,' said Kat, turning off the roundabout.

'We were actually going from a wedding ceremony to the reception. I'd only been driving a few months but it was Edwin's good pal from the bowling club getting married and he wanted to be able to have a drink. We were in the middle of nowhere past Selkirk and I took a wrong turning. Apparently it had been raining for weeks so the water was higher than usual. We ground to a halt right in the dip of the ford. Edwin was wearing his best grey suit and had to wade out to get help. It was in the days well before we had those mobile thingies. He had to walk two miles along a muddy track to get to the nearest farmhouse. He was *furious*!'

'I bet he was.'

'Stank like a cowpat throughout the reception. Eventually someone lent him a pair of red golfing slacks. I don't know how many people asked him whether the wedding party stipulated fancy dress. And so I told him I'd never drive again. "That's that!" I said. Do you like driving?'

'Not really,' Kat shook her head. 'Means to an end and all that.' She stretched her fingers, which were taut with tension.

'I expect we'll be stopping presently?' Dusty enquired mildly.

'Yes, not long now.'

'But it *is* beautiful scenery. I love these lush forests and the mountains with all that heather. Oh, look – there's a waterfall.'

'I can't look.'

'Hey, Kat, there's a hitch-hiker walking up ahead. Shouldn't we stop?'

'What? No way!'

'Why not? We've got plenty of space in the back. It seems a shame for some youngster trying to get to where they need to be.'

'Or some psycho-killer with an axe in their bag.'

Dusty tutted. 'Surely not. What would be the point in hacking off the head of a pensioner?'

'Speak for yourself! Anyway, it's the first rule of driving – never pick up hitch-hikers. Didn't Edwin teach you that?'

'No. I think he was more concerned with preserving the car's undercarriage. Anyway, what's the second rule?'

'Never drive through a ford.' Kat smiled.

They neared the young man who had his thumb stuck out. Dusty glanced back as they passed. 'Oh, but it looks like it's about to rain as well.'

'There's no point. Look – there's the House of Bruar. We're stopping now.' Kat indicated right and pulled off the road.

'Oh, good – I shouldn't have had that second cuppa this morning.'

Chapter 13

Kat opened the car door and stretched. Dusty was right – it had begun to rain and the wind gusted across the open moor. They hurried inside.

'Just nipping to the loo,' said Dusty. 'I'll meet you in the café.'

Kat browsed around the shop taking in the Scottish mugs, woolly jumpers, soft toys and handcrafted jewellery. She pulled out her phone and messaged her mum.

```
While we're away, find out what Arthur's
up to. Saw him doing something weird with
Dusty's ballgown.
```

Send.

A small girl bumped into the back of her legs.

'Watch where you're going, Christie!' her mother warned. 'I'm so sorry.'

'No problem,' said Kat, moving to one side.

'But I want that furry dog,' the girl insisted.

'This?' asked Kat. 'It's a Highland cow – see its horns?'

'Cool.' The girl beamed, her front teeth missing.

'I'm guessing you're Scottish? Do you live near here? The scenery is so fabulous,' the mother said, taking the girl's hand.

'Actually I'm from Edinburgh.'

'No way! That's where we're headed.'

'I'm sure you'll enjoy it.'

'Do you know J.K. Rowling?' the mother asked eagerly.

'Not personally.'

'Have you ever met her?'

'Not that I know of.'

'Christie and I are hoping to see her. We just *love* Harry Potter, don't we, sweetie?'

'Harry's my hero.' The girl began chewing on the Highland cow.

'Well, good luck,' Kat said, heading for the café.

'*There* you are,' Dusty said, approaching at speed. 'I thought I'd lost you.'

They picked up a tray and joined the queue.

'What can I get you?' a teenage girl behind the counter asked, wiping off the coffee machine nozzle.

'Can I have rhubarb tea and a flapjack?' Kat asked.

'A *rhubarb* tea?'

'Yes, please.'

'Anything else?' She looked at Dusty expectantly.

'I'll have a latte, please,' said Dusty. 'And do you have any scones?'

'Do you want a scone with raisins or without raisins?'

'Ooh, I'll have a scone without raisins, please.'

'We've only got scones *with* raisins,' the girl replied.

'I'm sure that'll be fine.'

They found a table at the window, where Kat could watch the cars manoeuvring around the car park. The surrounding hills had disappeared under a low cloud. Kat pumped out antibacterial gel on to her hands, rubbing them vigorously. She offered it to Dusty.

'No, thanks – smells like detergent. What's it for?'

'Germs,' Kat answered darkly.

'Oh, before I forget, you better have this.' Dusty handed a printed sheet to Kat.

'What's that?'

'Our booking.'

'Mill House? I thought we were staying in a hotel?'

'Cherie checked out *all* the local accommodation,' Dusty said apologetically. 'Apparently there is some Highland Games thing on. Everywhere is booked for miles around. It's a bit pricey on account of it being a *boutique* guesthouse – whatever *that* is. She was beginning to panic, thinking we weren't going to get anywhere.'

'So she didn't try the youth hostel, then?'

'I don't expect I'd be allowed in, dear. Hey, Kat, there's that hitch-hiker we passed!'

Kat peered through the steamed-up window. She watched as the young man, shoulder-length hair blowing in the wind, staggered between the cars under the weight of his bulging rucksack. He disappeared from view. Kat pulled on her jacket. 'Come on, we better get going.'

'And where will our next stop be?'

Kat rolled her eyes. 'Do you think we can make it to Inverness without a break?'

'How far is that?'

'About an hour and a half?'

'That'll be dandy. I'll be ready for lunch then.'

They were nearing the Volvo when Dusty grabbed Kat's arm. 'Look! There he is again. He looks so miserable in the rain. Ought we to help him?'

'That's not such a good idea,' Kat insisted. 'We don't know anything about him!'

'We could ask?' Dusty suggested. 'Why don't we ask what he does for a living? I always think that's a good reflection of a person's character.'

'I hardly think a lawyer or orthodontist would be hitching a lift up the A9!' Kat stood her ground. The slim man had stopped under a tree and was kneeling by his rucksack. He pulled woolly gloves out from one of the many zipped pockets.

'Tell you what,' said Dusty. 'Why don't we ask his name, occupation and where he's going, then we can make an informed decision?'

Kat's shoulders sagged in defeat. 'Fine.'

As the man stood up, they noted how young he looked – barely into his twenties. He had an earnest unshaven face, his hair a dirty blond. A waist-length jacket dripped rain on to his black jeans and trainers. Dusty strode up to him. 'Good morning, young man. My name's Dusty and this is Kat.' Kat stared at her boots.

The man looked up with surprise in his pale grey eyes. 'Oh, it's not so much what I'd call a *good* morning but I'm not one to start an argument.' He smiled. 'I'm Logan.'

'We were just having a discussion,' Dusty announced. 'And we wondered what your occupation is?'

'Really?' He tightened a buckle. 'No prizes for guessing I'm a student!' He adjusted his gloves. 'Professional scholar.' He bowed. 'At your service.'

'A student?' Dusty echoed with disappointment. 'I'd kind of hoped for a nice teacher or something.'

Kat couldn't help but laugh. Dusty inspected him closely. 'Shouldn't you be at university, then?'

'Not quite.' He waggled his hand back and forth. 'Another couple of weeks.'

'So limited funds to purchase a train or bus ticket, then?' Dusty concluded.

'I like to think of myself as being at one with the open road. Jack Kerouac and all that.'

'This is hardly California,' Kat remarked.

Logan gazed up at the slate sky. 'I'll give you that.'

'And may we ask,' Dusty continued, 'where you're headed?'

'I'm headed somewhere in that direction.' He made a vague sweep with his arm.

'We're travelling to Lochinver, if that's any help?' said Dusty, looking to Kat for approval. Kat shrugged.

'I'm sure it would be of tremendous help,' said Logan. 'I'd be forever in your debt.'

'Lovely!' Dusty clapped her hands. 'That's our car over there.'

Kat opened the boot for Logan, who pushed his rucksack into the corner. 'Hey, are you two *nuns*?'

Their car hugged the road as they wound through the craggy Highlands – lochs and hardy pines to their left, heathery moors to their right. The cheery radio lapsed into silence as they passed through Speyside.

'So, what's taking you up to Lochinver?' Logan asked from the rear. 'Assuming you're not making up the tug-of-war team?'

'It's a bit of a long story,' said Dusty, half turning in her seat.

Logan smiled. 'Well, I hope you don't mind me asking, but it's either that or *I Spy*?'

'I hate *I Spy*,' Kat muttered, overtaking a fuel lorry as it strained on the incline.

Dusty recounted the mystery of the ring.

Logan slapped his thigh. 'No way, man!' He craned forward. 'But I can help you!'

'How?' Dusty said.

'I'm studying forensic psychology,' Logan said with excitement.

'Forensic …?'

'Psychology. I'm studying the application of psychological theory to criminal investigation. It would be amazing if I can apply my theory to practice!'

'I knew we were meant to pick you up,' said Dusty with a smile. 'We've got a genius in the back.'

'I wouldn't say *genius* but you two don't exactly strike me as a couple of sleuths. Did you think you could track down the owner from over fifty years ago? How would you ever be able to do that?'

Dusty and Kat exchanged a quick glance. 'We hadn't really made a plan.'

Logan nodded in support, stroking his chin. 'I hear you. You thought you could just go with the flow? But, seriously, where are you going to start?'

'We thought if we maybe asked around the locals we could see if anyone remembers a Jess and Hamish and whether they got married or engaged. We're going to try the library, cafés, community centres …'

'Pubs?'

'If we have to.'

'That's my kind of research. But can I interject with some executive direction?'

'Of course,' Dusty nodded.

'Rather than getting hooked on this couple, why don't you make a list of all the Jesses that citizens mention, then all the

Hamishes? And maybe one will lead to the other?'

'That does make sense. It's not that big a community. We're sure that someone will know or remember one of them.'

'Can I see the ring?' Logan asked eagerly.

'Certainly,' said Dusty, reaching into her handbag.

'I don't think that's such a good idea,' Kat said.

Logan caught Kat's eye in the rear-view mirror. 'Quite right. You hardly know me.'

'We don't know you at all!'

'So ask away, driver.' Logan held his arms wide. 'What do you want to know?'

'Maybe we should start with where you're from?' Kat asked.

'Good question, caller number one. So I'm originally from Lauder in the Borders – and, yes, I'm aware that rhymes. I have a younger sister who's studying something to do with fruit flies. I'm about to go into my third year at Edinburgh University.'

'I hope you're not one of those students who does drugs?' Dusty commented.

'Hey, I'm not saying I'm squeaky clean – but, no, I generally turn to alcohol for light relief. All those exams we have – and the endless assignments! It's been some heavy stuff, which is why I'm taking a break.'

'Do you live in Edinburgh?'

'I had to give up my flat for the summer – it gets rented out to tourists at three times the price. I didn't want to go home so I've been kipping down with mates.'

'A squat?'

'I like to think of it more as a commune. It's pretty basic but I can't afford anything else.'

'You could get a job,' Kat suggested.

'I have a job! Well, I like to think of it as a craft – a vocation. I need to hone my skills. Maybe this is fate for me too? A chance to test out what I've learnt so far.'

'And have you always wanted to be a … whatchamacallit?'

'Oh yes, although I didn't know what it was called back then.' Logan gazed out at the passing scenery. 'As a teen I desperately wanted to be Alex Rider! And then Clarice Starling – without the heels, obviously. Now I'd settle for just getting through the course.'

'I'm sure you'll be just fine. And it would be *wonderful* if you can help us track down Jess or Hamish.'

'No pressure! But what will you do if you fail?'

'How do you mean?'

'What will you do if you can't find Jess or Hamish? I'm guessing you can't spend the rest of your lives searching for them?'

Dusty shook her head. 'I think I'll just return the ring to where my husband went panning. Throw it back into Loch Assynt.'

Logan pursed his lips in agreement. 'The circle of life. Cool.'

Chapter 14

Kat indicated to pull off the main road. 'We're at Inverness but, rather than getting caught up in the town, this might be a better place to stop for lunch.'

'Look, there's a Costa – shall we go there?' Dusty asked, gathering up her bag and coat.

Kat shrugged. 'It's as good as anywhere I suppose. Logan, are you going to join us?'

'If you don't mind, I think I'll just wait here. I have some water and may still have a pasty left from yesterday.'

'I'll buy you lunch, if you're short?' Dusty offered. 'Don't you want a hot drink?'

'That's very kind of you but I'm happy to sit in the car, if that's alright? Just in case someone tries to steal your habits.' He winked.

'But it's such a miserable day,' Dusty persisted. 'You should have something to warm you up.'

'Well, perhaps a coffee wouldn't go amiss.'

'Of course! A latte? Cappuccino? Macchiato? Americano?'

'Get you, Mrs Barista! I'll take anything.'

'Got your meds, Dusty?' Kat asked.

Dusty patted her bag. 'I'm all sorted.'

Kat appeared in the car park, a steaming cup in one hand. Logan had his hood pulled over his head, his eyes closed. Kat rapped on the car window and his eyes sprang open.

'Present from Dusty,' said Kat as Dusty picked her way through the puddles.

'Tell your grandma thanks.'

'She's not my grandma!'

'Isn't she?'

Dusty shook off her coat before fastening her seat belt as Kat exited the car park. Logan leant forward. 'So, you're not her grandma?'

'Heavens, no!' Dusty laughed. 'We're neighbours.' She patted Kat's knee. 'Although I wish she *were* my granddaughter. I have one grandson but he lives in Leighton Buzzard. He's apparently high up in drainage but I don't get to see him much except if Arthur Skypes him for me.'

'Anyway, we were just wondering,' said Kat. 'How far up north are you going?'

'Ah, back with the questions.' Logan swept a hand through his damp hair. 'And I thought I was the expert in scrutiny.'

'Don't we have a right to know?'

'I guess … well, I plan to spend some time at the Loopallu Festival in Ullapool.'

'How lucky! Ullapool's near where we're going,' said Dusty.

'The what?' Kat asked.

'The Loopallu? You never heard of it?'

'Can't say I have.'

'It's an awesome music festival that happens every year.'

'I've heard of Glastonbury,' said Dusty. 'Is it like that? Lots of mud and no toilets?'

'Sure. But it's a great gig for me. I can earn a few quid behind one of the bars and hear some crazy music. You should come.'

'Is it held in a concert hall?'

'More like a big-top tent.'

'I haven't camped in years,' Dusty said. 'I don't think my knees would like it.'

'The offer's out there,' said Logan, closing his eyes again.

'My mother used to say it was "coming down like stair rods",' said Dusty peering into the gloom.

'It's certainly not making it easy to see the road,' Kat complained. 'I'm sure we should have turned off miles back.'

Dusty smoothed out the map. 'What road did you say we should be on?'

'We need to be on the A837.'

'And where do you think we are?'

'I'm thinking the A839?'

Dusty ran her finger over the crease. 'Oh dear, I'm not very good at this. Are there any towns I can look for to see where we are?'

'We've just passed Stronechrubie?'

'Ah! Yes, I see it. When we get to Loch Assynt we're heading left along the A837.'

'Can I be of any help?' Logan asked from the rear.

'Sorry, Logan, but we've driven past Ullapool,' said Kat. 'I didn't want us to get lost by going off-piste.'

'No problemo. I said I'd give you a hand. I can easily get to Ullapool from here.'

Kat flicked on the full beam. 'This road's a nightmare.'

Their journey continued in tense silence. 'There!' cried Logan. 'Loch Assynt – up ahead.'

Kat followed the winding route, her shoulders hunched. A

white van accelerated and overtook on a short expanse of straight tarmac. 'Idiot,' she muttered. 'Dusty, what do the instructions say to get to the house?'

'I thought I gave them to you?'

'So you did. Logan, can you find them in my coat pocket?'

Logan fumbled in the dark, pulling out a printed sheet. '"*Take the A837 until you reach the T-junction marked Bridge-of-Cuil. Turn left and continue for about a mile. You will pass a small forestry outpost on your right. Take the next right and follow a single track (watch for the sharp bend in the road). At the end of the road you will come to Mill House. If you keep going, you will end up in Loch Inver!*" Have we come to a T-junction yet?'

'Don't think so,' said Kat.

'I could do with a tea junction,' Dusty said. 'I'm gasping.'

The wipers sped up as the rain came down in torrents, looking like snow in the headlights. Kat slammed on the brakes as the road split two ways.

'There's the sign,' Logan offered. 'Turn left.'

A car blared its horn from behind. Kat waved her hand in apology. 'Someone's in a hurry.'

'That looks like the forestry post,' said Logan. 'Either that or a very large pencil factory.' They bumped along the pine-lined track, the car slipping on the mud.

'Mill House!' announced Dusty in excitement. 'We're here!'

Kat pulled into a gravel courtyard surrounded by low stone buildings on three sides. 'Shall I check we've got the right place before we unload our stuff?' Kat suggested. 'Chuck my jacket over, will you?'

'I'm coming as well,' said Dusty, zipping up her raincoat. She opened the car door.

'Might as well come too,' Logan added.

The three huddled under a timber canopy as Kat pressed the bell. The door was thrown open by a tall, dark-haired man dressed in olive tweed jacket and trousers. He had a tea towel flung over one shoulder. 'Come in, come in! Let's get you out of that foul rain. I'm Aubrey, one of the owners – so pleased to meet you.' He held out a warm hand to Dusty.

'Dusty Harris. My daughter booked us for three nights?'

'That's right. We've been expecting you.'

'I'm Kat.' She flicked her wet hair out of her eyes.

'Logan.'

Aubrey frowned. 'I thought your booking was only for two people? Of course, it's fine – I can give you youngsters the honeymoon suite. It's more for catering requirements we ask.'

'Oh no! We're not together,' Kat protested, taking a step away from the group.

Logan grinned. 'I'm just extra baggage they picked up along the way. I don't need a room, mate – I have my tent. If there's somewhere you don't mind me pitching?'

'In this weather?' Aubrey gave a theatrical shudder. 'I can't possibly have you camping in this monsoon. I wonder …'

'Hey, it's really no problem,' said Logan, holding up his hands. 'I'm quite used to camping in Scotland.'

'Really? I can't think of anything worse!' Aubrey laughed. 'But if it's the outdoor life you prefer, you're more than welcome to pitch your tent round the back. Gregor keeps a small herb and vegetable patch but there's a decent piece of lawn. And there's a WC here off reception you can use. Let me show you round then I'll give you a hand with the bags.' Aubrey pushed a door to their right, which led into a spacious sitting-dining area. An open fire sent up a flare of red sparks as he threw on a couple of logs.

'I love that smell of burning wood,' Dusty sighed.

The tartan carpet and mulled-wine painted walls gave a cosy feel to the low-ceilinged room. Heavy velvet curtains were closed against the late afternoon darkness. One long wooden table and ten chairs stood in the centre; two well-worn leather settees were placed either side of the fire. A laden bookcase leant against a corner. Aubrey indicated to a door at the far end. 'This will take you to your rooms.' He crossed the sitting room and opened another door. 'And this is the kitchen. Say hi to our guests, Gregor.'

Gregor, dressed in full kitchen whites, wiped his hands on his apron. 'Afternoon.' He solemnly shook hands with each individual. He was slightly built with sandy hair and an anxious expression. 'So glad you found us. We were getting worried, weren't we, Aubrey?'

'We were. So Gregor is responsible for all our hospitality, aren't you, love?'

Gregor held up his hands. 'Guilty as charged!'

Aubrey pointed to a noticeboard on the wall. 'And here we have tonight's menu. Plus any other items of useful information.' He waved his hand at the leaflets pinned on to the board. 'Anyway, let's get you settled and then perhaps you'd like a coffee?'

'Oh, yes, please.' Dusty nodded.

'Or something stronger?' Aubrey winked. 'We don't have a licence but stock a small bar in this fridge and use an honesty box.'

'Whoa!' said Logan. 'Even better.'

'You can help yourself to any of the drinks in the fridge or in the cabinet but please don't go near Gregor's whisky.' He nodded to a crystal decanter. 'He only shares that on special occasions.'

'Indeed I do. Anyway, please excuse me.' Gregor ducked back into the kitchen. 'Those onions won't chop themselves!'

Aubrey insisted on carrying both Kat and Dusty's luggage in from the car. 'The gate to the back is over there.' Aubrey nodded his head as Logan stumbled across the courtyard with his rucksack. 'Will you be joining the ladies for dinner?'

Logan shook his head. 'I haven't budgeted for extra meals. I have a wee camp-stove that does the job.'

'Oh, I think I can cover that,' said Dusty. 'Especially if you're helping us with our assignment.'

'Sounds intriguing,' said Aubrey. 'So see you inside when you've got your tent up?'

'How can I refuse?'

Chapter 15

Dell sawed a slice off the charred sirloin steak and popped it into her mouth. 'Heaven!' she grinned. Ron nodded in agreement. 'Thompson's the butcher is definitely the best.'

'Nice home-made chips too.'

'Thank you, dear.' Ron lifted a beer bottle to his lips.

'But I feel so guilty,' Dell said, putting down her cutlery.

'Why? Kat's not here and we haven't had steak for months. Tuck in while it's still hot.'

'I don't mean dinner – I know she doesn't care what *we* eat. I meant about Dusty. Maybe I shouldn't have forced her to go. Pass the mustard.'

'She'll be *fine*. It'll do her good to get out of her bedroom for once. She can't spend the rest of her life wedded to those bloody books.'

'I know.' Dell sighed. 'But it's such a long drive. And what if Dusty takes a turn for the worse? What if taking her out of a familiar environment sends her even more barmy?'

'Kat knows she can call us at any time,' said Ron, removing a piece of gristle from his mouth. 'She's a sensible girl. And when was the last time she went anywhere?'

'She went to Dundee with Shelley in the summer.'

Ron snorted. 'Hardly the Costa Blanca!'

'But what do you make of her text?'

'Show me it again?'

Dell turned the screen so Ron could read the message. 'I've no idea!' he puffed out his cheeks. 'What does she mean, "doing something weird with Dusty's ballgown"? Surely she doesn't mean he was *wearing* it, does she? Of course, I don't know the bloke well but he always seemed okay to me.'

'Not like your average transvestite,' Dell agreed.

'I wouldn't know. And I can't see how the moustache fits in.'

'But think about it, Ron,' said Dell. 'He came round here in person to ask if Kat could take Dusty up north. It didn't come from Cherie. Maybe he *is* up to something?'

'Like what? You've got sauce on your chin, love.'

Dell shrugged. 'Maybe he's going to use the house for something this weekend?'

'You mean throw a party? Why would he use an old lady's house for that? Her chintz three-piece suite is hardly fitting for a rave.'

'What if,' Dell whispered, 'he's got a fancy woman and he's using the house for a dirty weekend?'

'Don't be daft, Dell! Surely that risks us seeing them both. Look, if it makes you feel any better, I'll drop by tomorrow and see if he's about. Now, guess what I bought us for dessert?'

'Chunky Monkey?'

'You got it in one!'

Chapter 16

'*Organically-reared Aberdeen Angus ground steak paired with locally-sourced smashed and buttered baby potatoes, in a rich beef gravy sauce and home-grown Mill House shelled peas,*' Dusty read out loud.

'Mince and tatties,' Logan whispered in her ear.

'I better tell them it's just peas and potatoes for me, then,' said Kat as they inspected the noticeboard. She tapped on the kitchen door.

Gregor whipped open the door in irritation. 'Isn't Aubrey around?'

'I'm sorry to bother you – maybe I should have said something earlier but I didn't book the accommodation …'

'And?'

'I'm vegetarian.'

'Oh, I see.' Gregor frowned. 'Yes, that would have been helpful to have known in advance of your arrival.'

'But don't worry,' Kat insisted. 'I'm more than happy with peas and potatoes.'

'Surely not! I can easily prepare you a cheese and mushroom omelette at least?'

'It's fine. Actually I'm not that hungry. It's been a long day and I'll be heading for an early night soon.'

'If you're certain? I would hate it to enter the public domain that Mill House can't cater for alternative requirements.'

'Don't worry. It can be our wee secret.' Kat turned to leave.

'I'm not happy about it but, at such short notice, what can I do?' He called after her. 'I make a fabulous spring vegetable roulade!'

'Perhaps tomorrow?'

'Absolutely.'

'Have you seen the *House Rules*?' Logan smirked, sipping from a can of cider. 'I hope you weren't considering slapping any foundation on for dinner?'

'*Please remove all traces of make-up before sleeping in the beds as any mark on the pillows incurs an additional laundry cost.*' Kat pulled a face. 'As *if*! What about this one? *Please don't feed the local birds with bread as we're trying to encourage a family of tits with flaked maize and sunflower seeds.*' Kat stifled a giggle.

'What are you two in cahoots about?' Dusty asked from the settee. She stirred her coffee.

'Nothing, Dusty,' Logan replied. 'I just hope you weren't planning to throw toast at the local tits?'

'Excuse me?'

'Or wear your boots in your bedroom?'

'Ah!' said Aubrey appearing with a glass of red wine in hand. 'I'm glad to see you're observing the house rules. It makes for a much more pleasant experience for us all. Perhaps now provides an apt opportunity to draw your attention to our coaster policy?'

'Sorry?' Kat said, puzzled.

Aubrey slipped a square mat under Dusty's mug. He gave a slight bow. 'Now, if you'd like to take your seats at the table, I will serve supper.'

By nine o'clock Kat was relieved to close the bedroom door and sink into the plush, four-pillowed bed. She snuggled under the covers and lifted *Anna Karenina* from the bedside table. After two pages she switched off the light and fell into a deep sleep.

'Help yourself to tea or coffee from the breakfast table,' said Aubrey. 'I've put out a selection of cereal and fresh fruit too. Your cooked breakfast will be ready shortly. And thank you for ticking your preferences last night. Gregor likes to get everything all lined up and tickety-boo for your convenience.'

'Any sign of Logan?' Kat asked as she perused the tea selection.

'I expect he's having a nice lie-in,' Dusty replied. 'Coffee is lovely and hot.'

'Have you taken your tablets?' Kat asked.

'Yes, Mum.'

Kat sat at the table. 'Only I was hoping we could get out into Lochinver early and get started as soon as possible. We can't hang around all day waiting for him to get his act together. You know what students are like.'

'Academic?'

'Slothful!'

Dusty sipped her coffee. 'It's certainly a smashing day for it. Clear blue skies and sunshine after all that hideous rain.'

Kat gazed out of the window. The sun peeked above a gorse-covered knobbly hill that rose steeply from beyond the foot of the garden. Logan's faded tent was pitched on a rectangle of wet grass. No sign of life.

'I hope he was okay,' Dusty fretted. 'I felt so sorry for him having to leave this cosy room and sleep under canvas. It was still chucking it down when we went to bed.'

Kat shrugged. 'It was what he was going to do anyway. The free hot meal must have been a bonus.'

Aubrey burst out from the kitchen backwards, holding a plate in each hand. 'Now, I have one scrambled egg on toast and one bacon and eggs?'

'That's mine,' said Dusty. 'Bacon and eggs, please.'

'Watch out, the plates are *very* hot,' said Aubrey, lowering them on to the table with white-gloved hands. 'A little trick I learnt from Gregor,' he said, waving his hands like royalty.

Dusty and Kat were finishing their breakfast when they heard the front door opening. Logan entered the dining area wearing his coat, with an armful of items that he dropped on to the table.

'What's all this?' Dusty asked. 'Have you been out shopping already?'

'Shopping is for the bourgeois!' Logan grinned, helping himself to coffee. 'I have been out *procuring* materials that will support our cause.'

'Oh yes?' Kat asked. 'A roll of old wallpaper?'

Aubrey returned from the kitchen with a plate of toast. 'Logan, can I get Gregor to make you anything?'

'Toast is grand,' Logan replied, picking up a triangle. 'And would you mind terribly if we used that wall?' He nodded to the wall without the windows.

'It depends. What did you have in mind?'

'I need to put this up.' Logan unfurled the wallpaper. 'I'll use Blu Tack so it won't leave a mark.' He winked at Kat.

'It's not really our kind of colour,' Aubrey frowned. 'It's a bit garish – but show me what you mean.'

Logan turned the paper over and stuck a long length on the wall. 'Voilà!'

'A piece of white paper?' Kat said, unimpressed.

'It's our Link Chart Investigation Board!' announced Logan triumphantly.

'It is?' said Dusty.

Logan strode back to the table and selected a black felt pen. In the centre of the paper he scrawled JESS AND HAMISH then drew a crude ring with three jewels. On one side he wrote JESS and the other side HAMISH. 'Now, we make a list of all those we hear about. Then when we track them down, we can cross them off.' He chewed the top of the pen. 'We need to be strategic about this. There's no point rushing around like headless chickens. We need to do this *systematically*.'

'If you say so, Dexter,' said Kat, saluting.

'I prefer to think of myself more as Detective Inspector Jimmy Perez.'

'Well, you've certainly got the accent.'

'And the Post-it Notes!' Logan waved a handful of pink pads.

'Where did you get all this?' Kat asked.

'I'll settle up with you,' said Dusty. 'I can't have you being out of pocket.'

'Nonsense! You bought me dinner last night. In any case, I got these free from a wee hardware shop on the front.'

'The Iron Man?' Aubrey asked.

'He had them in some backroom.'

'So what's this all about?' asked Aubrey, sitting at the table. Dusty recounted the story yet again. 'How intriguing,' he mused. 'Of course, Gregor and I aren't what you'd call local. We only moved up from Chipping Barnet eight years ago. But now I think about it, there may be a Jessie that leads the women's group at the Lochside Community Centre. The only reason I know that is because we got a call from her asking if we could donate any prizes to her raffle. I think we happily regifted a bottle of Chardonnay.' He made a sour face.

'Good! This is what we need,' said Logan, hurrying over to the board. He jotted JESSIE – COMMUNITY CENTRE on a Post-it and drew a line from the ring to the pink square.

'*Gregor!*' Aubrey yelled. Gregor came bustling out from the kitchen, spatula in hand. 'What is it? Has Captain Rooster escaped on to the road again? Oh, what's going on here?'

'Have you come across anyone called Jess or Hamish in this area? Likely to be aged seventy or eighty?'

Gregor concentrated for a minute. 'There's an old boy who sits on the bench smoking a pipe most days down at the harbour. I see him when I'm collecting from the fish market. I'm pretty sure he's a Hamish or a Harry.'

'Shall I do this one?' asked Dusty. 'This is exciting!' She put on her glasses and carefully wrote HAMISH – FISH MARKET before sticking it up on the paper.

'And Jess McGonagle sometimes works behind the bar in the Lobster Pot,' Gregor suggested. 'I know she's only in her twenties but, in my experience, people are often named after parents or grandparents.'

'Bang on!' Logan agreed, scribbling furiously. 'So shall we split up and see what we can find out? Maybe rendezvous at lunchtime?'

'How far's the village?' Kat asked.

'If you hop over the fence at the back, it's about a ten-minute walk down to the harbour,' said Aubrey.

'But we'll need the car,' Kat said. 'Especially if we're visiting lots of places.'

'In that case if you drive back along the single track, take a left then follow the road into the village.'

'Would you mind if I took a photo of the ring?' Logan said. 'It's a long shot but someone might recognise it.'

Dusty reached for her bag. 'Of course.' She opened the envelope and tipped it on to her palm. 'Kat, why don't you put it on for the photo? It might jog a memory.'

Kat shrugged, slipping the ring on to her finger.

'Wow! It fits perfectly,' said Logan. 'Hold out your hand.' He zoomed in on her finger.

'Oh, that's *gorgeous*!' Aubrey agreed. 'Suits your delicate hands.'

Kat smiled, admiring the diamonds as they twinkled under the lights.

'Look, why don't you just keep it on?' Dusty suggested.

'Do you think?'

'Yes! It's probably safer anyway. You know me – I might leave my bag in some café and it'll be gone forever.'

'If you're sure?'

'Of course I am, dear. Come on, then, let's get going.'

'Where shall we meet for lunch?' Kat asked. 'Aubrey? Any suggestions?'

'I'd recommend the Sailing Boat on the harbour. You can't miss it. They do wonderful falafel wraps and salted caramel brownies to die for!'

'Right, let's go,' said Logan. 'I'll try all the places around the harbour.'

'We'll ask at the community centre, the shops and try to track down the mobile library,' said Kat.

'Have fun!' Aubrey stood at the front door and waved them off with his tea towel.

Kat manoeuvred the Volvo into a half-empty car park at the far end of the village. A row of white painted shops and houses curved along the shore of Loch Inver, which sparkled in the morning sun. Several fishing boats were dotted around the stone harbour that jutted into the mouth of the loch. Dusty climbed out of the car and took a deep breath. 'What it is to breathe clean air! It's exactly how I remember it from fifty years ago. The village looks just the same – although there might be a few more gift shops. And there definitely wasn't a Spar when we were here. Edwin had forgotten to bring his shaving foam and we had to drive all the way to Lairg.'

Kat stood on the gravelly shore of the sea loch, the pebbles crunching under her feet. 'It really is beautiful up here,' she said, taking photos with her mobile. She reached into her pocket and held up the tiny Highland cow to the sun, taking a shot.

'Of course, we're lucky with the weather,' Dusty remarked. 'It rained for the entire two weeks of our honeymoon – not that we were caring about *that*!' She winked.

'Dusty!'

'But I was determined we'd go on a wee trip around the loch on a pleasure boat. Edwin booked a three-hour wildlife cruise that took us up to the Hermit's Castle and back. The water was like this.' She made a wave with her hand. '*Well!* Some poor lassie was terribly sick and – let me tell you - there's no *pleasure* in jumping aside every time the boat lurches and it comes your way.'

'I don't think we'll have time for a boat trip on this occasion,' Kat said, heading for the first shop.

'Pity. I do like the idea of being at sea.'

'Let's try here,' said Kat. '*Cath's Craft Cave.*'

Kat removed a small notebook and pen from her backpack. As they entered the shop a bell above the door tinkled to announce their arrival. The shop contained a number of revolving glass cases housing silver jewellery and gem-stoned trinkets. Wooden shelves displayed hand-thrown mugs and miniature white crofts with thatched roofs. A rosy-cheeked woman wearing a grey wool suit was sitting behind the counter, knitting. From somewhere the sound of a harp was being played through speakers. 'Good morning, ladies! How can I help? Just browsing or are you after something in particular? A present, perhaps?'

Kat and Dusty approached the counter. 'Actually, we're on a bit of a quest,' said Kat.

'Sounds interesting.' The woman raised her eyebrows, pushing the knitting to one side. 'I'm Cath, by the way. Of *Cath's Craft Cave*. Now, what's this quest of yours?'

Kat flicked open her notebook. 'We're looking for a lady called Jess or Jessica and a man called Hamish, who we think live or lived in this area – around Loch Assynt. Hopefully they are or were married to each other. They would be about seventy to eighty years old?'

'*Heavens!*' Cath gasped. 'Have they broken the law? Are you the police? Are they on the run like Bonnie and Clyde?'

'Police? *Me?*' Dusty laughed. 'I know they're short of officers but I'm not exactly in my prime.'

'Oh no! It's nothing like that,' Kat added. 'We think we have something that might belong to one of them.'

'Like a dog? Or a purse? A painting?'

Kat shook her head. 'An engagement ring.' She held out her hand. 'We're trying to find the owner of this ring.'

Cath clasped Kat's slim fingers and scrutinised the ring. 'That's *fabulous*! I love the setting. Come with me.' She scurried around the side of the counter heading for the door. Kat and Dusty followed in bemusement. Cath opened the shop door, flipping the OPEN sign to CLOSED.

'Oh, we really didn't mean to put you to any bother,' Kat protested as Cath locked the gift shop.

'It's no bother,' said Cath, striding along the road. 'Believe me, this is the most interesting thing that will happen to me today. Probably all week! We'll ask my mum. Come on, she's just in here.' She opened a gate to a whitewashed bungalow, the pretty front garden still full of wildflowers in bloom. Kat breathed in the waft of a buddleia's perfume. A couple of butterflies fluttered over their heads. Without knocking Cath barged straight into the house. '*Mum!*' she bellowed. 'Got visitors! Like a coffee? I'm having one.' Cath hurried into the kitchen and filled the kettle. 'Have a seat in the living room.' She nodded her head. 'Go on – in you go.'

Kat and Dusty entered the damp-smelling front room where Cath's mother had her armchair placed about one foot from a TV screen. The gas fire was on full, the curtains half drawn.

'Oh good, is it lunchtime?' she asked, not taking her eyes off the screen.

'Hi, I'm Kat and this is Dusty,' Kat said, standing awkwardly.

'Have you come to make my lunch?'

'Don't be daft, Mum, it's only ten o'clock in the morning. Sit!' Cath waved at the settee as she sank into an armchair on the other side of the fire, mug in hand. 'Bloody hell, Mother – it's like the *Towering Inferno* in here.'

'No, Cath, it's about this young man and he needs to cook dinner for three different girls, then he gets to pick the one he likes the best.' She shook her head. 'But I don't think he's going to impress them much. He served the first lassie beans on toast – for her *dinner*! Did you ever see the like?'

'Mum, I'm switching down the volume so we can talk.' Cath reached for the remote control.

'What? You'll need to turn down the volume. I can't hear what you're on about.'

'Mum, these ladies have something they want to ask you.'

Disgruntled, Cath's mother turned her attention to Kat and Dusty. 'Aren't you here to make my lunch? I like a Scotch pie.'

'They want to ask you some questions,' Cath announced in a loud voice.

'Oh? And about time too. Well, it started about six months ago. Bob that lives behind me turned up with a rehomed Alsatian. Now, I don't blame him in some ways. His wife died nearly five years ago and he's never been the same since. Seemingly he can't pass the butcher's without blubbing like a bairn. But, for the love of God, - it would drive you demented! If that mutt hears so much as a car driving along the road or a bird chirping *good morning*, it's bark, bark, bark. Can you not get it taken away?'

'Mum – these ladies aren't from the council.'

'Aren't you? Well, what do you want? I'm not giving any bloody money to any more charities! Tell them, Cath – I give plenty to the church, don't I? Who do you think paid to get the organ repaired after James Turner's youngest tipped milk all over the keys? *Me!*'

Kat took a deep breath. 'Actually, Mrs …?'

'Mrs Donaghue. And get the spelling right.'

'Thank you, Mrs Donaghue. We were just wondering whether you know anyone called Jess or Hamish living near here? Likely to be late seventies or eighty?'

'Jess or Hamish?' Cath repeated in a loud voice.

'Are you talking about Jess Watt? She died last year. Lost her leg to diabetes. Then poor soul fell out of bed and was taken off to Raigmore. We never saw her again.' She shook her head as Kat made notes.

'Do you know if she was ever married?'

'Aye! Did you not hear about that? Jess was married to Jock for forty years, then the bastard suddenly took up with a teacher and now I do believe they have a smallholding in Drumbeg. He had the nerve to come to her funeral. No shame! Any chance of some soup while you're here? I fancy a drop of chicken noodle.'

'What about Hamish?' Kat persisted.

'What about him?' Mrs Donaghue scowled. 'Don't tell me they've let him out?'

'Er,' Kat stammered.

'What are you on about, Mother?' Cath asked.

'You remember Rob Mantle with the webbed toes?'

'Of course I remember Rob – I was at high school with him, wasn't I? He won the swimming gala every year.'

'Yes, but did you ever hear about his uncle Hamish?'

'Can't say I did.'

'Hamish Mantle ...' Mrs Donaghue made sure she had their full attention. 'Have you not noticed that Mr McCreavy from the bank walks with a limp? Well, Hamish used to live north of Ullapool. He was on very trying times after his family lost the paper shop. He was drinking hard and had no money to support his family. God knows how he thought it would help to buy a gun and attempt a hold-up at the local bank. Mr McCreavy – a loyal employee – tried to stall Hamish with some nonsense about a *special code*. Hamish was many things but he wasn't stupid. Shot McCreavy in the kneecap and legged it with about three hundred quid. He got five years in Barlinnie – silly bugger. But then there was a rumour about him tackling a prison officer with a serving spoon. Have you got an update?' She leant forward in her chair.

'Sorry – no,' said Kat. 'That doesn't sound like the sort of man who might engrave an engagement ring for his fiancée.'

'Engraving?' Mrs Donaghue scoffed. 'He might have scored the prison walls right enough. But, och, no, Hamish never cared for anyone but himself. His poor weans grew up with nits and nae shoes. I think even his wife gave up on him when he went inside.'

'So are there any others?'

'Any other whats?'

'Anyone else called Jess or Hamish?' Kat said, her pen poised.

Mrs Donaghue shook her head. 'The best person to ask is Agnes.'

'Agnes!' Cath cried. 'Of course – why didn't I think of that myself? Come on, let's go and speak to Agnes.'

'What about my lunch?' Mrs Donaghue complained. 'It's been hours since my porridge.'

Cath rose briskly. 'Don't worry, I'll be back shortly.'

Chapter 17

Arthur opted for the train, boarding at Dalgety Bay along with families, dogs and pushchairs. He resented travelling to Edinburgh on a Saturday, with the centre being rammed with shoppers, but knew he had a better chance of Sid being on hand. And at least he could enjoy a few pints before Cherie started getting antsy. It had only just gone eleven but he stopped for a quick pint in the Halfway House. He leant against the bar, hoping to catch the Premier League punditry, but soon got fed up with being elbowed in the back by an animated Italian. He shuffled along to the corner of the bar, where an old man with no teeth lifted a glass of house whisky. '*Slàinte mhaith!*' the drinker announced, spraying spittle over Arthur's hand.

Arthur downed his pint and headed towards the cobbled Howe Street. He stepped past a wild-haired busker who sat cross-legged on a piece of cardboard strumming a lyre. A crowd of pink-wigged girls teetered past in St Trinian's outfits. The leader threw a handful of glitter over Arthur as he waited at the crossing. 'Cheer up, Carrot-Top!' she slurred as they stumbled into a themed pub.

Brushing glitter off his shoulders, Arthur pushed on the heavy door to the antique shop. He cursed, noting no sign of Sid. While a customer in a tatty raincoat haggled over something in his hand, Arthur hovered by a solemn grandfather clock. He gripped the briefcase as he shuffled around the glass cabinets; watches, necklaces and bracelets all ticketed and on display. An entire case of armoury, dating back to the eighteenth century, caught his eye – as did the price tags. Bloody hell! He was pretty sure he remembered his old uncle boasting of having a Lee-Enfield in his basement. Maybe he would ask whether he'd hung on to it. Could be worth something now. He kept one eye on the deal being brokered as a couple entered the shop. Finally! He strode up to the Victorian counter, where the suited shop assistant was squirrelling away whatever Mr Hard Times had released from his grip.

'Good morning, how may I help you?' He wiped his hands on a soft cloth.

'Is Sid working today?' Arthur asked, hoping he might magically appear from the back room.

'Day off – fishing on the River Tay, I believe. May I be of assistance?'

Arthur hesitated. Sid gave *mates' rates* but he couldn't afford to wait until next Saturday. With reluctance he placed the briefcase on the counter and retrieved Edwin's coin collection. He presented each of the four trays in a row.

'Lovely!' The man gave an appreciative nod. He removed a magnifying glass from a top pocket and scrutinised each coin individually. 'You must be parting with these with some regret?'

'That's right,' Arthur said. 'But in some ways I'll be satisfied if a genuine collector can enjoy them the way I have.'

'Of course.'

'Are they worth something?' Arthur asked, a little too eagerly.

The man frowned. 'Well, I'm sure you know their value but naturally we're both looking to turn a profit.'

'Indeed.'

'These two here,' the man tapped both index fingers on

individual silver coins. 'Are worth more than the rest of the entire collection. But you'll know that, of course.'

'I do,' Arthur said, feeling his armpits dampen. 'But I feel they should remain within the set. Keep the family together, so to speak.'

'Hmm.'

'So are they of interest to you?'

'Let me make a quick call,' the sales assistant replied, smoothing down his hair. 'I'll be back in a jiffy.' He stepped into the rear of the shop. Arthur could hear him on the phone as he waited impatiently. He felt his phone buzzing in his pocket.

`How are you getting on at the estate agents?`

`Fine` he texted back.

The salesman swept back a velvet curtain, appearing with a resigned expression on his face. 'Such a pity,' he said with tight lips.

'What?' Arthur demanded.

'Just got off the phone to my coin dealer in Leicester.' He shook his head. 'If only you'd come in last month.'

'Why?'

The salesman shrugged. 'Seemingly he attended an international antique fair in London last month and a dealer from Taiwan was making enquiries about a similar piece.'

'That's good, then?' Arthur said. 'Means there's a demand for it?'

'Timing is everything.'

'Well, do you want to buy them or not?'

The salesman frowned in distaste. 'Sir's tone is not appreciated. I'm merely providing the landscape. Of course, it is a most acceptable collection.'

'And? What are we talking about?'

'Four fifty?'

'What!' Arthur exploded. 'I checked online and it said they were worth eight to nine hundred.'

'A collection is only worth what someone is willing to pay.' He slid the trays back towards Arthur. 'Please don't feel obliged to part with your precious reserve.'

'Five hundred?' Arthur felt the sweat trickle down his back.

'Fine. I will prepare a credit note.'

'I need cash,' Arthur blurted.

The salesman hesitated before heading to the till. He took his time counting out twenty-pound notes into a neat pile. Arthur scooped it into the briefcase and bolted for the door.

'A pleasure doing business,' the salesman said sourly.

Arthur leant against the pavement railings and drew a deep breath. He knew five hundred wasn't going to be enough. *Shit!* He'd have to go back for more.

Chapter 18

Logan cut down a narrow hedged path behind Mill House, appearing between a garage forecourt and a short terrace of houses. He turned right, heading for the quayside. A stone jetty, extending into Loch Inver, housed a spacious depository where crates of fish were being moved around on trollies. Black-eyed gulls swooped across the bay, squawking with irritation as they assaulted the moored boats in the harbour. The sun glinted off the clear water like a spray of stars. Logan dodged a teenager on a bike who was performing wheelies through the Saturday morning bustle. He spotted Gregor's bearded old man reclining on a wooden bench, surveying the scene with half-closed eyes.

Logan brushed off shards of broken glass and perched on the edge of the bench. The old man squinted at him from beneath a cloth cap. He was wearing a stained woollen overcoat, baggy trousers and scuffed leather boots. Logan opened his notebook and clicked his biro pen. 'Good morning, sir – my name's Logan.'

'Good for you, son.'

'Can I ask – is your name Hamish?'

'Nope.'

'Oh,' Logan said, disappointed. 'I thought you might have been called Hamish.'

'Well, I'm not. Would it help if I was?'

'Maybe.'

'It's Harry.'

'Oh,' Logan repeated. He wrote HARRY BY THE HARBOUR in his notebook, underlining the name.

'So who's this Hamish you're looking for?'

Logan turned to face Harry. 'I'm trying to find out if there was a Hamish who lived in this area that was married to a Jess.'

'Are you now?' Harry pulled a quarter bottle of Lamb's Navy Rum from a pocket and took a sip. He offered it to Logan.

'Does that ring any bells?'

'Nope.'

'What about any Hamishes? Do you know anyone called Hamish?'

'Dead or alive?'

'Either.'

Harry closed his eyes, turning his face to the sun. 'I was at school with Hamish Bennett. He was quite a character – had lost an eye as a child and loved nothing more than popping out his glass eye and making the girls scream.' He chuckled to himself.

'And what happened to him?'

'How should I bloody ken? It was sixty years ago, son.'

'Any others?'

Harry let out a grumpy sigh. 'There was a Hamish that skippered the *White Angel* aboot twenty-five years back. He was a *great* skipper – always knew the best place to land a catch. Used to drive aboot in a big silver Merc.'

'You say "used to"?' Logan asked, scribbling notes.

'Aye, well everyone kens the *White Angel* went doon the winter of ninety-five.'

'I didn't – sorry. Did he have any relatives? A wife? Kids?'

'Aye, he was married to Margaret for nearly thirty years.

What did you say this is for? You're not from one of they daft TV programmes, are you? *Long Lost Bloody Families* or the like?'

'No,' Logan smiled. 'I'm just trying to find a Hamish who may have lived around Loch Assynt about fifty years ago.'

Harry snorted out loud. 'That's a bit vague, laddie – if you don't mind me saying.'

'What about a Jess or Jessica?'

'Help ma Boab! I thought you were on aboot a Hamish? Now you're asking aboot a Jess? You're no the polis, are you?'

'Do I *look* like the police?' Logan asked hopefully, puffing out his chest.

'No really, son. With that haircut?'

'Fair enough. So what about a Jess?'

Harry took another gulp of rum. 'This is my Saturday, by the way.'

'I understand,' Logan said. 'I do appreciate your time.'

'Aye, well, it's double rates.'

Harry concentrated on the skyline. 'I did ken a lassie once. Some might even say we were winching. She had the most stunning red hair and fiery temper that went with it – and could draw whistles just hanging oot the washing. Of course,' Harry said, 'I cut a bit of a dapper figure myself in those days.'

Logan listened with his pen poised. 'I'm sure.'

'The thing that she loved to do best was to take the long way round the cliffs – see way over past the end of the loch.' He pointed his bottle towards the horizon. 'She made me humph a picnic all the way up there, even in the bloody winter. Said she could see our future in the loch.'

'And was she a Jess?'

'What? No, she was Helen – why?'

'But I—?'

'Look, son, I've had enough of your nonsense. Clear off and leave me in peace. Away!'

Logan pocketed his notebook and made for the warehouse. Surely someone would know something – he just needed to find a local with a bit of history.

Cath led the way between neat gardens through a meandering alley that rose sharply away from the shoreline. Dusty slowed as the footpath narrowed to irregular stone steps. Slated-roof cottages with deep-set windows were dotted at intervals. A tabby cat sprawled across their pathway, enjoying the warmth of the sun.

'Are you okay?' Kat asked Dusty.

'Fine,' she panted. 'Is it much further?'

'Just here!' Cath declared, unlatching a painted gate. She strode up the path and, once again without knocking, opened the front door. 'Agnes, love! I've got some visitors.' Kat and Dusty followed uncertainly. A broad woman wearing a patterned housecoat and knotted headscarf appeared in the hall, feather duster in hand. 'Oh, hello, Cath, I thought I recognised your voice. Who's this, then?' She peered behind Cath.

'This young lady is – did you say Katy was your name?'

'Kat.'

'And this is …'

'Not such a young lady.' Dusty held out her hand. 'I'm Dusty.'

'*Are* you now? Just as well I've got this!' The woman waved the feathered stick with a coarse laugh. 'I'm Trish, the cleaner. Agnes is just finishing up in the bathroom – she's had a hell of a time since she switched to Bran Flakes. Come and have a seat in the front room.' She held the door open into a compact room that was crammed with a flowery settee and three armchairs. An oak coffee table filled the remaining floor space. Trish flapped the duster over the settee. 'Go on, have a seat. I'll make us some coffee.' She backed out of the room. 'Oh, you're done now, are you? I'll get in and blitz the bathroom after I've made your coffee.'

Agnes, a sprightly lady dressed in a Fair Isle jumper and black slacks entered the room in surprise. Her hair was presented in a neat bun and a pair of glasses hung on a chain round her neck. She slipped into one of the armchairs, crossing her slim legs. 'Oh, my gosh! It's unusual for me to receive any surprise visitor, let alone three. Please tell me this isn't anything to do with my son's insistence on me being referred for a mental health assessment?' She glanced at Dusty. 'Well, perhaps not. Oh! I do hope it's not because I was late settling the invoice with the gardener ... but he absolutely did *not* trim the hedge like I asked him to! He might have skimmed over it with a butter knife but he most certainly did not take off the six inches as I requested. Poor Frances next door has to sit in the shade after lunch all because of my ungainly bush and it's simply not fair on her. Especially since her budgie contracted the flu.'

'Hold your horses!' Cath said. 'I just—'

'Here we go,' Trish announced, slapping a tray on the table. 'Shall I be mother? I should say I'm pretty well qualified with *four* boys. *Four*, I said. Count 'em!' Trish slopped coffee into china cups.

'Not for me, thanks,' Kat said.

'Right – there's milk and sugar. Now I need to get a shove on. Dennis will be looking for his Scotch Broth any minute.'

'Fine, off you go,' Agnes said, waving her hand. 'By the way, I'm out of Toilet Duck.'

'Right, Agnes,' said Cath. 'Please let me introduce you to Kat and Dusty. They came into my shop this morning and I think you might be able to help them.'

'Really? Sugar?' said Agnes, stirring her coffee. 'How so?'

Kat took a deep breath and recounted the story, fiddling with the ring on her finger as she did so. Agnes listened intently while sipping her coffee. 'So,' she mused. 'I should say the first thing I can do is call all my contacts in our women's worship group. We have representation from all five of the local Church of Scotland parishes. I can also make a request to the Free Churches through Ishbel. What you're looking for is the register of any wedding around about nineteen sixty-six or just after?'

'If you could?' Kat said. 'That would be brilliant! I suppose if they had been planning to get engaged then it's most likely they'd have got married soon after—'

'I should say so,' Cath interrupted. 'In those days people got married as quickly as they could. There was none of this living-together malarkey.'

'I agree,' said Agnes. 'Shortbread?' She offered up the plate.

'Thank you,' Dusty said. 'This detective work builds an appetite.'

'We also need to consider the other possibilities,' Kat said. 'I mean, it's feasible that Hamish had planned to marry Jess but anything could have happened to him.'

'Or *her*,' Cath added. 'Maybe your ladies should be checking for deaths too?'

'Hmm.' Agnes wiped her mouth with a napkin. 'But you say you checked for any announcements in the press?'

'I did,' Kat agreed. 'There was nothing in this area and I searched from nineteen sixty.'

'So we're back to tracking down local knowledge,' Cath said. 'Agnes, you've lived here your whole life and, with your father's shop, must have known everyone in the area?'

'True. At least I used to,' Agnes nodded. 'There have been so many incomers, though – I hardly know any of the families over at Burnside. Okay, let me think.' She closed her eyes. 'Who was here in the sixties? I'd have had my two by then but still helped out in the shop. Now there *was* a Hamish Urquhart who used to come in quite regularly for his mother, who never left the house on account of her fear of seagulls.'

'And did he ever marry?'

Agnes shook her head. 'Not as far as I can remember. He did take up with a lass from Achmelvich but she was right flighty and his mother didn't approve. The girl had grand ideas to move down to Glasgow to run a guest house.'

'So perhaps he intended to propose and when his plans were scuppered he threw the ring into the loch?' Dusty suggested.

Kat frowned. 'It's a pretty fancy ring to be throwing about.'

Agnes shook her head. 'And I don't expect Hamish had that kind of money. His father died leaving them with very little. I believe he even got into bother for poaching.'

'What about a Jess?' Dusty asked.

'Yes, there have been a few Jesses I've known over the years. We can rule out Jess Mather – she's still married to old Alex although, God knows, he doesn't deserve her. You know,' Agnes leant forward, 'that miserable old sod inherited his father's boat. A grand one too – the *Merlin*. When his father passed, he never put another foot on that boat and frittered it all on whisky. Drank a boat's worth of the stuff!'

Kat jotted down JESS AND ALEX.

'There's also Jess Crearer. She was a most eccentric lass that grew up on White's Farm. Mind you ... hardly surprising. The girl came from a long line of nutters. They kept themselves to themselves and never really mixed with us in the village. She used to ride about town on a cow.'

'Oh, I remember my mother talking about her!' said Cath. 'Didn't she take it to school and give all the kids milk at playtime?'

'That's her,' Agnes nodded. 'She must be about seventy by now. I think she moved away to Aberdeen.'

'And did she ever take up with a Hamish?' Kat asked.

Agnes shrugged. 'Now that, I can't say. As far as I recall she had a bit of an altercation with her folks. But I think her brother still lives up there – it's on the road to Strathan. Might be worth a visit?'

Kat flipped back a page. 'I heard there may be a Jess McGonagle that works in the Lobster Pot?'

Cath shook her head. 'That's *Jenny* McGonagle.' Kat scored through the name and stood up to leave.

'*Hammy MacPhedran!*' cried Trish, bursting back into the room. 'Sorry, but I couldn't help overhearing your conversation. Surely Hammy's your man?'

'Of course!' Agnes nodded. 'How could I forget about *him*?'

'Well, it was a long time ago,' Trish agreed. 'Right, I'm off. Just had to throw that one in. So I'll see you next week? I might be a wee bit late as I've got to go and get my thingy checked out?'

'What *thingy*?' Agnes said. 'Your boiler?'

'No! My *down below*,' Trish whispered. 'You know – after I had that episode in the post office?'

'Oh yes. Well, see you when you get here.'

'Nice meeting you folks! Good luck.'

'So who's this Hammy?' Kat asked, turning to a new page.

Agnes leant back in the armchair. 'How could I forget young

Hammy?' she repeated. 'His family owned a whole lot of land over by Baddidarach and he was spoilt rotten. I don't expect you know Suilven Lodge? I heard it has an indoor swimming pool. Anyway, it's a bit of a cliché as Hammy was a right wild child. Tore around on a motorbike just to wind up his folks. Then he got arrested on some kind of drugs thing, which his father managed to make *disappear*. Mind you, it *was* the sixties – probably half the constabulary was on something—'

'And did he know a Jess?' Dusty interrupted.

Agnes held up a hand. 'Just when his family thought he could do no worse he took up with Phyllis Bryden.'

'Is that spelt Bry*den* or Bry*don*?' Kat asked.

'Bry*den*. She was married to Cecil – the school's headmaster. It caused such a stir in the village. Everyone knew except Cecil. Or perhaps he did know but wouldn't admit it. They didn't exactly keep it private. Hammy owned a yacht.'

'A *yacht*?' Dusty echoed.

'I told you he was spoilt. He would sail up and down the loch with Phyllis lounging on the deck drinking champagne. She told people she was helping him learn French. Must have thought we were all buttoned up the back!' Agnes tutted. 'I'm not even sure what he saw in her. It wasn't as if she was particularly pretty and she was twice his age. I actually thought he just did it to yank his father's chain. Anyway, when Cecil turned up at the lodge with a shotgun Hammy had little choice but to back off.'

'And did he?' said Kat.

'He did. But in another show of defiance he pursued every girl in the area. I heard he proposed to one lass after only a few weeks of courting. He knew his family would disapprove. And Trish is exactly right – he *is* the most likely person to buy a flashy ring.'

'And throw it away without a second thought?' Dusty suggested.

'So where is he now?' Kat asked.

Agnes shrugged. 'I've no idea. When he reached the age of twenty-one his family sent him off to France – said if he was so keen on learning the language he should go and live there.'

'Oh,' said Kat, crestfallen.

'His sister died a couple of years ago but her son, Alastair, still lives up at the lodge. Now, what's his surname again? Can you remember, Cath?'

'You mean Alastair Aitken? He'll make a bit of a catch for someone. I keep on at my Ellie to get her hooks into him.'

'Of course, he'll be well tied up with the Highland Games this weekend. *He's* into guns too. I'm sure you'll find him there.'

Cath checked her watch. 'Oopsy! Mother will think I've forgotten all about her.'

'We must be off too,' said Kat. 'We've taken up enough of your time. Thank you so much, Agnes. You've given us lots to think about.'

'And I'll get right on to my worship ladies now.'

'That's most helpful,' said Kat. 'Can I write down my number for you?'

'Will you jot it down for me too?' Cath said. 'I'd love to know how you get on. And I can ask around the village too – see if anyone remembers anyone else. Will you be staying long?'

'We'll be here until Monday,' said Kat.

'Gosh! Not long. I hope you find an answer.'

Cath, Kat and Dusty stood up to leave.

'You don't mind seeing yourselves out?' said Agnes, reaching for her phone. 'What time is it? I need to catch Nancy before she gets going with the Brasso.'

Chapter 19

Dell bumped the vacuum cleaner up the stairs and shoved open the door to Kat's bedroom. She straightened the curtains and opened the window wide. Why on earth was one of Dusty's kitchen chairs propped against that tree? Maybe Arthur was using it to stand on for some pruning?

She soon got to work on hoovering the carpet with vigour, shifting piles of books from one side of the room to the other. Kat's absence provided a rare opportunity to get the polish out – she gave the windowsill a good scoosh. It was amazing that Kat didn't suffer from asthma with all this dust around! Next she stripped the bed, pulling the duvet on to the floor. Dell lifted the pillow, revealing a flattened T-shirt underneath. She shook it out, immediately recognising the faded white and red logo. It was Jack's. A knot in her stomach tightened. Sinking on to Kat's bed she held the T-shirt to her face. Memories of Jack with his floppy hair and boundless energy came flooding back. How he used to call her 'Del Boy' and Ron 'Rodders'. And his favourite party trick was to sit Kat on his knee, hold the back of her neck and sing 'Let It Go' through gritted teeth while Kat mouthed the words. She sighed, folding his T-shirt carefully.

Chapter 20

Logan approached a gnarled man in PVC dungarees and wellington boots, a filleting knife in his hand. 'Excuse me,' he said. 'Is there someone here who knows everyone?'

'Why?' the man replied, swinging the knife round. 'You're not from Revenue and Customs, are you?'

'Certainly not.' Logan laughed nervously. 'I'm just trying to track someone down and it would make my life easier if I could speak to the boss.'

'You asked for someone who knows everyone and now you're asking for the boss. Which is it to be?' he asked, irritated.

'Er,' stammered Logan. 'S-someone who knows everyone?'

'Right,' the man nodded. 'Then you're looking for Skipper. He's out on the dock. Look for the *St Andrews*.'

'Thank you – much obliged.' Logan backed away from the knifepoint. He retraced his steps into the bright sunlight where a line of fishing boats was moored in the harbour. Gangs of gulls swirled and screeched overhead. A handful of locals haggled over fish prices as tourists in sunglasses queued for shellfish in plastic pots. A hand-painted sign on a shed announced PRAWNS AND A PINT. Logan leant over the dark water, trying to pick out the boat names. He found the *St Andrews* near the end, a rope looped through a sturdy iron ring sunk into the stone dock. A bearded man in green overalls and peaked cap was throwing lobster pots on to the deck, where a teenage lad was rearranging them in stacks.

Logan waited until the man paused. 'Are you Skipper?'

'Depends who's asking.'

'My name's Logan. I'm looking for some information.'

Skipper turned sharply, eyes blazing. 'If you're from the tax office you can fuck off!'

'No!' Logan protested, hands in the air. 'Honestly, I'm not. I'm actually a student at the University of Edinburgh.'

Skipper snorted, resuming the pot throwing.

'Anyway,' Logan continued, 'I'm looking for a Hamish and the chap inside said you know everyone round here.'

'Which Hamish?'

'Well, I'm not entirely sure,' said Logan, pushing his hair behind his ears.

'You don't have a surname?'

'No, sir.'

'Then you're on a bit of a lost cause, son. Going around Scotland asking random strangers if they know anyone called Hamish, are you? Because you've got a job for life there, pal. In fact, it wouldn't surprise me if you had a bloody government grant for it.'

'No, it's nothing like that,' said Logan. 'It's more of a local thing. I'm trying to find a Hamish who might be around age seventy to eighty, who may or may not have once been engaged to a Jess.'

'Whit in heaven's name are you havering about?'

Logan took a deep breath and blurted, 'Do you know an old man called Hamish!'

'Aye, I do, as a matter of fact. Old Hamish Gillies.'

'And do you know where I can find him?'

'Of course I do. I'm no soft in the heid!'

'Great! I mean – great that you know him, not great that you're not soft … anyway!'

'He lives over on Strom Island.' Skipper jerked a thumb towards the loch.

'And does he ever come over to Lochinver?'

'Aye, he does. Whenever he runs out of the whisky.'

'Do you think I can get out to speak to him?'

Skipper shrugged. 'If you can persuade someone daft enough to take a boat across. It's about twenty minutes in that direction.'

'Do you know anyone that can take me?'

'Listen, pal, I'm a busy man. I don't have time for this carry-on. Away and ask some other patsy.' Skipper released the rope and jumped on to his boat, leaving Logan standing on the dock. He saluted with a grin then ducked into the cabin.

Logan glanced around the harbour in search of possible assistance. Beyond the fishing vessels a handful of painted cruise boats bobbed next to a wooden kiosk advertising LOCHINVER BOATS TRIPS. A board listing times and prices for trips leant against the empty kiosk. A young couple debated the merits of the seabird versus the islands cruise while their two kids kicked stones into the lapping water. Further along, a curly-haired lad in jeans and hoodie was cleaning the bottom of a small dinghy with a bucket of soapy water. Logan ventured down the stone steps to where the dinghy was tethered. 'Hi, there,' he called. The lad peered at him through thick lenses. 'Me?'

'Yes,' said Logan. 'I'm wondering if there's anyone around here that can take me to Strom Island.'

'Why?' The lad stopped working, sponge in hand.

'I'm trying to find someone.'

'So you said – someone to take you in a boat.'

'Well, I need someone to take me to the island to find someone else.'

'So – two people?'

'Exactly!'

'Are you the Polis?'

Logan reached into his rucksack, flashing his university student card. 'I'm Logan. What's your name?'

'Craig.' He pushed his glasses up the bridge of his nose.

'Nice to meet you, Craig. I see you've got a cracking wee boat there.'

'It's mine.'

'Splendid! And can you take me across to Strom Island?'

'Can I or will I?'

Logan gave what he hoped was a winning smile. 'You'd be doing me a massive favour, Craig. I really need to speak to Hamish Gillies.'

Craig frowned. 'What's he done now? Has he got into trouble again? I heard he fell into a fight with Robbie. Are you one of those bounty hunters? I've seen them on TV – they chase people all over the country and sometimes there's a shoot-out.'

'It's actually more for research purposes. So will you take me?'

'I normally charge people.'

Logan pulled out his notebook and pen. 'I'll tell you what, Craig. I'm going to take a note of your name and address and I'm going to recommend that you get a special mention in my report.'

'Cool,' Craig grinned. 'It's Craig Cormack and I live with my mum at twelve Main Street – above the coffee shop. It always smells nice in our flat. Not that I drink coffee – I don't really like the taste. I prefer Coke.'

'Fantastic,' said Logan. 'You've been most helpful with my

enquiries. Shall I …' He took a step towards the bobbing boat.

'Here,' said Craig, passing the bucket. 'Shove that up there.'

Logan left the bucket on the dock and stepped into the rubber dinghy, which rocked with alarming instability.

'I've got a girlfriend,' Craig announced, unknotting the rope.

'Good for you.' Logan gave a thumbs up.

'I took her out last night for a wee trip down to the castle but she was sick. Threw up all over my boat.'

'Right,' said Logan, examining his boots.

Craig pressed a button on the outboard motor and shifted the throttle. The engine chugged to life as he pushed the tiller away and the dinghy nosed out of the harbour. Logan gripped the handles either side as the light craft bounced across the marina. Craig grinned, the wind whipping through his curls.

As they neared, the island emerged as scrubby terrain dotted with deformed pine trees, warped by harsh winters. Logan could make out a whitewashed croft wedged on the top of a low rise. As a cloud flitted by the sun a dark shadow was cast over the rock. Craig steered towards an inlet where a shabby rowing boat languished alongside a crumbling jetty.

'This is the part where two people arrive and only one leaves the island,' Logan joked.

'Are you staying?'

'I hope not! What's this Hamish like, anyway?'

'Mad.'

'Mentally-ill mad or psycho-mad?'

Craig shrugged, fastening his dinghy to the jetty. 'He lives on his own island – he can do whatever he likes.' They clambered on to the jetty and headed in the direction of the house. Waist-high gorse bushes snagged at their clothes as they pushed through the overgrown path. From nowhere a bull of a man with a wild, grey beard and eye patch burst through the undergrowth. '*Ginger!*' he bellowed, stumbling past. He wore a holey black jumper and army trousers tucked into turned-down galoshes.

'Hey, Hamish!' Craig shouted to his retreating back. Hamish whirled round, pinning his one eye on the lads. 'Jeeso! Where did you two spring from? Never mind, help me find Ginger.'

'Who's Ginger?' Craig asked as they tried to keep up with Hamish's bumbling stride. A thorny branch flicked back into Craig's face. '*Aya!*' he yelped.

'Ginger – my goat. She chewed through her rope *again*. I'll give her such a kicking when I catch her.'

On cue a mournful bleat could be heard coming from a clump of ferns. Hamish pushed the leafy greenery to one side to reveal a skinny off-white goat pulling at the roots with square teeth. She jumped in surprise, springing up from four hooves. 'No, you don't!' Hamish roared, grabbing at her with clumsy hands. She bleated in protest, kicking him swiftly in the groin. Hamish dropped to his knees like a felled oak. He clutched at his crotch. 'My nuts!' he wailed. 'Get that bloody pest before I kill her.' Craig and Logan left Hamish rolling in the undergrowth as they set off after Ginger. Having been offered a reprieve, the goat skipped away in delight, vaulting through the ferns with the agility of a Russian gymnast.

Logan jogged around the small island, taking high steps over the terrain. He finally caught up with Craig, who was crouched on the path. Craig put a finger to his lips and indicated for Logan to stay low. The sound of satisfied munching could be heard. Craig motioned for Logan to keep still while he planned to make a wide circuit of the absconder. A few minutes passed as Craig tiptoed behind the animal, which chewed on in blissful ignorance. Suddenly Craig yelled '*Yar!*' and surged forward, arms outstretched. Ginger leapt in the air, dropping a turd in fright. She landed awkwardly as Craig pounded towards her. She shot forward, darting through Logan's widespread legs. '*What?*' Craig gasped in disbelief. 'Pay attention, mate!' They both set off in pursuit of Ginger as she zigzagged towards the jetty. She trotted over the wooden slats before coming to a halt at the end. The loch's water slapped at the timber structure.

'*Gotcha!*' Craig cried, grabbing at Ginger with both arms. He carried her back over the jetty.

'Baa,' Ginger protested, nibbling at his hair.

Logan arrived, panting heavily. 'Thank God for that! I don't think I could do another lap of this island.'

They walked back to where Hamish was still lolling on the ground, massaging his manhood. He glared at Ginger with one eye. 'No supper for you tonight,' he growled.

Logan waited until Hamish had scrambled to his feet. He held out a hand. 'Good morning, sir – my name's Logan.'

'Is it now?' Hamish studied him with distaste.

'He's a kind of detective,' Craig added. Logan didn't contradict him.

'You can tie her up next to her wee hoose,' Hamish instructed Craig as he entered his own property. They followed him into the barren kitchen where a Formica table was flanked by two wooden chairs, one leaning at an angle. Food-encrusted saucepans lay abandoned on the cooker. An antiquated fridge with a rusty handle hummed in the corner. The room reeked of cooked fish. Hamish collapsed on to one of the seats, folding his arms on the table. He kicked out a chair – which Logan took as a sign of acceptance – while Craig reclined awkwardly against the Belfast sink. A frustrated bluebottle buzzed against the dirty window.

'Tea?' Hamish barked.

'Yes, please,' said Logan.

'I'm asking you to make tea, laddie.'

'Right,' Logan said, jumping to his feet. 'Of course.'

Craig watched in silence as Logan filled the stained kettle and switched it on. A single cracked mug lay on the draining board. Logan found a shop-brand box of teabags and popped one into the mug. He pulled on the fridge lever but it was rusted shut. A half-empty bottle of milk sat in the sink. He daren't check the sell-by date. With the tea made, Logan resumed his seat.

'You two not joining me?' Hamish stirred in two heaped spoons of sugar from a bag on the table.

'I'm fine,' said Logan. 'Just had breakfast.'

'Humph. I never invited you to my island. You've no business here.'

Logan retrieved his notebook and pen. 'I'm sorry, I won't keep you long. Mr Hamish Gillies is it? I just have a few questions for you.'

'*He* started it,' said Hamish with a loud slurp.

'Who?'

'Robbie.'

'Started what?'

'He said I stank like a cow in labour. So I said, "You're not exactly as fragrant as a bunch of flowers!". Then he thumped me. Right here – in my good eye.'

'Oh, I haven't come here to ask about that.'

'Why not, man? I was blinded for the rest of the night. Had to row back here hoping the moon would direct me. Write that in yer wee book.'

'Well, what I really wanted to ask you about was whether you ever knew a girl named Jess or Jessica?'

'*Who?*'

'A Jess or Jessica.'

'Which Jessica?'

'That's the problem – I don't know her second name.'

'And you think *I* do? Hell's bells, man! What do they teach you polis these days?'

'Perhaps if we can go back to the sixties?'

'My sixties? Laddie, that was twenty years ago. I cannae tell you what I did last week, never mind twenty years ago. Except what happened with Robbie – I remember *that* alright!'

'Actually, I meant the *nineteen sixties,*' Logan began. 'Can we go back to the nineteen sixties?'

'Eh? Mebbe – I can't really say, son. But if they can put a man on the moon, I've no doubt they can go back in time.'

Craig stifled a giggle. Logan tried a more direct approach. 'Do you mind me asking if you ever got engaged? Did you ever ask anyone to marry you?'

'Marriage? Oh aye! I asked plenty of lassies but they all turned me down. Well, all except one.'

'Who was that?' Logan asked eagerly.

'Och, how am I supposed to remember? It was years ago. I was a lad no' much older than you. It was when I was oot on the boats.'

'Did you buy her a ring?'

'Who?'

Logan took a deep breath. 'The girl you wanted to marry. Did you buy her an engagement ring?'

'D'yer think I'm made of money? Is *that* why you've come out here?' Hamish suddenly pushed himself up from the table. He snatched a nearby tin opener and wielded it in Logan's face. 'If you've come to rob an old man, you've come to the wrong place.'

Logan jumped up, knocking his chair to the floor. Craig backed towards the door, his hands raised in surrender. Hamish uttered a snarling sound, making an arc with the tin opener. 'I think it's time you two wankers got off my island, don't you?' He glared with one eye. 'And who taught you to make a cup of tea that tastes like goat's piss?'

'I'm sorry, I didn't mean to upset you.'

'I'm not upset,' Hamish growled. 'You'd *know* if I was upset. You'd be having to change your breeks in Lochinver. Now be off!'

The two scrabbled for the door as Hamish chased them towards the jetty. 'Thanks for that, mate,' Craig muttered as he fired up his dinghy. 'I'll be next on the list when he gets ashore.'

'Sorry,' said Logan. He watched over his shoulder for signs of Hamish following them into the loch. 'I guess that's one more Hamish off my list.'

Chapter 21

Kat set off at a pace down the steep incline towards the harbour. The air felt unseasonably warm for September as she carried her jacket in one hand.

'Hold up,' Dusty said, panting. 'What's your hurry?'

'What are we doing?' Kat asked, coming to an abrupt halt. She waved her arms in despair. 'This is crazy! We're never going to find Hamish or Jess. They could be anywhere in the world by now. Maybe they're not even alive any more. We've got no chance!'

'But we have to try,' Dusty said, wringing her hands.

'Why?'

'Well, I ...'

'What?'

'I feel I need to do it for Edwin. He must have hung on to the ring with the intention of returning it.'

'But he didn't. And now *we're* lumbered with it.'

'He probably didn't know where to start.'

'So how has *his* problem become *my* problem?' Kat shook her head. In her pocket her hand gripped the little cow so tightly the horns almost pierced her skin. 'I can't believe I let all of you talk me into doing this trip. It's such a waste of time.'

'Do you think *I'm* a waste of time?' Dusty accused. 'Because I'm old and useless?'

'I didn't mean that. Anyway, you're not useless.'

'But I *am* old?'

'Hey! I can't change the maths.'

Dusty put an arm round Kat's shoulders. 'I know this isn't how you wanted to spend your weekend – with a fuddy-duddy like me. But I *do* appreciate what you're doing. And Edwin would have given you a big hug.'

Kat kicked at the dirt on the pavement. 'It's just going to be harder than I thought – I mean, what did we expect? That the first person we asked would say, "Oh yes – Hamish and Jess live in that house over there. I'm sure they'll be so chuffed you bothered to return their ring!"'

'I know life's not like that but we need to try. And we at least have a few more names to check.'

'I suppose.' Kat began walking towards the main street. 'Come on – let's go and find Logan. See if he's had better luck than us.'

Kat nudged open the door to the Sailing Boat – a brightly painted café overlooking the harbour. They were greeted with the aroma of ground coffee and the hiss of steamed milk. Only two tables were occupied, both by single customers who each nurtured a hot mug. A chalkboard advertised SOUP OF THE DAY – TOMATO AND BASIL and WRAP OF THE DAY – TUNA CRUNCH. Kat chose a seat by the window so she could keep an eye out for Logan while Dusty wove through the tables to the Ladies.

'That's better,' said Dusty, removing her coat. 'I've drunk so much coffee this morning I'll be what you youngsters call *buzzing*.'

'I wouldn't know. I only drink herbal tea.'

'Oh, I like my coffee – it's the only drug I take these days. Apart from Night Nurse, of course.'

'Here he is,' said Kat as Logan entered the café. 'Inspector Poirot.'

Logan collapsed on to a chair and whipped off his jacket. He swept his untamed hair back with both hands. 'Boy, are you two a sight for sore eyes.'

'Ah, that's nice,' said Dusty, patting his hand. 'Oh – you're freezing!'

'How come?' asked Kat.

'There are some right loons in this place. Proper nutters. Anyway, I'm starving – shall we order some food?'

The three looked expectantly at the spotty lad perched at the till, who announced, 'You need to order at the counter.'

'Fine,' Kat muttered. 'What are you having?'

'I'll have the soup of the day, please,' said Dusty, 'and a flat white. Might as well keep on my high.'

'Maybe I'll just have a coffee and a ...' Logan rummaged in his pocket, pulling out a fiver. 'A buttered roll.'

'Have something more substantial than that,' Dusty chided. She handed Kat a twenty-pound note. 'My treat.'

'Thanks, Dusty,' Logan grinned. 'In that case – pie and beans for me.'

Kat returned to find Logan with his notebook open. 'What've you found out?' he asked. 'I've got three Hamishes. One died at sea – but was married to a Margaret. One had a glass eye and is who knows where ... and one is a completely mad Hamish who lives on a deserted island out in that loch. That's where I've been most of the morning.'

Kat nodded, opening her book. 'We've got a Jess Watt who has died, but she was married to a Jock. Another Jess – still married but to an Alex. A Jess Crearer who was a bit eccentric and now, we think, lives in Aberdeen but we can possibly ask her brother.'

'How about any Hamishes?'

'So, there's a Hamish who shot a bank teller and, as far as we know, is still in prison.'

'I told you they were all loons!'

'And there was a young Hamish who went off with a local girl but had no money for a fancy ring – so it seems unlikely—'

'But,' Dusty interrupted excitedly, 'maybe a possible Hamish known as Hammy.'

'Hammy?' Logan mused. 'I never thought to ask about a Hammy.'

'No one asked for ham,' the server grumbled, unloading plates from a tray. 'You asked for two soups and a pie.'

'That's right,' said Kat.

'I can't change orders once you've asked for stuff or it comes out my wages. Cutlery's over there.'

'Is that my chamomile tea?' Kat asked.

'We didn't have any so I just gave you a green one.'

Logan grabbed a fork and scooped beans into his mouth. 'So tell me about your lead.'

'By all accounts this Hammy was a right character,' Dusty replied. 'A bit of a playboy – from a family with land and plenty of money. He was still a teenager when he had an affair with the headmaster's wife – and when *he* found out he came at Hammy with a shotgun. Nice soup, by the way – with just a hint of basil.'

'When he was warned off the headmaster's wife he apparently went around pursuing all the girls in the area until he got packed off to France,' Kat added.

'And he had loads of dosh for a flashy ring and would have thought nothing of throwing it into a loch if things didn't go his way.'

Logan pondered over their words. 'That does sound promising. So where is this Hammy now?'

'There's the rub,' Kat said. 'We've no idea. But,' she checked her notes, 'although his sister died, seemingly her son still lives in the same family home.'

'So we could ask him?'

'Precisely.'

'Great work, team! We're making progress.'

Dusty gave Kat a sideways look. 'I think we've made a start but we've got other people helping too.'

'Oh yes?'

'A nice lady called Cath, who owns the craft shop, is asking around the village. And her contact, Agnes, has links with all the parishes. She's going to call and ask them to check their church records.'

'Cool.' Logan nodded. 'You ladies are on it! So,' he pushed his plate to one side, 'what's the plan of attack for this afternoon?'

'We haven't yet been to the community centre where Gregor thought we could ask about a possible Jessie there. Then we've got two that we need to drive to – Suilven Lodge to ask about Hammy, and White's Farm to find out about Jess that moved to Aberdeen.'

'But remember Agnes said Hammy's nephew would most likely be at the Highland Games this weekend?'

'There's not much wrong with your memory is there?' Kat asked.

Dusty smiled. 'I am doing well, aren't I? I don't normally even know what day of the week it is.'

'Are the places near each other?' said Logan.

'I can check on Google Maps. I'll just ask about the Wi-Fi.'

She approached the counter. 'Excuse me – can you tell me

the Wi-Fi code?' The server, engrossed with his phone, pointed silently to a handwritten note next to the till. Kat returned to the table. 'Hmm.' She frowned. 'So it looks like the two places are actually in opposite directions. Baddidarach is north of here but Strathan is to the south. I don't know that we'll have time to do both today.'

Logan glanced at his watch. 'Why don't we all check out the community centre then maybe we can try the one that's more likely to be at home?'

'That would be White's Farm. I wonder where the Highland Games are?'

Kat approached the server once again. 'Really?' he demanded. 'What now?'

'We were wondering where the Highland Games are held?'

'Do I *look* like a tourist information office?'

'Sorry, it's just that we're trying to locate a man who—'

The server held up his hand. 'Listen – I don't need your whole life story. The games are held down at Culag Park – take the road towards Inverkirkaig. I'm sure not even you can miss it. Is that it? Are we done?' He turned back to his phone.

'Thanks,' Kat muttered.

The three put on their coats and headed out of the café.

Chapter 22

Dell snapped the tongs in anticipation as she flipped the bacon. A rasher split and she popped a sliver of unsmoked into her mouth. She buttered four rolls – generous with the ketchup on to two and brown sauce on the others.

'Ron!' she shouted from the foot of the stairs. '*Ron!* Lunchtime.'

Dell returned to the kitchen, serving the bacon rolls on plates. She placed a neatly folded paper napkin either side of the table and poured freshly squeezed orange juice.

'Ho, ho!' said Ron, rubbing his hands in glee. 'It's been a while since this kitchen has smelt bacon.' He placed his peaked cap on the table and unbuttoned the dark grey military jacket, which he hooked over the back of his chair.

'Mustn't get any sauce on this uniform. Mo will kill me.'

As Dell bit into her roll, brown sauce squirted in a fountain across the table.

'*Dell!* Watch it,' Ron warned.

'Sorry, love, I'm starving.'

'So do you think you can take it in a wee bit this afternoon? We've got the dress rehearsal this evening and Mo is so pernickety. She sent Burt home last week just because his boots weren't polished enough. She said the Nazis would have shot him rather than let him turn out with scuffed footwear.'

'Course! But straight after lunch do you mind nipping round to Dusty's? I'm sure I spotted Arthur going in just now and I want you to catch him before he heads off again.'

'What? Why me?'

'You can ask him? Man to man, like.'

Ron wiped his mouth. 'Ask him what? Whether he gets a kick out of parading around in his mother-in-law's ballgown?'

'I don't know! But I told Kat we'd do a bit of rooting about to see what he's up to.'

'I hardly know the man,' Ron protested.

'Neither do I,' said Dell. 'I've only ever really spoken to Cherie and I always find her a bit up her own arse.'

'How do you mean?'

'It's just a feeling. I remember one year when you were putting up the Christmas lights outside and she made some comment about how she thought that garden decorations really lowered the tone of the neighbourhood. And another time when I took some scones round to Dusty's I offered her one and she told me that she never accepts other people's home-baking as she couldn't be confident of their hygiene regulations.'

'Really?'

Dell licked her finger and rubbed at the sauce mark. 'Yes, proper snooty she was.'

'Nice lunch, love.'

'Thanks. So off you go – have a quick word with Arthur.'

'What about a cup of tea?'

'I'll put the kettle on. Go on – I need to hang the washing out anyway. It's a gorgeous afternoon.'

Ron grumbled as he slipped on his uniform jacket and headed next door. Dell pulled the washing from the machine and carried the laundry basket into the garden. She gave Ron's pyjama bottoms a shake and pegged them on the line.

Ron pressed the doorbell. Nothing. He held his finger on for ten seconds before releasing it. The door sprang open and Arthur's flushed face appeared. 'What is it?' he demanded, scowling at Ron's uniform. 'I didn't realise Edinburgh Council had ramped up their traffic wardens' jurisdiction!'

'My apologies,' said Ron, adjusting his gun holster. 'I've got a rehearsal this evening.'

'What for? A firing squad?'

'Look, I'm Ron from next door. Dell's husband.'

'Oh, right. Dell.' Arthur kept the door half closed.

'I wondered whether I could come in for a minute?'

Arthur pursed his lips. 'Now's not really a good time. I'm … er, I'm—'

'It won't take long,' Ron insisted, placing a hand against the door and applying pressure.

Arthur relented, taking a step backwards. He led Ron into Dusty's lounge, where a wall-mounted clock marked the seconds with a resolute knocking.

'Have a seat,' said Arthur, without any grace.

Ron inspected the floral settee and doughy armchairs before selecting a more upright wingback chair. The room had an old-fashioned feel of comfort with its patterned wallpaper and paintings depicting Scottish lochs and castles. A decanter of whisky sat on a sideboard with four upturned crystal tumblers.

'Edwin always did like his wee nip of whisky,' Ron commented.

'You want one?' Arthur asked stiffly as he leant against the ornate mantelpiece, oblivious to the ceramic urn. He tried for casual but his face portrayed a patient undergoing a prostate examination.

'No, thanks – far too early for me. Anyway, I'm driving later.'

'Right. So?'

Ron sorely wished he had rehearsed what he was going to say. It was all very well for Dell to say 'just pop over' but he couldn't think of any plausible excuse for this intrusion. 'It's about Dusty …' he began.

'I assumed it would be. What's she done now? I hope she hasn't bothered you with her tiresome forgetfulness. It's really becoming quite a worry for Cherie and I – which is why we have offered up our home to her.'

'No, it's nothing like that. Although Kat did kindly find where she'd misplaced her toaster.'

'You see – that's what we're concerned about. She might leave a saucepan on the cooker and it could burn the whole house down.' Arthur gave a dramatic wave of his arms.

'Well, she certainly hasn't been herself these last few weeks.'

'The sooner we can get the house on the market the better. In fact the estate agent should be sending round a photographer this weekend.'

'I see … So, I'm just wondering whether … whether …'

'Whether *what*, man? Look, I'm really busy here and I can do without this distraction.'

'Busy doing …?'

'Well,' Arthur blustered. 'I'm helping Dusty get packed for the move, obviously.'

Ron made a deliberate show of scanning the room. 'Yes, I can see you're up to your eyes.'

'Actually, I've made a start upstairs, if you must know. Bloody hell – you're really taking this Gestapo role seriously!'

'Ha ha,' said Ron, nodding. 'So, when you say making a start, would that be packing up Dusty's clothes?'

'What on earth are you getting at?'

Ron squirmed in the armchair. 'I was just meaning whether you were perhaps sorting out her dresses? Maybe getting rid of any she doesn't want?'

'I think that's entirely my mother-in-law's business what she does with her outfits, don't you? If you're angling for some of her cast-offs I think you've got a bit of a cheek!'

'*Me* wearing her cast-offs – what about *you*?'

'Right, I've had enough of this nonsense! I think it's time you left before I—' A jangling ringtone sounded from Arthur's pocket. He checked the screen before darting out of the room. Ron followed but Arthur dodged through the kitchen and shot through the back door.

Dell untangled one of her lacy black bras that had ensnared Ron's chinos. She was reaching down into the peg bag when she heard Dusty's back door fly open.

'*Look,*' she heard Arthur growl. 'I told you to stop phoning me! You *know* why. I can't risk Cherie overhearing this conversation.'

Dell held her breath, not daring to move on the other side of the fence. She heard Arthur take a few steps into the garden.

'Fine,' he muttered. 'If you really need to meet, then we'll meet. *Tonight?* That's a bit short notice. You know I can't give you what you want. Oh, alright, if you insist – let's meet this evening. I don't want anyone to see us. Do you know Calton Road – just at the back of Waverley? What time? *Ten o'clock?* That's late, isn't it? Right, see you then. And in the meantime – leave me alone!'

Arthur slammed the back door shut as Dell straightened up. 'Oh my!' she exclaimed.

At the sound of Arthur's return Ron bolted down the stairs. He reached the bottom step, breathless, as Arthur appeared in the hall.

'Well, I better be off,' Ron panted. 'Let you get on with the packing.' He jogged out of Dusty's house and back into his own. He entered the kitchen, slumping on to a chair just as Dell burst in.

'I think Arthur *is* having an affair!' she gasped.

'What are you on about? Where's this come from?'

'I just heard him on the phone. He was furious that she'd rung him – said he didn't want Cherie to find out. But the best bit is – I know where and when he's meeting her tonight! They're having a tryst at the back of the station.'

'Dell! We can't go interfering with whatever's going on between them.'

'I'm not talking about interfering. I just thought we ought to know what he's up to. We said we'd find out for Kat. So did *you* discover anything of interest?'

Ron shook his head. 'I don't know what he's up to but he's skulking around next door, saying he's helping Dusty get packed. The only thing I did find that's a bit odd, is that he had torn the month of September off the calendar. We're only halfway through the month, aren't we?'

'No wonder Dusty's getting her weeks muddled if he's deliberately confusing her.'

'I don't know about that but when he took the phone call I hurried upstairs and there's not a single packing crate to be seen. Not even a drawer open or cupboard emptied.'

'You see? I think we both know why he's skulking! He's hiding out from Cherie – meeting his fancy woman. And poor Cherie struggling around on crutches as well.'

'I thought you said she was "up her own arse"?'

'No one likes to see someone kicked when they're down.'

'Humph. So what will you tell Kat?'

'Perhaps you're right. Maybe we better not blow the whistle until we've laid eyes on this woman. We could gather some evidence.'

'Who for?'

'You never know! What if there's a dispute and they separate and Cherie is left homeless. Where would that leave Dusty then?'

'Calm down, woman. You're getting ahead of yourself. Let's just try to establish the facts first.'

'So shall we follow them to their secret rendezvous tonight?'

'Tonight?' Ron puffed out his cheeks. 'But I've got my dress rehearsal tonight. And you know I need to be there until the bitter end. Mo won't be chuffed if the von Trapps escape Austria and I'm not there to be furious. It's hardly a showstopper if they pull off a daring getaway and no one gives a—'

'Tea?'

'Oh, that'd be grand.'

'Don't worry, I'll pick you up from rehearsals.'

'I can see I'm not going to win this one.'

'Not a chance.'

Chapter 23

'Where do you suppose we'll find the community centre?' Dusty asked.

'Follow me,' said Logan, holding up his hand. 'I'm sure I saw a sign to it on my way from the harbour.'

'It's such a beautiful day,' said Dusty. 'I've hardly been out at all this summer, except for pottering in the garden.'

'Why's that, then?' Logan asked, setting off along the narrow pavement.

'Oh well, my daughter says I shouldn't go far in case I get lost or something.'

'And is that likely?'

Dusty shrugged. 'They seem to think I'm a bit of a liability. I *do* keep misplacing things. And what's worrying is, when I find them again, I've no recollection of putting them there.'

'You give the impression of doing fine to me,' said Logan, hand on heart. 'In my not-quite-qualified opinion.'

'Ah, but you're keeping me right.'

'So if we ran off now and left you alone, you'd what? End up in the loch?'

'Who knows?' Dusty laughed. 'I might find myself at sea aboard a fishing boat!'

'There it is,' Kat said. 'Lochside Community Centre. Oh, it looks like something's on.'

They approached the single-storey rectangular building that occupied a corner of the street. A paved path divided a neat front lawn. The same tabby cat they'd seen earlier now lounged on the grass, swatting at a bee. A small queue jostled towards the front door. Dusty tapped an elderly lady on the back. 'Excuse me, is there something on this afternoon?'

The pensioner turned and peered at them through smeary glasses. 'Aye, it's the bingo, of course! It's on every Saturday.'

'And would you know if there's anyone called Jessie that works here?' Kat asked.

'You mean Jessie Paterson? Aye, she runs the bingo.'

'That's smashing!' Dusty smiled. 'Thank you.'

The queue shuffled forward. A red-faced woman, her fringe stuck to her forehead, guarded the entrance. She was dressed as a pineapple and, from a hole cut in the side, stuck out a sweaty hand. 'One book or two?' she asked Kat.

'Sorry?'

'*One* book or two? One book costs fifty pence; two cost a pound.'

'Well, they would, wouldn't they?'

'I'm not getting you?' The Pineapple squinted beyond the three visitors to the agitated regulars. 'Look, are you coming in or not? Poor Peggy's trying to get past and her legs'll not hold her up much longer.'

'We wanted to speak to Jessie Paterson,' Kat said in a rush.

'Then you'll need to pay.' She shook the bucket hooked over the other arm. 'She can't talk to you until the bingo's finished. Is it about the blocked sink? I didn't think the council worked on a Saturday.'

'No, we're—'

'Get a move on!' someone shouted from behind.

'We'd better just pay it,' Logan said. 'Here, I've got fifty pence.'

The Pineapple accepted the coin with a grunt, handing over a book of bingo cards.

'We only do Full House on a Saturday,' she informed Dusty. 'If you come on a Tuesday we count lines as well.'

'I'll bear that in mind,' said Dusty, scurrying in.

The community centre consisted of a reception area, with double doors propped open into a spacious wooden hall, where trestle tables had been placed in rows. A couple of the tables were already taken by chatting women. A young girl sat on her own, pushing a pram back and forth with one hand.

'You should be right at home here, Logan,' Kat commented.

'I'm going to study this occasion for research purposes.'

'In case there's ever a murder in a bingo hall?'

'It could happen!'

'Especially if anyone else takes me for a council employee,' said Kat.

'But you are, dear, aren't you?' Dusty said.

'Yes, but I didn't think it was that obvious,' Kat muttered.

'Shall we sit here?' Dusty suggested, choosing an unoccupied table.

The minute they sat down, two misshapen women in matching grey tracksuits and pudding-bowl haircuts made their move.

'I'm Vicky,' said the first, winking at Logan.

'And I'm Velma.'

'We're sisters,' they said in unison.

'That's nice.' Dusty smiled at them both as Logan selected a chair furthest away.

'Where are you lot from, then?' Vicky asked. 'Have you been to the Highland Games? We get a lot of visitors this time of the year. Normally it chucks it with rain but it's been top notch weather today.'

'Did you get tired of standing? I do,' Velma added. 'Goes right for my back.'

'We've come up from Edinburgh,' said Dusty.

'Oh, really? Fancy that! For the week? Taking your grandchildren on a wee holiday? The sun will do them good. They just sit inside playing those video games all day. I mean – she's right peaky, isn't she?' Vicky pinched Kat's cheek.

'We're neighbours, actually,' Dusty replied.

'*Are* you now?' The sisters scrutinised the threesome as though they were the most fascinating people they'd ever met.

'We would never go to the bingo with our neighbour, would we, Velma?'

'No, we absolutely would not!' Velma folded her arms with indignation. 'Our neighbour stinks to high heaven. He never has a bath! Says when he was on a submarine they never bathed for six months at a time. *And* he has a dog.'

'*Smells* like a dog.' Vicky sniffed.

'So, can I ask a silly question?' Logan interrupted. The ladies swung their heads round and fixed him with a grin. 'Yes, of course!'

'What's with the lady dressed as a pineapple?'

'Oh, that's just Ruth having a bit of fun,' said Vicky, squeezing Logan's arm. 'It's Fruit Bingo this month. *Yawn!*'

'Yes, we prefer December, don't we, Vicky?'

'We do – Chocolate Bingo all month long!'

The PA system crackled into life. 'Settle down, ladies!' A stout woman wearing slacks and a blazer was sitting behind a battered bingo machine.

'And gent!' Velma shouted.

The woman on the stage searched the faces with a frown. 'Oh yes! Well, good afternoon ladies and gent. Now this afternoon's bingo has been kindly sponsored by Bargain Buster on Main Street.'

'That's Jessie,' Vicky whispered. 'You better get ready because she won't wait for you.'

'Eyes down for a Full House.' The machine whirred and a ball popped up into Jessie's hand. 'Garden Gate – number eight.' A pause. 'Four and seven – forty-seven. Staying Alive – eighty-five.'

Kat frantically scanned her cards, scribbling off the numbers with a biro.

'Here,' Vicky pushed a fluorescent marker across the table. 'It's quicker just to dab it with this.'

'Kelly's Eye—'

'Number one!' the crowd retorted.

'Duck and dive – twenty-five.'

'Did she say thirty-seven?' Dusty asked.

'*Forty*-seven,' Kat hissed.

'Knock at the door – number four.'

'What came after forty-seven?' said Dusty in despair. 'I can't keep up.'

'You pair'll be getting chucked out soon,' Vicky whispered.

'Torquay in Devon – eighty-seven. Quiet, please, you lot.'

'Quiet, please?' Dusty echoed. 'What's that? All the threes? Thirty-three?'

'Did you say thirty-three?' a voice asked.

Jessie tutted. 'Not thirty-three. Eighty-seven, I said.'

'Eighty-seven? We've already had that!'

'*Please, now* – everyone settle down,' Jessie warned. 'I don't want to declare a null game like we had on Tuesday.'

'Cindy McCabe's phone went off in the middle of a game,' said Velma. 'There was chaos. Her ring tone is Shakira's "Hips Don't Lie".'

'Final warning!' Jessie said in a firm voice. 'Man at the door – fifty-four.'

'I should be so lucky!' Vicky snorted.

'Bingo!'

All heads turned to the back of the room where a frail lady bent double held up her card.

'She can't have bingo yet, the daft sod,' Vicky announced in a loud voice.

'It's Miss Tranter,' Velma added.

'It's *Saturday*, Evelyn!' Jessie called from the stage. 'We don't do lines on a Saturday.'

'Oh, is it?' Miss Tranter mumbled. 'Saturday, you say?'

'Give her a prize!' Vicky shouted.

'Prize! Prize! Prize!' the crowd chorused. Jessie shrugged, nodding her head to the Pineapple, who leapt off the stage. She awarded Miss Tranter a tin of peaches. 'For me? How lovely.'

'What'd she get?' Vicky asked, peering over her shoulder.

'Peaches,' Velma replied.

'Nice. You can never have too many peaches.'

'Okay, let's get started again. Eyes down for a Full House.'

A hand shot up. '*Are* we playing for a Full House only—'

'That's what I said, isn't it?'

'Yes, but she got a prize for a line.'

'Mrs Brown, you know the rules better than anyone. I don't expect this type of attitude from a fellow bridge player. Now, young and keen – fifteen.'

'I give up!' Dusty said, throwing down her pen in defeat.

'Can I have your book, then?' Vicky asked, snatching at the card.

'Help yourself.'

'What numbers are you waiting for?' Dusty whispered to Kat.

'Sixteen and thirty-one.'

'Get up and run – thirty-one.'

Dusty dug her nails into Kat's arm. 'You only need one more number!'

'And she'll be the proud owner of a tin of fruit cocktail,' Logan muttered.

'Danny La Rue – fifty-two.'

'House!' A young girl jumped up from her table, waving her card in the air.

'Not that Linda again,' Vicky grumbled. 'She wins every flipping week.'

The Pineapple once again stepped down from the stage, presenting the winner with a hamper of fruit. Several of the bingo players stood up and wandered over to a trolley, where a helper wearing a tabard poured from an oversized teapot.

'Tea break,' Velma advised, taking a packet of cigarettes out of her pocket.

'Here's our chance,' said Kat, hurrying over to the stage. Dusty and Logan followed dutifully. Jessie was indicating tea with one sugar to someone in the queue.

'I'm sorry to bother you,' said Kat, stepping up on to the stage with Dusty in tow. Jessie inspected the three with a frown. She gripped the lapels of her blazer.

'Well, you're no bother – *yet*. But if you so much as question my judgement over the rules of bingo I'll be obliged to deploy my Ruth.'

'I've never been apprehended by a pineapple before,' Logan remarked.

'She has surprisingly sharp spikes,' Jessie declared. 'Thanks.' She gratefully accepted a mug of tea.

'This isn't about the bingo,' said Kat. 'We're trying to track down anyone in this area called Jessie or Hamish, who may have been in a relationship during the nineteen sixties – particularly around nineteen sixty-six.'

'Hamish?' Jessie said, startled. 'What about Hamish?'

'You knew a Hamish?' Kat asked with excitement.

'I should say so! He was bloody gorgeous. Hang on a mo, though – *which* Hamish are you talking about?'

'We don't really know,' answered Kat truthfully. 'But can we be really cheeky and ask if you dated a Hamish?'

'How do you know about that?' said Jessie with suspicion. 'It was more than fifty years ago!'

'Oh my goodness!' Dusty cried. 'We've found our Jess and Hamish.'

'What's this all about?' said Jessie, biting into a Rich Tea biscuit. 'Honestly, you'd think they could keep a biscuit from going stale from one week to the next.'

Kat waved her hand in Jessie's face. 'Is this your engagement ring? Were you ever engaged to Hamish?'

'Engaged? You've lost me, lass – what's this all about?'

Dusty stepped forward. 'I was clearing out my attic when I came across this ring. My husband seemingly pulled it out of Loch Assynt when we were on our honeymoon in nineteen sixty-six. Now, I've no idea why he hung on to it for all these years, but we're looking to return it to its rightful owner.'

Jessie examined the ring in detail. 'I've never seen it before in my life. It's a cracker, though. What's it got to do with me? Ruth. *Ruth!* Stop that child swinging from the emergency exit bar.'

'Well,' Kat persevered, slipping the ring off her finger. 'There's an inscription inside that says, "Marry me, Jess? Love Hamish".'

Jessie looked blankly from one face to the next. 'And you think?'

'We think you're Jessie!' said Kat with a grin.

'No, it can't be.' Jessie shook her head. She turned pale. 'It can't have been *my* Hamish.'

'Why not?'

Jessie continued to shake her head. 'Because my Hamish was *already* married. Sad to say but true.'

'Oh,' said Kat, deflated.

'Can you tell us a bit about the circumstances around your relationship?' Logan asked in earnest, ready with his biro and pad.

'This isn't really the place for it,' Jessie sighed. She lowered her voice. 'Dear Hamish. He was a sales representative for office supplies – came up from Edinburgh in a white Austin Morris. The original young gun in a smart suit a size too big. I was working in a newish office just outside the village. Our company provided admin support to a lot of the businesses in the area. For me it was just a wee earner after I left school. Anyway, when Hamish walked into our office and asked if he could speak to Mr Wright I thought I was going to faint on the spot! I'd never seen anyone so exotic-looking. His parents came over from Italy after the war and when they had a son, they wanted him to fit into the Scottish culture so they named him Hamish. I believe his younger brother was called Angus. Hamish Patrizio – can you imagine? In Lochinver? He was tall and dark and so very romantic. We spent every day for an entire fortnight in each other's company. I truly believed he was *the one.'* Her face crumpled.

'So what happened?' Logan urged.

'We both knew he was only in this area for two weeks. His next tour was down in Fort William. It was on our last night that he confessed to me he was married.'

'What a rat!' Dusty exclaimed.

Jessie gave a sorry smile. 'Maybe. He said he wanted to give us the fairest chance – to see if he could really be happy. And he was. I could tell I made him happy.'

'So, there was just the minor issue of him already being married?' Logan asked. *'Men!'* he tutted.

'Things aren't always as they seem,' said Jessie, finishing her tea. 'His wife was suffering deeply from depression. They'd already lost two babies through miscarriage. His poor wife was distraught. He once found her up to her neck in the Forth, which is when she got admitted to hospital. There was very little hope for her ever regaining her mental faculties. He had stood by her for more than a year while she was incarcerated. They tried everything to bring her back. But he himself was such a young man – just turned twenty-one. The irony was that they only got married because she was pregnant. When our paths crossed he saw a chance for happiness and grabbed it. I don't blame him at all. Would you?'

The three shuffled their feet and examined the floor of the community centre.

'Anyway.' Jessie regained her composure. 'You have your story now. What more do you want?'

'So he didn't propose to you?' Kat persevered.

'How could he? He was already married – and in a hopeless situation.'

'But,' Dusty ventured gently, 'do you think there's any possibility that he planned to return home and end his marriage?'

'Perhaps he *did* intend to propose to you?' Logan suggested.

'I doubt it.' Jessie shook her head sadly. 'I'd like to think so but I knew how much loyalty he felt to his wife. I knew he'd never abandon her.'

'And what about you, pet?' Dusty asked. 'Did you ever get married?'

'Och aye! Of course! The old bugger is still on the go. It's our golden wedding anniversary this October. Who'd have thought? Just shows you what a virtue tolerance is.'

'Would you know how we could contact your Hamish?' asked Logan.

'For what?' Jessie asked sharply. 'He can't know anything about what I've told you. He'd be horrified. I don't want you stirring up a lot of unhappy memories. Leave the man alone.'

'We wouldn't mention anything that you've shared,' Logan advised. 'We would just ask if he'd ever lost a ring. There'd be no harm in that?'

'I suppose not. Although I can't imagine where he could have bought a ring like that around here. But please don't tell me his answer. I couldn't bear it if he had made any kind of plan for us.'

'Jessie! Put the bingo machine back on – we need to get going. There's Welsh Pilates for Beginners at three o'clock.' The Pineapple jabbed Logan in the back. 'You lot – get back to your seats. Tea break is over.'

Jessie gave a rueful shrug. 'Aye, tea break's over.'

'We might as well go,' said Kat. 'We found out what we needed to know.'

The Pineapple hurried them towards the tables. 'Stop dawdling, you lot. If I don't clear this room by three I'll have the Bendies on my back. Come on, shoo!'

The three found themselves back on the pavement, where the tabby had progressed to licking itself with a satisfied purr.

'What now?' said Kat. 'I was so sure we were on to something there.'

'And we might still be,' Logan replied. 'We must follow up on every lead. This is solid police work, you know. Can't make any assumptions.'

'Phew! But it's exhausting, though,' said Dusty. 'And so warm!' She removed her coat, slinging it over one arm.

'Come on, let's get back to the car and we'll decide our next move.'

They trundled along the empty main street and found their car as only one of two remaining in the car park. 'Looks as though everyone really does go to the Highland Games,' said Logan. 'It's hardly Piccadilly Circus.'

'Logan! Lochinver's population is about six hundred.'

'Is it?' said Logan.

'Yes … and I feel I've spoken to every single one of them.' Kat opened the car doors and they sat in contemplative silence. Dusty leant her head back and dozed. Logan caught Kat's eye in the rear-view mirror and winked. They stepped out of the car again. 'What now?' she asked.

'It's probably a bit late today to tackle the Highland Games. What was that other person you mentioned? The farm?'

Kat checked her notebook. 'Yes, someone mentioned a Jess Crearer. She grew up on a farm near here but we think moved to

Aberdeen. Apparently her brother still lives at the farm.'

'Shall we all go and check it out?'

'Might as well. Dusty's going nowhere.'

Chapter 24

Kat drove the winding road past Loch Culag to Strathan.

'I know you can't really look because you're driving,' said Logan, 'but that's an amazing view of the loch.'

'I'll take your word for it.'

'How much further?'

'Only a couple of miles, I think.'

'There's a sign there – Strathan, a quarter of a mile.'

Kat made the turning just as Dusty came to. She rubbed her eyes. 'Sorry about that – must have dropped off. What are we doing now? I shouldn't have had all that tea at the bingo. I don't suppose there'll be any public toilets out here, will there?'

'I doubt it,' said Kat. 'I shouldn't think the cows have much need of one.'

'There!' Logan cried from the back.

'A toilet?' Dusty asked hopefully.

'White's Farm.'

A weathered sign hung from a rusty post at an angle. Kat jumped on the brakes and took a hard left. The car smacked over the dirt track through overgrown grassy embankments. 'This is why all farmers own Land Rovers,' Kat grumbled. She gripped the steering wheel as the Volvo lurched from side to side. The trail opened out into a courtyard where a dented, mud-splattered truck was parked next to a corroded blue van, deserted on bricks with wheels removed. The farmhouse, a two-storey stone building with sagging roof and flaking window frames, looked abandoned. There was no sign of activity in the nearby ramshackle barn or empty cowshed. An outside tap dribbled water into a muddy pool.

'*Who* are we visiting here?' Dusty asked.

'We're looking for some info on Jess Crearer. She was the one who Agnes said was a bit eccentric and may have moved to Aberdeen. Apparently her brother still lives here.'

'According to whom?' said Dusty. 'This place doesn't look like anyone's lived here in years.'

'I agree,' said Kat, opening her door. 'But we might as well check it out since we're here. Do you want to just stay in the car?'

'If you don't mind?'

'I'll leave the radio on for you.'

'I'm coming out for the fresh air,' said Logan. 'Not that there's much fresh about it. Something smells like it's *died*.'

Kat rapped on the front door. A distinguished gent in a black velvet suit and red bow tie opened it with a flourish. His grey hair was slicked back and his beard neatly trimmed. Intense blue eyes twinkled with pleasure. 'Good afternoon and welcome to White's Farm.'

'Er …' Kat hesitated. 'We're looking for Jess Crearer's brother?'

'Yes, yes! That's right. I'm Thomas Crearer. Do come in – I've been expecting you.'

'Have you?' asked Kat. Agnes must have rung ahead and warned the locals. They followed him into a living room, where a worn leather settee wilted under their weight. Thomas fetched a wooden dining chair from the corner and sat cross-legged. 'Now,' he beamed, 'may I fetch you lovelies a cup of tea?'

'I think we're okay, aren't we?' Kat replied. Logan nodded in agreement.

'Fine!' Thomas clapped his hands. 'I can't tell you how excited I am about today.'

'G-good,' Kat faltered. 'I hope you may be able to help us.'

'Oh, I'm sure we'll all be able to help each other! Do you mind if I smoke? I'm so nervous! Where *is* the pretty lady?'

'Dusty's waiting in the car.'

'Quite right! I'd expect nothing less. It's your duty to check all is above board before progressing.' His hand shook as he lit a cigarette and he flapped at the offensive smoke. 'I wish I didn't but what's a man to do?' He laughed with a high-pitched squeal.

Kat found her notepad and pen. 'So, Thomas, can you tell us anything about your sister Jess?'

'Oh, I'm delighted that you're exploring my family background. Excellent!' He winked at Logan as he smoothed down his hair. 'What do you need to know about her?'

'Well,' said Kat, 'we heard from Agnes that she might have moved to Aberdeen. And we wondered whether she got married at all?'

'Actually, she's got a sweet little bungalow near Stonehaven – do you know it at all?'

Kat nodded. Thomas flapped his hands again. 'She had a terrible row with Father one evening. This was years ago – she was barely out of her teens. I don't even know what it was about … although I do believe it had something to do with her distilling her own moonshine in the barn. Anyway, the next morning she upped sticks and disappeared. Mother made a show of being distraught, but I do think she was just a teeny weeny bit relieved. Jess used to embarrass them rotten. She knew it wound them up. Jess once confessed to the Sunday School teacher that she was the devil. Poor Miss Lindle had a fit!'

'Are you still in touch with your sister?'

'Naturally!' Thomas looked offended. 'Although Jess and I were never that close. We were yin and yang. She was the wild to my prudence.'

'And *did* she ever marry?' Kat asked, crossing her fingers behind her back.

'It was a sorry affair,' said Thomas, shaking his head.

'How so?'

'Now what was his name?' Thomas mused. 'Ha … Ha …'

Kat and Logan waited in tortured silence.

'*Harold!* That was it. They got married in nineteen sixty-three. Mother, Father and I travelled across to Stonehaven. I don't think she really wanted us to be there – had a face like a skelped arse the entire day. We stayed one night in a deplorable B and B and travelled back the next. They were married all of two years. In fact, I think she only married him to ruffle Father's feathers. Harold was a Catholic, you see. Father would have been less furious if she'd married an Englishman. Anyway, there you have it – our family history laid bare.' He stubbed out the cigarette and popped a mint into his mouth. He passed round the packet.

'So, do you know if your sister ever *went out* with anyone called Hamish?' Logan asked impatiently.

'Hamish?' Thomas considered the name, letting it roam around his mind for a couple of minutes. 'I don't believe so. But then, what do I know? She'd hardly confide the details of every lover to her kid brother!'

'Perhaps you wouldn't mind if we contacted Jess?' Logan asked.

'I don't give a fig who you contact.'

'Then could you possibly pass on her contact details?'

'I can do better than that!' He gave an obsequious bow of the head, withdrawing a mobile phone from his pocket and jabbing at the screen.

'Jess, darling? It's Thomas. I know – it's been too long! I know … *I know.* Indeed! Anyway, luvvie, I've got company here. *Of course I have!* So, they want to know if you ever went out with a Hamish? Please don't ask—'

'Or were ever engaged to a Hamish,' Kat interrupted.

'Or were ever engaged to a Hamish,' Thomas repeated dutifully. 'I didn't think so. To be honest I'm not sure. I think it's all background information. *As if!* Well, I'll let you know the outcome of course. Bye, sweetie! Yes, yes. I'll send a photo. Bye, darling.'

Thomas leant back in his chair. 'So it seems there was never a Hamish on the scene. Happy?'

'Not really,' Kat sighed. 'A bit disappointing, actually.'

'In any case I'm not entirely sure this is *all* that relevant. When can I expect to welcome our good lady?'

They heard a knock at the door.

'That might be her,' Kat answered. 'She probably got fed up waiting.'

Thomas shot upright. 'How do I look?' he asked, spinning in a circle.

'Fine?' Kat shrugged, gathering her coat and bag. 'Anyway, we should be off.'

'No! Please stay. Wait a minute – at least until I get the door.'

Thomas took a deep breath before throwing the door wide open. Dusty stood on the doorstep wringing her hands. 'I'm so awfully sorry to bother you but I just wondered whether you minded me using your facilities?'

'Welcome! Welcome! And you're more beautiful than I could have imagined.'

'Oh my,' Dusty giggled. She patted at her outfit as she stepped into the farmhouse. Thomas took her hand and held it lightly to his lips. 'I'm so very delighted to finally meet you. I'm Thomas Crearer. *Enchanté.*'

'Hello, Thomas, I'm Dusty.'

'Of course you are! And how fabulous it is to have you here in my home.'

Dusty blushed. 'You're so very kind. But perhaps you could direct me to the bathroom?'

'Absolutely, darling! Please follow me – it's just at the top of the stairs.'

'Thank you.'

Thomas held the bathroom door open as Dusty slipped past him. He closed the door behind her.

'Missing you already!'

Thomas returned to the living room. 'I say! She is – as I had hoped – completely beguiling.'

'Well, we are rather fond of her,' said Kat. 'I take it she asked to use the bathroom?'

'Indeed.'

'Then we mustn't keep you any longer.'

'Agreed!' Thomas smiled. 'You've made me so happy. I can't thank you enough. Now, where do I sign?'

'Sign?' Kat repeated.

'Yes – I understand the agency requires us to sign to say that both parties are satisfied?'

'Look, mate, we're not with you,' said Logan. 'What's this all about? What agency?'

'Dearie me! What kind of amateurs have been sent to my home?'

'Hey! Less of the *amateurs*,' Logan objected. 'Come on, Kat, let's go.'

'But we need to wait for Dusty.'

'Okay, why don't we all just calm down,' said Thomas, waving his arms. He strode across to the table and returned with a form. 'Now,' he said. 'The contract clearly states that on my wife's arrival, both parties must sign here and here. Then I return the paperwork and Bob's your uncle.'

'*Wife?*' Kat and Logan said in unison. Kat leapt to her feet. 'Dusty's not your wife!'

'Oh, but she is,' said Thomas smugly. 'I paid two thousand pounds for her. Look – here's my contract with *Perfect Partners*. I've been waiting weeks for her to arrive.'

'She's not a bloody new cooker,' said Logan.

'Look, Thomas,' said Kat, 'you seem like a very lovely man but there's been some huge misunderstanding. We came here looking for a Jess who might have been married or engaged to a Hamish.'

'Yes, I told you all that.'

'But that's it. That's all we needed to know. We don't know anything about *Perfect Partners* or a wife.'

'That's right,' Logan added. 'I think you must have got our visits muddled. Hey, man – good for you in getting a new wife and all that but honestly, we're not who you think we are. We're just some random folk from Edinburgh on a bit of a quest.'

'No!' said Thomas, stamping his foot. 'That lady in my bathroom is my new wife. I've paid for her. Two thousand pounds! I don't have that kind of money. I've drained my savings and borrowed from my sister. I haven't eaten properly in six months. I've been drinking bloody supermarket gin since Christmas! And, apart from anything, have you any idea how lonely it gets out here on your own? Sometimes I don't see another living soul for weeks.'

'I'm sorry to let you down, Thomas, but she really isn't your new wife,' said Logan, heading for the door. Thomas grabbed his arm. 'You're wrong! Look at the letter she sent me – and the photo.' He waved a piece of paper in Logan's face. Kat squinted at the picture. 'Hmm, right enough it does actually look a bit like Dusty. But I'm telling you – it's not her. For a start, your wife's name is Sarah.'

'Hoots, lassie! Do you think I care what she's called? She's my wife and I'm keeping her!'

'Sorry, pal,' said Logan as he walked out into the hall. Kat followed. They heard a banging sound from the bathroom. '*Help!*' shouted Dusty. 'I'm locked in. Somebody help me!'

They turned to Thomas, who at least had the decency to look bashful.

'No way, Old Man!' Logan gasped. 'You unlock the door right this minute.'

'Oh my God!' Kat cried. 'I can't believe you'd lock a poor defenceless woman in your bathroom!'

'She's not just any woman,' Thomas protested. 'She's my wife. You two should stay out of my business. Now leave before I call the police.'

'*You* call the police?' Kat objected. 'How about *we* call the police?'

Thomas shrugged. 'She's my wife and I'm keeping her. This has gone on for months now.'

Logan shook his head. 'I'm really sorry, Thomas, but can't you see you've been duped? There is no *Perfect Partners*. You've been scammed. Someone has taken your money and you've got nothing in return.'

'No, *you're* wrong!' said Thomas, folding his arms. 'Johnny down at the Fat Trout did exactly the same as me and next thing you know he's got a bloody gorgeous wife from Belarus.'

'*Help!*' Dusty yelled again, rattling the door handle. Kat ran up the stairs. She called through the door. 'Hang on a moment, Dusty. There's just a wee thing we're sorting out and we'll get you out in a jiffy.'

'Oh, Kat – I don't know what happened. I shut the door but now I can't open it again. I told you my memory was getting me into trouble.'

'It's not your fault, Dusty,' said Kat. 'We're just going to find the spare key. We'll only be a minute.'

Kat sprang down the stairs, two at a time. 'Right, mister, you can hear her distress. Open that bloody door – *now!*'

Thomas slunk back to the living room and huddled on his chair.

'Thomas Crearer, you open that door *this instant!*' Kat insisted.

Thomas looked out of the window, brushing a piece of fluff from his velvet trousers.

'I swear I'll …' Kat growled.

'This is getting us nowhere,' said Logan, biting his nails. 'We need to think.' He jogged up the stairs and crouched at the bathroom door, squinting through the keyhole. He spied Dusty teasing her hair in the mirror and spoke through the gap, 'Hey, Dusty, how are you doing?'

She circled the small room before working out where the voice was coming from. 'Oh, it's you, Logan,' she said from the other side of the door. 'I seem to have got myself stuck.'

'Now don't you worry.' Logan gave a reassuring smile. 'We're just working things out at this side. Maybe you should have a wee seat on the side of the bath? The door does seem to be jammed so I'm just going to try to ease it. Are you over by the bath?'

'I am,' said Dusty. 'But do be careful.'

Logan took a deep breath and gave the door a mighty kick with his boot. The solid door didn't budge an inch.

'Oh my!' Dusty cried.

Taking a few steps back Logan ran at the door, throwing his shoulder against the wood. He bounced off it with a yelp.

'Do watch what you're doing Logan! I'd hate to get us into bother with the farmer,' Dusty fretted. 'He seems such a lovely man. We can't go kicking his house down.'

'Seemingly so,' Logan agreed. He thumped the door with his fist. 'Honestly, Dusty, this really isn't your doing.'

'Thank you, Logan, you're being most patient with me.'

'So just sit tight.'

'Will do. Over and out!'

Logan returned to the living room, massaging his bruised shoulder.

'Look sonny, what in heaven's name are you doing to my home?' Thomas frowned.

Kat loomed over him, hands on her hips. 'This is kidnapping!' she accused.

'Don't be silly,' Thomas retorted. 'I'm not asking for ransom money. In fact, I've paid *you*!'

'Okay – not kidnapping,' said Logan. 'But definitely abduction.'

'Again, I hate to be picky but where am I meant to have taken her away *to*? I haven't taken her anywhere.'

Logan groaned. 'Thomas, you're being ridiculous. You're clearly holding her captive.'

'Am I?' he asked, all innocence. 'I do believe she asked to visit my bathroom and entered the room of her own accord.'

'And now she wishes to leave the room. Bloody hell, man, this is *a crime*,' Logan insisted.

'Some would say the length of your hair is a crime, but let's not get personal.'

Kat held her phone at the ready. 'This is your last chance then I'm calling the police.'

'Go ahead,' Thomas smiled. 'I'm sure one of the lads will be more than happy to drop by – especially after all the steaks I've donated over the years.'

'A word, Kat,' said Logan indicating towards the hall. 'We're not achieving anything here – the man is obviously unhinged.'

'But what are we going to do? Surely we have to get the police involved?'

'I wonder whether we can get Dusty out another way?' said Logan.

'How do you mean? Find a spare key?'

'I mean, if there's a window? Do you think you can distract him long enough while I check whether I can find a ladder? I'll message you.'

Kat puffed out her cheeks. 'I don't know. He's a bit deranged.'

'Can you try?' Logan squeezed Kat's hand.

'Fine.'

Logan snuck out the front door.

'Hey, Thomas,' said Kat loftily. 'Is the offer of a cup of tea still open?'

'Ah! That's more like it! Let's all have a nice cup of tea. And then we can sign the forms.'

'Or not,' Kat muttered under her breath. She followed him into the kitchen where she observed, with a twinge of guilt, a table laid with one solitary knife and fork. A bucket of empty gin bottles stood at the back door.

'Yes, a nice cup of tea,' Thomas repeated, wiping a tear from his eye.

Logan hurried into the nearest barn, skidding on a patch of slurry. A mound of rusting machinery lay abandoned at the entrance – years since any of it had seen any action. A mouse shot out from under a trailer and he leapt to one side. Aha! Logan's eyes fixed on a wooden ladder that leant against the barn wall. He clambered towards it, cracking his knee against a solid tractor engine. 'Bloody hell!' he howled. A disgruntled pigeon flapped up into the rafters. The ladder was heavier than it looked, despite missing a couple of rungs, and he struggled to lift it above the dross. Slinging it over his shoulder he stumbled back to the house. He positioned it against the worn brickwork, giving it a good shake to test its sturdiness. The bathroom window was pretty grimy but he could see Dusty resting on the edge of the bath. He gave the window a gentle tap. Dusty looked up and down but saw nothing. Logan smacked the pane with urgency.

'Wah!' Dusty cried, her arms shooting in the air. She trotted over to the window, grappling with the stiff latch. 'Logan! What a fright! What are you doing out there?'

'I've come to get you out.'

Just as Thomas was carefully pouring boiling water into four mugs, Kat's mobile pinged.

`Found ladder – Logan.`

'Can I help you with that?' Kat asked Thomas. 'Have you got a tray?'

'Of course I have a tray,' Thomas sniffed. 'We're not all animals out in the country.' He reached beside the fridge and withdrew a metal tray depicting the Queen's Silver Jubilee, complete with twin thrones. He used a spoon to fish out the four teabags. 'I expect my new wife will prefer to use a teapot for guests – I'm sure she's much more refined than I am.'

'This is perfect,' said Kat. 'Have you got any milk?'

'I suppose you'll be wanting a milk jug too?'

'No,' Kat said. 'As it comes is fine.'

'As it comes is out of a cow but I'm sure that's a bit too real for you?'

Kat carried the tray back through to the living room and placed it on the table. Her phone pinged again. At the window now – Logan

'Where's that young man of yours got to?' Thomas asked with suspicion.

'Oh, he's just popped out for a cigarette,' Kat lied. 'He'll be back soon.'

'But I could have offered him one!' said Thomas. 'He never said.'

'He's a bit of a secret puffer.'

'I hear you, sister! The looks I used to get down at the Fat Trout when I pulled out a packet would make you wilt. Of course, I got fed up standing outside latterly.'

'Actually,' said Kat, stalling for time, 'I think Logan prefers coffee – would you mind?'

Thomas twitched in his chair. 'Right! Coffee it is!' He disappeared back into the kitchen.

Logan tugged at the window but it jammed.

'Are you joining me?' Dusty asked. 'Perhaps you can work out how to open this blasted door? I don't know how I managed it but I seem to have broken the lock. I'm so embarrassed.'

'You needn't be,' said Logan. He rubbed at his stubble as he thought. 'But you know what? I think there's a wee problem with the door. Apparently this has happened before.'

'So it's not my fault?'

'It's absolutely *not* your fault!'

'Thank goodness.'

'So, I'm wondering whether you could perhaps climb out of this window and I'll help you down the ladder?'

'Logan! Don't be ridiculous! I'm eighty-two years old. I can't possibly get down that ladder. I'll fall and break my neck! And probably take you with me.'

'No, you won't,' said Logan, panicking. 'I'll be here to help you every step of the way.'

'I can't,' Dusty insisted. She returned to the bath and plonked herself down. 'I'll just wait until that nice Mr Crearer sorts it out. I thought Kat said it was just a wee problem?'

Logan groaned.

Kat's mobile vibrated. Need more time — Logan

Thomas returned with a mug of coffee. 'There you go. Does your friend take milk?'

'Yes, please.' Kat frowned. 'And I wonder if I can bother you for some sugar?'

'But there's sugar in the bowl,' said Thomas, with a wave of his hand. 'Make yourself at home.'

'Actually,' Kat said, bracing herself, 'I think Logan really prefers *brown* sugar in his coffee. If it's no trouble?'

'Trouble?' Thomas replied through gritted teeth. 'Why, it's a pleasure.' He stomped off back to the kitchen.

Outside, Logan's mobile buzzed. Please HURRY! — Kat

Logan took a deep breath. 'Okay, Dusty, I'm just going to say it how it is. Your nice Mr Crearer seems to think that he's paid an agency for you to be his new wife.'

'Say wha …?'

'Exactly! I think he's mistaken us for someone else and now he's holding you captive. He says he's paid a sum of money and now he expects you to live with him in this house as man and wife. There you have it. That's our *wee problem*.'

'Wife?' Dusty repeated. 'Is he mad? Does he know I've been through the menopause?'

'I've no idea – to either of those questions.'

'And he's downstairs with Kat just now?'

'Yep – asking her to sign you away as his new bidie-in.'

'But I-I …' Dusty stammered. 'Is he *dangerous*? What will he do to us?' Dusty paced the bathroom.

Logan shrugged. 'I mean – he looks harmless enough …'

'Move aside, I'm coming out.' Dusty dragged a linen basket over to the window and knelt on it. 'I'm sure it can't be any harder than climbing down from the attic?'

'That's the spirit!' Logan nodded. She grasped the window frame and stuck one leg out of the window. Logan guided it on to the first rung. She swivelled her body round and stuck her bottom into Logan's face. He manoeuvred her hips through the narrow gap. 'Am I stuck?' she gasped.

'Not at all. I've got you. I'm going to move your foot down to the next rung. There we go. Well done, Dusty – you're doing grand.'

'Just get me away from this nutter!' Dusty said. 'I can't be his wife! What would Edwin say?'

149

'That's a girl – keep coming down. I'm right here.'

'I should have known something was up the moment he said I was beautiful. I mean, I know I'm no bag of spanners but *"enchanté"*? My mother told me never to trust a man who spoke French.'

'Let's keep it moving.'

Kat's phone pinged. `Nearly there — Logan`

'It was right at the back of the cupboard,' Thomas complained, thumping the bag of Demerara on to the table. He took a gulp of milky tea.

'Thank you, Thomas.' Kat gave a sweet smile. 'That's so kind of you. I feel I'm being such a pest but I would really love a biscuit if you have one? It's been quite an afternoon and I actually feel quite faint.'

'A *biscuit*, you say?' Thomas counted to ten.

'I'd be ever so grateful,' said Kat. 'Then maybe we can get down to business?'

Thomas narrowed his eyes. 'Let me see what I've got. You might be lucky if I can lay my hand on something other than oatcakes.'

'I'm a bit wobbly,' Dusty announced as she descended the ladder.

'You're doing a fantastic job,' Logan said, gripping Dusty's waist. 'We're nearly there – just a few more steps down.'

'Oh my!' Dusty cried as she landed on firm ground. 'I haven't been up a ladder that big since I was a lass – and that was to hang flower baskets for the local gala.'

'Great!' said Logan. 'But we really must hurry to the car.'

'Hurry? Is he coming after us? Oh, I hope he hasn't got a shotgun! Where's Kat?'

'She's on her way.' Logan took Dusty's hand and urged her

towards the car. He pushed her into the passenger seat and started the engine.

'We can't leave without Kat!' Dusty protested.

Logan reached for his mobile.

Kat's phone pinged in her hand.

      `Get out now — RUN! — Logan`

Kat leapt up and sprinted from the room. She opened the front door and ran towards the idling car. Logan revved the engine as she fell into the back seat. '*Go!*' she commanded.

Thomas appeared at the front door, a packet of Hobnobs in one hand. 'No – come back!' he wailed as Logan sped off down the track. 'But you've stolen my *wife!*'

Thomas let the biscuits fall to the ground as the tears flowed. '*Please,*' he begged.

'Oh – my – God,' Kat said with disbelief. 'What the hell just happened to us?'

'Logan said that man thought I was going to marry him!' said Dusty. 'What was that all about?'

Logan ran his hand through his hair as the car skidded back to Lochinver. 'The poor man has just been swindled out of two thousand pounds. It was a scam, Dusty.'

'But I feel terrible! I hope he doesn't think it was *us* that took his money.'

'I hope not too,' said Kat. 'Maybe he'll go to the police?'

'I doubt it,' Logan replied. 'I think, deep down, he knew what had happened. He probably just feels like the biggest fool.'

'Oh … and he seemed so nice as well.' Dusty gazed out of the window.

'Hey, I can take you back if you want?'

'No, Logan, just get me back to Mill House.'

Kat sighed. 'I'd give anything to be back in my own bedroom with a good book.'

Chapter 25

'Keep still, will you?' Dell muttered with her mouth tightly clamped on pins.

'Sorry,' said Ron. 'I'm not used to standing doing nothing.'

'You're not *doing nothing* – you're doing a pretty rubbish impression of a dummy.'

'Hey, less of the dummy. I like to think of myself as a male model.'

'Cheeky!' Dell pinched Ron's bottom. 'Anyway, how much do you want this tunic taken in?'

'I'd like it fitting a bit neater than it does at the moment, but not so tight that if I sneeze, a button will take out an eye in the front row.'

'How does that feel?'

'Fine.'

Ron's phone blared out the theme tune from *Dr Who*. He fumbled in his trouser pocket.

'Ron Carmichael here. Oh, hello, Mo.' He covered his hand over the phone. 'It's Mo.'

Dell rolled her eyes.

'Yes, Mo, I'm just getting my uniform taken in so that I don't look like I'm wearing my dad's cast-offs. Well, she's right here making the adjustments. Oh, I don't know – I'll ask her.'

Ron covered the phone again. 'Mo's asking what you're doing this evening.'

'You know what I'm doing this evening. I'm picking you up so that we can *you know what.*'

'I think she means before that.'

'It depends why she wants to know.'

Ron spoke back into the phone. 'She wants to know why. I see. Oh dear, oh dear. How unfortunate. Well, that *is* bad news. Will she get an emergency appointment? Right, I'll ask her then.'

'Ask me what?' mumbled Dell, removing a pin from her mouth and tucking it into the serge.

'Mo says that Donna was mucking about on her granddaughter's scooter when she fell and knocked out her front tooth. Her lip's up like a balloon.'

'Daft Donna,' Dell tutted.

'So Mo's asking if you can read her part tonight?'

'What's the part?

'She plays Mother Abbess.'

'What? I can't sing a note!'

'That doesn't matter. They just need you to speak the words and move around the stage so we can all get in our final dress rehearsal.'

'Why can't Mo do it?'

'Come on, Dell, you'll be great! Anyway, Mo's the director – she needs to watch what everyone's doing.'

'And what if Donna can't make the opening night?'

'Apparently she's seeing an emergency dentist tomorrow. And hopefully her lip will have gone down by then.'

'What was she thinking – fannying around on a scooter? You ought to introduce a clause banning such ridiculous behaviour so close to the performance!'

'So will you do it?'

'Oh, alright. But as long as we're finished in time for *you know what*.'

Ron resumed his conversation.

'Okay, Mo, Dell says she'll come along tonight. Ha ha – oh, she just means in time for cocoa.' He blushed as he hung up.

'I mean it,' said Dell. 'We must get away in time to see what that rat is up to next door.'

'Yes, love. We will. I'll make sure we speed up our search at the end. You never know, we might even catch the von Trapps!'

Chapter 26

Logan parked the Volvo in the driveway of Mill House, noting an additional car that hadn't been there when they left that morning.

'Eh-up – looks like we've got company.'

'Well, I'm shattered,' said Dusty. 'All that shimmying down ladders has taken it out of me. I think I'll have a wee catnap before dinner.'

'I'm going to my room too,' said Kat. 'This day has just been too weird.'

'In that case, let me fill in what we know on the chart,' said Logan, holding the front door open for the ladies. 'See you for an aperitif?'

'Sure,' Kat said. 'Here's my notebook so you can see what intel we gathered.'

Kat and Dusty trailed off to their rooms as Logan threw his jacket over the back of a chair and kicked off his boots. The smoky smell and crackle of burning logs made him feel sleepy and he was tempted to crash out on the settee. Damn! The pens and Post-its were waiting expectantly in a pile in front of the wallpaper map. He rolled up his sleeves and began scribbling under JESS and HAMISH.

'I say!' a female voice cried behind him. 'That looks frightfully interesting. What on earth are you up to?' An eager young woman with straight mousy hair and plenty of teeth bounced into the room. She wore a flowery green pinafore dress, her hands fidgeting in the air.

'What this?' replied Logan nonchalantly. 'It's a Link Chart Investigation Board.' He stuck a THOMAS CREARER Post-it on to the paper, writing JILTED HUSBAND underneath.

'How fascinating! What's it all about? Do you mind me asking? I'm Felicity, by the way.'

'Logan,' he said, shaking her hand. He lowered his voice. 'We're on a quest.'

He flipped the lid off a bottle of craft beer while he explained the story of the ring.

'But that's so romantic,' Felicity gushed. 'Imagine if, after all these years, you can reunite Jess with her fiancé's symbol of bethrothal?'

'Ah, but there's a darker possibility,' Logan warned.

'Such as?'

'For example, what if young Hamish was beaten and robbed of the ring? The ring later discarded as evidence? Perhaps something tragic happened to the lad before he had time to propose? What then? Will we find Jess pining on the edge of a cliff where she has held a vigil for the last fifty years?'

Felicity's hand flew to her mouth. 'Oh my! I hadn't thought of that. How ghastly!'

'Or,' Logan ramped up the drama. 'What if some dire catastrophe befell dear Jessica? Perhaps she *was* engaged to Hamish but, before they could exchange their vows, she was struck down by some incurable disease?'

'How sad! And poor, darling Hamish left without his sweet bride!'

'Precisely!' Logan gulped from his bottle, stifling a burp. 'We have a massive responsibility here to uncover the truth. To put right a wrong.'

'And have you?' Felicity enquired with hopeful eyes.

'Not yet,' Logan sighed. 'But! We have ruled out some possibilities. We know we haven't yet found the right Jess or Hamish. Here let me show you.'

'Yes, *please*,' she breathed, moving in closer.

'By the way, do you want a drink?' Logan indicated the drinks cabinet. 'Did Aubrey explain about the honesty box?'

'He did. Now, I wonder if they have a dry sherry? Oh, they do – hurrah!' Felicity poured herself a glass and carried it across to the wall chart. Logan launched into an explanation of all the Jesses and Hamishes they had uncovered throughout the day, over-egging his violent encounter on Strom Island.

'How brave of you to manage such barbarism,' said Felicity, sipping at her sherry.

'It's kind of what I'm trained to do – we never know what we might confront in the field.'

'Of course.'

'Anyway, there are endless scenarios,' he summed up.

'And you can't make any assumptions.'

'That's a fundamental principle of policing,' Logan agreed, stroking his unshaven chin.

'I mean,' said Felicity. 'What if they *had been* engaged, this Jess and Hamish? What if they'd been deliriously happy with their whole lives ahead of them. And then, say, one day, Jess returned home after an Adele gig in London to find that Hamish had spent the weekend with Jess's best friend? What then, eh? And what if Hamish was so bloody egocentric that he denied the whole thing and it was only when Jess's best friend confessed to their despicable affair that Jess uncovered the ugly truth – that he was a complete bastard? What, *then*, eh? Perhaps Jess threw the ring into the loch in a fit of rage and self-loathing and perhaps she might actually throttle you at the mere mention of Hamish. Have you thought of *that* scenario?'

'I ... er ...' Logan wiped his sweaty brow. 'Gosh, it's warm in here.'

The kitchen door swung open and Aubrey breezed in, a glass of red wine in one hand. 'Ah, Logan, I see you've met our new guest. And how you've made tremendous progress with your map!'

'Yes to both,' Logan nodded in gratitude.

'And were we any help at all?'

'Well, you *were* right about Jessie at the community centre, although she's married to someone else.'

'Oh, that's a pity.'

'Yes, but she did briefly go out with a Hamish – unfortunately he was already married and unlikely to propose to her. But we will follow up that lead.'

'Good man.'

'And Gregor's reference to the old boy that sits on the bench on the harbour is actually a *Harry*.' Logan emptied his bottle and reached for another.

'Sorry about that.'

'But he did lead me to a Hamish Gillies.'

'Of course! Hamish on Strom Island. Now I have heard about him. Didn't he get into a bar brawl recently?'

'The very man. I cadged a boat ride across to the island. He was – how can I put it – less than patient with my line of questioning.'

'You are most certainly taking this seriously.'

'Oh yes,' said Logan. 'Actually, don't mention it to Kat but, this summer, I was supposed to have done a uni project based on a theoretical investigation. I didn't quite get my act together – but this is perfect. I just need to write it up.'

'*Oh my!*' Felicity swooned. 'So you're an empirical as well as intellectual scholar, then?'

Logan nodded awkwardly. 'I'm not sure that's how my fellow students would describe me.'

'And who's Kat?'

'I am,' said Kat.

Felicity twirled round. 'Oh.' Her face fell. 'Are you with Logan?'

'I'm not sure that *with* is how I'd describe it. I gave him a lift here.'

'I was hitch-hiking,' Logan added.

'Marvellous!' said Felicity. 'So you're not an item?'

'If by *item* you mean we're more than an occasional car ride – then, no, we're not.'

'Harsh,' Logan shrugged.

'Now, Felicity,' Aubrey began as he rubbed an eye with his spare hand, 'I'm not sure that I drew your attention to our house rules over there?'

Felicity frowned. 'I did see mention of the hot water-slash-shower parameters.'

'Excellent! And I have jotted an additional one this afternoon requesting that you wipe down the basin after each use – it saves a build-up of detritus. You wouldn't believe how much scrubbing it takes to remove excess globules of toothpaste.'

'Right.'

'Well, I'll let you youngsters mingle. Must check on Gregor. BTW, I've posted this evening's menu on the bulletin board.' Aubrey ducked back into the kitchen.

'*Locally brewed beer-battered haddock with twice-fried wedges and a mousse of crushed garden pea,*' read Kat.

'Sounds like fish and chips to me,' said Logan.

'Oh, you're such a wit,' Felicity giggled.

'With a silent *T*,' muttered Kat. She poured herself a glass of water from a cucumber-infused jug.

'And what's on *your* menu tonight?' Logan enquired.

'Seems like Gregor's determined that I should sample his spring vegetable roulade.'

'Yum,' said Felicity. 'I almost wish *I* were vegetarian. You know, I did try it once and I lasted for nearly six months.'

'Oh, really?' Kat asked.

'Yes, I was doing so well. And then one evening I came home to the most fabulous aroma of cooking meat and that was it – I was a goner!'

'People often say they cave at the first whiff of a bacon roll,' said Kat. 'Was that what blew it for you?'

'Actually, it was a roast pheasant with tarragon and cherry dressing.'

'Of course it was,' Kat smirked.

'Daddy had completely forgotten I was a vegetarian!'

'Did I hear someone mention Daddy?' A beaming man with outstretched arms swept into the room. He wore a cream linen suit and Panama hat. His ruddy face and portly build gave the impression he enjoyed the good life.

'Daddy, you must come and meet these super people,' Felicity gushed, embracing her father. 'This is Logan – he's doing splendid detective work!'

'Is he now?' the man boomed, extending a fleshy hand.

'Well, it's more a personal crusade-type thing.'

Kat snorted.

'And this is his driver – sorry, what did you say your name was again?' Felicity continued.

'Kat,' she supplied, keeping her hands in her pockets.

'Kat short for Katy?'

'Katharine.'

'Of course. Well, it's a pleasure to meet you. My name's Darwin – as in *Darwin Flockhart*.'

'Hi,' Logan said.

'Daddy, not everyone's heard of you!' Felicity gave her father a friendly punch on the arm.

'I'm sure they've *heard* of me, but I do acknowledge that perhaps my face hasn't graced the screen in recent months. Unless perhaps you caught an episode of *Take the High Road* from two thousand and four? I played Hugh Tankton, a businessman set on purchasing a plot of derelict land to turn into an amusement park? No?' He turned sideways to show his profile. 'Some people say I have an air of Simon Callow ...'

'From *The X Factor*?' Kat asked doubtfully.

'No!' Darwin tutted. 'My thespian colleague most notable for crashing out in *Four Weddings and a Funeral*.'

'I love that film!' said Kat. 'My mum watches it all the time.' She squinted at him across the room. 'Okay, I guess I see who you're talking about. So do you know him?'

'I'm not sure that I would be wholly truthful if I claimed close kinship but I did once spot him in the BBC canteen when I was interviewed for *Britain's Building Cowboys*. To let you understand, I had commissioned an extension that went horribly wrong and now I'm forced to house any overnight guests on a camp bed—'

'Drink, anyone?' Logan interrupted. 'Oh, here's Dusty.'

'Evening, everyone!' Dusty smiled as she entered the living room. 'You know I lay down my head for a wee catnap and if it hadn't been for my medication alarm going off, I do believe I would have slept until Sunday!'

Darwin guffawed in Dusty's direction. He removed his hat and bowed graciously.

'Oh … aren't you that actor?'

'Yes, I am, dear lady!' Darwin grinned. 'Recognition at last!'

'I loved you in *A Room with a View*,' said Dusty. 'Although that scene when you took all your clothes off and jumped into the pond … my! It was a bit too racy even for me.'

'If only,' he grunted. 'Now where can I get one of those beers?'

'Sorry, did I say something wrong?' Dusty apologised. She took refuge on the settee. 'I've only just come to.'

Logan placed a hand on her shoulder. 'You're fine, Dusty. I think we're all ready for some food.'

The kitchen door swung open and Aubrey breezed into the room. 'Ah, good – everyone's here. If you could please be seated?' He rubbed his hands together. 'Gregor has been hard at work all day preparing your supper; I'm sure you'll enjoy it. However, I do have one tiny caveat.'

'Oh yes?' Logan asked. 'Are we doing the washing-up?'

'Heavens, no, dear boy,' said Aubrey. 'I'm just warning you that the haddock this evening is fresh out of the water and – while Gregor makes every effort to retrieve any evidence of bony material – there is a natural risk that the odd fragment may have escaped his scrupulous attention.'

'Can we get that in writing?' Darwin said with a mock frown.

'Well, earlier this year, we did have the most unfortunate frightful episode when we received online feedback pertaining to a single bone found in Gregor's fish dish … so I'm just mitigating the risk and covering all bases.'

'Get on with it, man!' Darwin protested. 'The fish will have swum back upstream by now!'

'Of course,' Aubrey backed out of the room again, returning with a tray held at shoulder height. 'Now please be mindful of the hot plates.'

'Looks lovely,' said Dusty. 'What's that green splodge?'

'That'll be the *mousse of crushed garden pea*,' Logan whispered.

'I prefer mushy peas,' Dusty replied. 'I've never seen a *mousse* pea before.'

'Then you've never been in a Canadian forest – *boom boom!*' Logan laughed.

'See what I mean, Daddy?' Felicity giggled uncontrollably. 'I told you what fun these people are.'

'I do my best,' said Logan. 'The world would be a miserable place without the *Commonus Punnus*. Wait until breakfast, I'll be cracking *yolks* left, right and centre.'

'Stop!' Felicity screeched. 'I'll get a stitch.'

'And the spring vegetable roulade for Madame,' Aubrey placed the plate in front of Kat.

Out of the corner of his eye, Logan observed Kat placing a tiny toy in front of her plate and taking a photo.

Aubrey rubbed his hands together. 'Enjoy. Now, does anyone need anything else?'

'I don't suppose you have ketchup?' Logan asked.

'*Ketchup?* Oh, I shouldn't think Gregor would want you tainting his flavour combinations with sugar-based colouring,' Aubrey sniffed.

'You're right,' said Logan. 'This is perfect.'

'You'll be sent back to your tent if you're not careful,' Kat warned.

'Is that your tent out in the back garden?' asked Felicity.

'It is.'

'So you prefer the spiritual bond with nature? The lure of the great outdoors and all that?'

'And it's free,' Logan quipped.

'You're such a card!'

'I hope it's not this roulade making me nauseous,' Kat muttered to Dusty. 'Would be a shame to waste Gregor's effort.'

Logan munched on a chip. 'So what brings you up to Lochinver, Darwin?'

'Ah! Well, I'm glad you ask,' Darwin grinned. 'I'm producing, directing and starring in a one-man theatrical performance of Shakespeare's soliloquies.'

'Wow! Ambitious.' Logan nodded in appreciation as he scooped at the mousse.

'It's called *Just Me, or Not Just Me*,' Felicity added proudly.

'Clever,' said Logan.

'Why, thank you. It's been a soul-searching voyage for me; one which started when I was nine years old and witnessed Romeo's, "What light through yonder window breaks". I tell you, Logan, I felt a stab right here.' He punched his chest. 'And I knew then that my mission in life would be to share such tenderness and torture with the world. Even at such a young age, I understood it was my *raison d'être*.'

'Really?'

'Indeed. Throughout my career I've been learning and honing my craft – making the performing arts arduous journey …'

'*Taking the High Road?*'

'Exactly! And so here am I. On a grand tour of Scotland.'

'That sounds wonderful,' said Dusty. 'I can't believe I'm having dinner with a famous actor. Wait until I tell Cherie! Didn't I see you in *Death in Paradise*? I love that programme – it makes me feel all hot and summery even in the middle of winter.'

'I … er—'

'Daddy was in the Edinburgh Festival Fringe last year,' Felicity interrupted. 'Weren't you, Daddy?'

'Cool,' said Logan. 'Which venue were you playing?'

Darwin's fork hovered over his battered haddock. 'Well, there's actually quite a traumatic narrative relating to last year's Fringe.' He sawed at the fish.

'Tell them, Daddy!'

'It was in truth quite distressing. So,' he paused while swallowing a mouthful, 'I had been corresponding with a company called Straight Fringe for months; negotiating dates and costs et cetera. You know how it is?'

'Of course.'

'I paid an extortionate sum of money to this company and arrived in Edinburgh with such excitement and trepidation. It was to be my first solo venture. So it transpired that I arrived as an eager beaver at my venue – with my dear stagehand Luke in tow – only to discover that my theatrical venue was, in fact, someone's front room!'

'Can you believe it?' Felicity demanded. 'A living room! And the woman didn't even know it had been booked out.'

'You're kidding!' said Logan, clearing his plate.

'Not at all, young man. I wish I were. So the property belonged to a Mrs Ross and, while she skedaddled off to Australia to visit her son in Cairns, her unscrupulous lodger booked out her front room to me.'

'And where was this?'

'That's another bloody thing. Excuse my French,' he apologised to Dusty.

'Eh?'

'It wasn't even *in* Edinburgh. The flat was in Dalkeith! I mean, talk about rural! On my final evening's performance, the audience couldn't actually hear my monologue owing to the herding of the milk cows back into their shed!'

'Oh dear,' said Logan, finishing another beer.

'*Oh dear?*' Darwin echoed. '*Oh dear* is what one says when one steps in a puddle in ones brogues and one has damp feet all day. *Oh dear* is not what you say when you've paid three thousand pounds to have your lifelong ambition presented in the corner of a sitting room in *frigging* Dalkeith, with the audience perched on a set of pine dining chairs circa nineteen seventy and, during the final moments of my epiphany, the doorbell is rung by a delivery boy grasping a *frigging* Chinese carry-out!'

'Now, Daddy, – watch your blood pressure. Remember what your doctor told you.'

'Go easy on the cheese toasties?'

'And the other thing … you know? *Stress?* Take deep breaths.'

Darwin pushed his chair back and sighed. 'Felicity is quite right. I really should just let it go. Anyway, this is another year and a new tour. So … here's to me!' He raised his bottle of beer.

'Can we see your show?' Dusty asked, putting down her cutlery.

'Now you're talking!' Darwin saluted Dusty with his bottle. 'My good lady I would be nothing short of delighted if you were to partake of one of my performances tomorrow.'

'Where is it on? I haven't seen a theatre in Lochinver but we were at the community centre today – is it on there?'

'Daddy's playing the Highland Games.'

'What – all of them?' Kat asked.

'No, silly! He has a pop-up theatre over by the Scots Pine bar.'

'Yes, I thought the games would provide an excellent opportunity to harvest from a large spectatorship. I've been given a pitch for the three days. So plenty of time to catch a performance tomorrow!'

'And how has it been going so far?' Dusty asked. 'Have you been playing to a packed audience?'

'Actually, the pop-up only seats twenty,' said Felicity.

'Oh, what a shame,' said Dusty. 'I expect you have to turn people away?'

'Hmm, not so much.' Darwin wiped his mouth with a napkin.

'So we'll be able to see the show? I wouldn't want to take up someone's place.'

'I'm front of house,' Felicity declared. 'So I'll make sure we reserve your seats. It'll be good to have some class in the audience. I put on my cheerful face and try to drum up business but the locals aren't exactly open to culture. Perhaps being next to the bar wasn't the smartest move. I touted myself around a bit today but was told to piss off at least twice. And one youth in a football top asked me if "Shakespeare was the wanker in tights?"'

'Sorry, darling. I know you're doing your best.' Darwin patted his daughter's hand.

Aubrey appeared from the kitchen to remove their plates. 'Now, for dessert Gregor has created a poached apple and cinnamon compote with a topping of browned, crumbed granola.'

'How delicious,' Dusty said. 'It sounds like an apple crumble!'

'There are some culinary similarities,' Aubrey agreed. 'And it is served with a warm milk vanilla sauce.'

'A bit like custard?'

Chapter 27

After clearing away the dessert dishes Aubrey nodded with his head. 'Help yourself to tea and coffee. And then we have a wee surprise for you.'

'Ooh! Exciting.' Dusty clapped her hands together. 'The last time anyone said they had a surprise for me was when Sadie passed on a two-for-one voucher for M and S underwear. As if I needed any more bras at my age! I wonder what kind of surprise?'

'Let's hope it involves alcohol,' Logan suggested.

'Here, Logan, give me a hand,' said Aubrey, making to shift the long dining table up against the wall. 'Now let's push the settee back.'

'Are we having a party?' Dusty enquired. 'I used to love it at Hogmanay when everyone had to take a turn at giving a party piece. Mine was always playing the spoons; my speciality was "The Bonny Banks of Loch Lomond". Do you remember, Kat? All the neighbours came round.'

'Sort of.'

'Your mum used to make you play the fiddle.'

'God, yes!' Kat groaned. 'That flipping violin. How painful must that have been for you?'

'Not at all! It was just in the spirit of New Year's Eve.'

'And talking of spirits?' Logan gazed at the whisky decanter with longing.

Aubrey checked over his shoulder. 'What the heck!' He

reached for two whisky tumblers and poured a generous measure into each. 'Shh! I won't tell if you don't!'

'Bottoms up!' Logan grinned.

'Indeed. Anyone else for a wee sample?'

'Go on then – if you insist!' Darwin nodded.

'So what's this surprise?' Dusty asked, snuggling into a corner of the settee. Kat brewed a mug of peppermint tea and sat next to her.

'Well …' Aubrey began. 'I might be looking for a couple of volunteers.'

'For what?' Felicity asked with an expectant face.

'Tonight is our *Saturday Night Jive*. Let's just say there's a bit of dressing up involved.'

'Well, why didn't you say so, man!' Darwin cried. He stood to attention. 'Dressing up is what I do for a living.'

'And can I help?' Felicity said. 'I love a pretty frock.'

'Right, let's have you two.' Aubrey stuck his head into the kitchen. 'Come on, Gregor, love, it's Saturday night!'

Gregor burst out of the kitchen, throwing his apron on to the floor. 'I'm here! Let's get this party started!'

Kat sank low. 'I'm scared,' she muttered.

'Off we go.' Aubrey herded Darwin and Felicity towards a door marked PRIVATE.

'We won't be long!' Gregor winked at the audience of three.

After five minutes of silence had elapsed Logan pushed himself up from the settee. 'Might as well prepare myself for the worst.' He poured another whisky. 'This is a good malt.'

'What's the worst?' Kat asked. 'I couldn't bear it if they come back wearing kilts and force us into some lame *ceilidh* dancing.'

Logan shuddered. 'For me the worst would be if they launch

into an hour-long fancy-pants poetry rendition.' He threw back the whisky.

'I'm not so keen on magic,' Dusty confessed. 'They always think they're so clever but I just wish they would tell us how they do the trick. I mean – we all know magic doesn't exist. So why not just tell us how they did it. It drives me mad!'

Logan snorted. 'You tell 'em, Dusty.'

Behind the private door Darwin and Felicity were bundled into another room. Aubrey flicked on the light switch.

'Oh my!' Darwin breathed. 'What's all this? I take it you're fans of Blondie?'

'May we welcome you to the official headquarters of the Scottish men's Debbie Harry fan club,' Aubrey said, sweeping his arm in an arc. Gregor clapped his hands together. 'We're the Deborah Hairies!'

'I used to *love* Blondie,' said Darwin.

'What do you mean *used to*?' Aubrey demanded. 'They're as strong as ever.'

'Of course. I just meant—'

'Wow!' Felicity squealed. 'You really are mega-fans. Look at all this stuff! Photos and CDs and outfits and mugs and models and ...'

'Is this genuine?' Darwin asked, pointing to a dummy dressed in a torn T-shirt and yellow striped trousers.

'Oh yes,' said Aubrey. 'This is a lifetime's pledge to memorabilia. I bought 'Denis' when I was eighteen years old and I've been collecting ever since.'

'And what about you, Gregor? Are you a fan too?'

'I should say so! In fact, that's how we met, wasn't it, sweetie?

At a Blondie gig in Munich.'

'So are these all hers?' Felicity asked, peering into an illuminated glass cabinet displaying black boots and red stilettos. 'Actually *hers*?'

'They are,' Aubrey nodded proudly.

'And are these all *yours*?' Darwin waved his hand at a corkboard sagging beneath the weight of concert tickets from around the world.

'They are. I reckon I've seen Blondie perform in –' Aubrey counted in his head – 'six … no *seven* countries!'

'My, that *is* devotion,' said Darwin. 'I wish I had such a dedicated fanbase.'

'No offence, Mr Flockhart,' said Gregor, 'but you might have had a different experience in life if you had the looks of Debbie Harry.'

'Granted.'

'Hey, Daddy, *look* at all these selfies. You should start collecting some too!'

'Hardly,' Darwin grunted. 'So what did you mean by *headquarters*?'

'Aubrey and I run the fan club in Scotland – it's mostly men. Hence the "Hairies". We have our own wee Hall of Fame.'

'But what about the women?' Felicity objected.

'Oh, we're not the only Blondie fan club in the UK. But we serve a purpose up here in Scotland. We take a lot of this merchandise on tour – maintain a presence at some of the pop fairs that take place around the country.'

'That's super!' said Felicity.

'Yes, we close the guesthouse over January and February. That's our "us" time,' Aubrey said. 'In fact, last year we ran a tour of France, Italy, Poland and Luxembourg. They're *huge* in Luxembourg.'

Darwin inspected the turntable and vinyl collection. 'This is immense.'

'So what do you need us to do?' Felicity asked.

'Ah! Well, it's just a bit of fun, really,' Aubrey smiled. He opened a wardrobe. 'Don't worry – these aren't the real deal.' He wafted his hand through the costumes. 'These are Debbie Harry outfits through the ages, from punk to the noughties. Let's just have a bit of a laugh.'

'Quite right!' Darwin nodded.

Aubrey selected a blonde wig and fitted it over Darwin's balding head. 'Perfect!'

Darwin ran his hand through the long hair. 'I feel like a princess!'

'Felicity? Would you care to choose an outfit?'

'Oh … there are so many. Hey, I love these!' She grabbed a pair of thigh-length black boots.

'Then you'll need this to go with those.' Aubrey handed her a ripped leather jacket.

Felicity kicked off her pumps and pulled on the boots, tying her pinafore up with a belt. She threw on the jacket and tucked her hair under a blonde bobbed wig. 'How do I look?' She pouted into the mirror.

'A final touch, I think,' Aubrey said, reaching for a scarlet lipstick.

'Can I borrow that after you?' Darwin asked.

'Daddy!'

'I want to look the part. You know me – I'm a method actor.' Darwin rolled his shoulders and took a few deep breaths.

Gregor swished through the dresses. 'It might be a bit of a long shot but what about this?'

'Oh *yes*!' Darwin exclaimed. 'That's got my name all over it. Don't mind me.' He unzipped his trousers and kicked them across the room, unfastening his shirt at the same time. Gregor passed him the pink and cream striped Lycra jumpsuit.

'I don't ever recall seeing her in this but it's so comfy,' said Darwin, looking like a bloated Mr Whippy. He ran his hands over the stretched material. 'It's very forgiving.'

'Forgiving but not forgotten,' Felicity protested. 'Honestly, Daddy, you look *ridiculous*.'

'None taken!'

Aubrey and Gregor threw on sombre dark T-shirts and jeans and matching shades. 'I suppose we'll be the band this week seeing as our guests ought to have the limelight. Well … don't you two look fabulous? Right, let me run you through a few Debbie moves. Gregor can fire up the music from here. We'll go in first and do the warm-up to the introductory medley. When you hear the opening bars of "Call Me!", come charging on to the stage. Take these mics.'

Aubrey and Gregor exited the room, slinging guitars over their shoulders.

'Golly, Daddy, I never thought we'd be doing this in a back room in the middle of the Scottish Highlands.'

Darwin did a few bends to the side and marching on the spot. He waved his arms in big circles as though doing the backstroke.

'Well, Felicity, I suppose I take this type of spontaneous entertainment in my stride. It's what makes me a professional. You could throw me into the deepest ocean and I'd surface reciting, "Now is the winter of our discontent".'

'*Wah!* That's us, Daddy – we're on!' Felicity gave her father a shove in the back as they burst into the living room. Darwin pranced in a circle as Felicity belted out, 'Colour me your colour, baby, colour me your car!'

Kat, Dusty and Logan shrank back into the settee with their mouths open. Their eyes flew from Felicity's thrusting hips to Darwin's Jagger-like strutting in front of the fireplace. Aubrey and Gregor strummed their stringless guitars in the background, scowling moodily at the meagre audience. Music blasted from wall-mounted speakers, vibrating around the room. Darwin paced up and down the carpet, flicking his blonde hair and pouting his red lips at Logan, who swallowed the last of his whisky. Felicity posed in front of the settee and bent forward, pushing her rear into their faces.

'Oh my goodness!' Dusty cried. 'What was in that apple crumble?'

Logan slapped Felicity playfully. 'It's at times like these when you need a dollar bill – it's just not the same slipping you a one-pound coin.'

'Unless you need a shopping trolley,' Kat added.

Darwin ploughed back and forth across the carpet until sweat dripped from his chin. Felicity attempted to dance through the instrumental, her ankles buckling in the high boots. 'Ow!' she complained, hanging on to a dining-room chair. The song eventually faded and the four band members bowed with a theatrical flourish.

'Thank you so much!' Aubrey shouted. 'We've been the Blondies – good night!' He bustled the band members back through the private door.

A minute passed.

'What – the – hell?' Kat said, blinking. She rubbed her eyes. 'There are some things you just can't un-see.'

Logan got up silently, poured another whisky and drank it in one. He poured another and sank back on to the settee. 'I'm too young,' he murmured.

'Who …?' Dusty said. 'What …?'

Logan patted her knee. 'And you thought you'd seen it all?'

'Actually, I don't know what I *have* just seen. What was that? At least with an M and S voucher you know what you're getting.'

The three were still sitting in shock when the Blondies returned a few minutes later – back in their everyday attire.

'How good were *we*?' Darwin demanded, wiping the sweat off his face with his linen shirtsleeve. He ran over to the settee to high-five each individual.

'I'm a bit lost for words,' Kat mumbled. 'I can honestly say that I've never seen anything quite like it before.'

'Dusty?' Darwin prompted.

Dusty shook her head. 'Was that *nylon*?'

Logan sprang up. He gave Darwin's hand a mighty shake. 'Ha! That was stupendous! *Loved* it.'

'Really? I do like to please. I'm hoping for a five-star review.'

'How did you like me as a blonde?' Felicity simpered, perching on the arm of the settee. 'Do you think it suited me?'

'Er … I …' Logan faltered. 'Well, you definitely had more fun.'

'We did!' Felicity agreed.

'More than us, at any rate,' Kat whispered to Dusty.

'Drinks all round!' Gregor announced as he returned to the room. 'Now, would anyone like to try my special malt?'

'Oh, I wouldn't mind trying some,' Logan slurred. He could see two Gregors but reckoned that was still an improvement on Darwin in a jumpsuit.

Finally exhausted by Aubrey's *Saturday Night Jive* all except Darwin retreated to their bedrooms, Logan heading for the garden with a swagger. Darwin strode around the room as he refocused on the more pressing performance of the following day. He leant his hands on the wide windowsill and gazed out into the darkness. '*Tomorrow, and tomorrow and tomorrow, creeps in this petty pace from day to day.*'

Chapter 28

'Wardrobe malfunction!' Ron shouted across the hall to Dell. 'My zip's stuck.' His hands fiddled at his crotch.

'Up or down?' Dell asked.

'Down! I can't go on stage on Monday with my flies down. It'll make front page news if I'm accused of indecent exposure.'

'It's hardly press night on Broadway.'

'Still, Dell. It'll cause more than a titter amongst the eagle-eyed.'

'Can't you cover it with your gun?'

'Eh? Then it'll look like I'm wearing a codpiece!'

Dell knelt down in front of Ron's groin and poked at the zip with her finger.

'Please, Mrs Carmichael, this is a *family* show!' Mo protested as she swept past pushing a bicycle. 'The curtain will be going up in five minutes.'

'Five minutes!' Ron wailed.

'Quick, let me grab a safety pin but you'll need to stand still.'

'Don't worry about that! The last thing I need is you pricking my—'

'*Ron!*'

Mo shouted from offstage. 'Places now, everyone. Curtain is going up in two minutes. That's *two* minutes. Chris, will you please stop using your braces to catapult Haribos at Sandy? Nuns, you'll need to stand further back – the audience will be able to see your habits flapping around on the edges ... at least a foot back.' She clapped her hands loudly. 'Come on, people, we've got a show to put on! Good luck, everyone!'

In his final scene Ron marched around the stage ordering his minions to check every corner of the abbey. He couldn't fail to miss Dell's frantic waving from stage left and histrionic jabbing at her watch. So he picked up the pace and half of the von Trapp children were still mucking about behind the curtain when he called off the search and they were expected back on for the finale. Dell whispered her excuses to Mo and pushed Ron towards the exit. '*Come on!*' she hissed. 'It's half past nine! We need to get a move on if we're to catch that bugger Arthur with his pants down.'

'I hardly think he'll be fornicating at the back of the station,' Ron protested as he fumbled for the car keys. 'I wish we had time to get changed. This uniform is killing me – I'm like a stuffed pig with these buttons done up.'

'There's no time,' said Dell, jumping into the passenger seat. 'Which way are you going? Through the Grassmarket and down the Royal Mile?'

Ron swung the car on to Murrayfield Road. 'I was thinking about going along Queen Street and round by Picardy Place?'

'Whatever – just get a shifty on.'

'Move your head back, Dell – I can't see the traffic past your bloody veil.'

'Why is it so busy tonight? There are cars everywhere – it's mobbed.'

'I think there was a gig on at Murrayfield ... maybe the Rolling Stones?'

'Don't ask me!'

Ron sped along Queen Street, tutting at every red light. He drummed his fingers on the steering wheel. 'I'm just going to park somewhere along New Street, then we'll need to walk along.'

'Walk? We'll need to run at this rate.'

'I can't run in these trousers. They're stiff as a board.'

Ron abandoned the car half on the pavement and they bolted towards Waverley Station. In the darkly lit street Dell stumbled off the kerb, twisting her ankle. 'Aya!' she cried, grabbing at Ron.

'What've you done?'

'I think it's sprained. Ow! Ow!' Dell hobbled a few steps.

'Here, take my hand,' Ron offered, hurrying along the pavement. They turned the corner and the rear of the station came into view. Ron forged ahead, dragging Dell behind as she limped as quickly as she could.

Alec was leaning back in his chair, balancing on two legs. His eyes were fixed on a European football game, the volume turned down. He reached for his mug of coffee – the third of the evening – and took a bite from a steak-bake, still in its paper bag. His phone vibrated and he grinned at the video clip his pal had just posted. A cat, dressed as Darth Vader, swiping at a mouse. nice one he messaged back.

'*Unit three-four-oh to control,*' his radio transceiver crackled. '*Do you read me? Over.*'

Alec tipped his chair forward as he spoke into the transmitter. 'Three-four-oh receiving. What's up, Cam? Over.'

'*What's the score? Over,*' Cam asked.

'Come off it, Cam, you know we're not meant to use these for that. One – nil. Over.'

'*Nah, I'm only joking about the footie. Couldn't give a stuff who beats Man City. Over.*'

'Get lost, then. Over.'

'*No, I need you to take a wander down to the taxi pick-up. Some joker has stopped a cabbie saying there's some kind of military geezer dragging a woman along the pavement. Over.*'

'You're kidding, right? Over.' Alec threw the pasty on to the table and reached for his torch.

'*No – wish I was, bro. And to make matters worse the caller said he thought it was a nun. Over.*'

'Sorry – did you say "nun"? Repeat – nun? Over.'

'*Yes. I repeat. There's a report of a serviceman possibly abducting a nun at the back of the station. Over.*'

'No way, man! This is police business. I'm not equipped for that carry-on. What if he's armed? Over.'

'*Don't be a dick, Alec. Just check it out. Over.*'

Alec cursed as he pulled on his high-vis jacket and stuck a cap on his head. *Why me?* He jogged down the iron staircase that led to the taxi rank, which stood empty. There was little light coming from the quiet street. He checked to his left, where a group of lads were jostling along the pavement into town. Turning to his right he immediately spotted the couple in question – a sturdy male in Nazi uniform tugging a middle-aged nun behind him. She was clearly in pain and resisting his abduction. *Shit!*

'Slow down!' Dell protested. 'You're going too fast.'

'You're the one who's desperate to stick your nose in.'

'Yeah, but I can feel my ankle swelling up. I'm going to—'

'Shh!' Ron said. 'I think I can see him. Is that Arthur over the road standing in that archway?'

'It's too dark, I can't see. Maybe.'

'Perhaps we should wait here,' Ron said, pulling Dell back into the shadow of the station. 'We don't want to get too near.'

'Fine,' Dell agreed, leaning on a low wall. 'I can't believe what a cheating swine he is.'

Alec took a deep breath and approached the couple with his arms held wide. 'Right then, you two, what's going on here? Madame, can I ask whether you are alright?'

'Not really,' Dell whimpered. 'I think I've sprained my ankle.'

Alec turned to Ron and shone the torch in his face. 'What, may I ask, is your business with this poor woman?'

'None of *your* business, anyway. Who are you?'

'*Shh!*' Dell urged, nodding over the road. 'Keep your voice down.'

Alec drew himself up to his full five-foot-eight height and puffed out his chest. 'My name's Alec Donald and I'm Senior Security Officer for Waverley Station. I have every right to investigate any person of questionable motive, who may be behaving in a suspicious manner within the parameter of the station.'

'Only *just*,' Ron commented, stepping towards the kerb.

'Stay where you are! Now, I'm asking you again – what is the nature of your business with this woman? I observed you forcing her against her will to progress along this street and—'

The transceiver crackled on his lapel. '*What's the story, Alec? Do you require backup? Over.*'

'*Shh!*' Ron whispered, checking to see whether the sound had carried over the road.

'Don't you "shush" me,' Alec objected.

'Look, this is my wife and we're just out for a quiet stroll of an evening.'

'Give over, man! Is it normal in your world to be dressed like Hitler and to force your wife to dress as a nun? What kind of sick life do you lead?'

Dell caught a movement in the archway, where Arthur had been hiding. She couldn't quite make out anything other than a shadowy figure. She twirled Ron round so that he was facing that direction while she patted Alec's arm in an effort to distract him.

'Honestly, Mr Security Man, this is my husband, Ron Carmichael. We've been rehearsing for a musical you see – *The Sound of Music*. Ron plays one of the Nazi soldiers and I'm standing in for Donna, who fell off a scooter and chipped her front tooth. I'm Mother Abbess – *Climb Every Mountain*,' she half-sang in a stage whisper. She quickly checked over her shoulder.

'*The Sound of Music*? Ah, well that explains the costumes,' said Alec, hugely relieved. 'But it doesn't explain why you are skulking around the back of the station on a Saturday night, now, does it?'

Alec's transceiver burst into life again. '*Come on, Alec – what's going on? Please report now! Over.*'

Ron winced as Arthur retreated into the archway. But then another shape emerged. It stepped in closer to Arthur, who was backed against a wall. The stranger's arm came up, one hand leaning against the wall, pinning Arthur to the spot. The shadow bent in closer, speaking into Arthur's ear. A car turned down Calton Road, temporarily flooding the scene with light. Ron jolted upright. 'It's another man!' he cried.

'*What?*' Dell asked in disbelief.

'His secret tryst is with another man!'

Dell frowned. 'Oh dear, this is worse for Cherie than I thought.'

'But maybe explains why Arthur has been rummaging around

in Dusty's wardrobe – maybe he's going through some kind of trans-thing?'

'Maybe,' Dell mused.

The car passed with a roar and the street fell into darkness. Ron surveyed the archway but it was empty.

'What are you pair on about?' Alec asked in bemusement. He flashed his torch up and down the pavement.

'Look, are we free to go?' Ron appealed with his hands open.

'And I really must elevate this ankle,' Dell complained. 'It's agony. I need to get some ice on it.'

Alec shook his head. 'You know, I've been doing the night shift for the last five years, but this really takes the biscuit. So, you're telling me that soldier-man here is your husband and you're happy to go with him of your own free will?'

'I am,' said Dell. 'Although if he were to reappear as George Clooney, I wouldn't object.'

'Right – well, be off with you. And – a word of advice – if you're really into cosplay, can I suggest you enjoy it in the comfort of your own home? Please stay away from public arenas.'

'Yes, sir, advice noted,' Ron nodded, leading Dell back to the car.

'*Alec – please respond now or I'll be forced to escalate the situation. Over.*'

'Relax, Cam, it's all under control. Just a pair of dafties trying to spice up their marriage. Over.'

<line space>

Arthur scrambled up the stone stairs in the dark, desperate to get away. He had known a thousand wasn't going to do it. It was barely worth the effort of turning out by either party. But he *had* hoped it would buy him another week. *Curses!* He'd have to come up with another plan. He strode towards London Road, where he waited impatiently next to a teenage couple who had clearly mistaken the bus shelter for a double room.

Chapter 29

'My apologies,' said Darwin. 'I think with all the excitement I forgot to fill in your wee chitty.'

Aubrey's pencil hovered above his notepad. 'Not to worry, I can take your order now. Never let it be said that Mill House doesn't have a relaxed attitude to customer requirements. So – scrambled, boiled, poached, fried or an omelette?'

'I'm a poached man myself,' said Darwin. 'Although, after last night, some might say I should be *toasted*!'

'And white or brown bread?'

'White ... but don't tell my daughter I asked for that!'

'Very good. Now please do help yourself to cereal.'

Dusty wagged her finger at Darwin. 'You know what's good for you.'

'Bran is good for me, but I'm not a bloody horse.' Darwin guffawed at his own joke.

'Anyway, I expect you need some energy for all your dramatic performances today?'

'Indeed,' said Darwin, spooning cereal into his wide mouth.

'Morning, Daddy!' Felicity said as she pulled up a chair next to her father. 'What are you doing eating that sugary nonsense? Aubrey's laid on some splendid muesli and you've opted for Choco-tripe!'

'Oh, I never noticed the other stuff. I just went for the nearest.'

Darwin winked at Dusty.

'Morning,' Kat yawned as she made herself a mug of rooibos tea.

Aubrey appeared with Dusty's bacon and eggs in one hand and Darwin's full Scottish breakfast in the other.

'Really, Daddy,' Felicity tutted, 'you'd think you had the perfect cholesterol level.'

'Ach, I just keep taking the tablets. Isn't that what they're there for?'

'It's like fighting a losing battle.'

'But your father has a full day ahead of him,' argued Dusty. 'A man needs his food.'

Felicity shook her head. 'But energy doesn't need to come from solid fuel – it can come from lighter sources. More energy-efficient fuel.'

'Like wind?' Darwin laughed. 'Because that's what'll happen if I live off bloody muesli.'

'Language, Daddy.'

'And talking of language,' Kat enquired, 'how many performances do you have today?'

'I've got two this morning and two this afternoon.'

'Gosh, that's quite a lot,' said Kat. 'You do the same show four times a day?'

'Well, that's where I'd like to correct you,' said Darwin, dunking a sausage into the egg. 'Yes, on paper – granted – it might appear to be the same show. But let me tell you, young lady, *every* performance is unique. Every single time I recite the same lines I give it a piece of myself.'

Felicity rolled her eyes.

'I'm absolutely at the mercy of the ebb and flow of the audience. *Their* mood is *my* mood.' Darwin sipped his coffee. 'I'm sure you'll be astonished to hear that at one of my performances earlier this year, I couldn't even bear to utter a single word. I sensed an atmosphere in the place and simply felt I could not progress until we – as a united group – had confronted the elephant in the room.'

'Gosh,' Dusty breathed. 'You're such an artist. What did you sense was wrong?'

Darwin nodded his head as he relived the experience. 'It all stemmed from the back of the crowd where a young infant had filled its nappy. I sensed the tension in the auditorium but was not afraid to say, "Hey, guys, let's resolve the issue before we move on!". And they agreed. That nappy needed changing.'

'Good for you,' said Kat. 'There's many a Fringe show I've been at that was shit.'

'Morning, all,' Logan murmured as he slipped off his jacket. He kept his sunglasses on.

'I've saved a seat for you here,' Felicity said, patting the chair next to her. 'How did you sleep in the great outdoors?'

'Eugh,' said Logan, holding his head in his hands. 'I have to confess, I much prefer the comfort of a double bed. Especially with a hangover.'

Felicity blushed. 'I feel rather guilty having booked the king-size for myself.'

'Now, I never said anything about not being king-sized!'

'Oh – ha ha,' Felicity twittered.

'Glad you've retained your sense of humour, young man. Despite the heavy-handedness with the whisky,' Darwin said, slapping butter on to his toast.

'Urgh, I'm never drinking again,' Logan groaned. 'My body is clearly not used to such fine malt. Now a litre bottle of Lidl's own brand I can handle.'

'How would you like your eggs?' Aubrey enquired.

'Excuse me!' said Logan, bolting from the table.

'Oh dear,' Kat smirked. 'The demon alcohol.'

'Now, now,' Felicity tutted. 'One mustn't jump to conclusions. Logan may very well be suffering from a virus. September can give you a chill if you're sleeping outdoors.'

'You're quite right,' Kat agreed. 'And if Logan has a wee cold, perhaps a hot toddy might be the answer. I'll suggest it when he comes back. Sorry, Aubrey, can I have the *locally foraged mushrooms on toast*, please?'

'Of course.' Aubrey rubbed his eyes with nervous vigour. 'And did you enjoy the Saturday Night Jive?'

'We did!' Dusty said. 'I can honestly say that I've never seen anything quite like it.'

'Why, thank you! Gregor will be delighted.'

Logan slunk back to the table, wiping his mouth.

'So,' Kat began, 'what's the plan, Stan?' She let Logan gulp down some black coffee before raising her eyebrows.

Logan coughed. 'Right – the plan. It'll be all about the Assynt Highland Games today.'

'Ooh! Can I help?' Felicity waved her hand in the air. 'I'm going to be there with Daddy but I'd love to help. It will be so exciting to assist with a forensic investigation.'

'Em …'

'*Please* – I promise not to get in the way.'

'I guess we could use all the help on offer?' Logan looked at Kat, who shrugged.

'It will be *amazing*!' Felicity beamed.

'Will it?' Logan asked. 'It feels like looking for a needle in a haystack.'

'Or a Hamish in a haystack,' Felicity laughed.

'Now, dear, remember you're front of house for me four times a day,' said Darwin, wiping a crust of toast around his plate. 'Delicious! Nothing quite beats a Scottish breakfast.'

'Ah, but I've been thinking,' said Felicity. 'How about if I interrogate each person that comes into your show? I could ask, a) *Is your name Hamish?*, b) *Is your name Jessica or Jess?* and c) *Do you know anyone of that name?*'

'That may well work,' Logan mused. 'Just toast for me.'

'No problem,' Aubrey said, presenting Kat with her mushrooms.

'Well, I don't want my paying customers to feel as though they have to pass some type of inquisition before they're allowed to enter,' Darwin objected. 'I'd much rather you greeted them with a sweet smile, perhaps a Shakespearean curtsy and the offer of a discounted programme. Some of my fans will have travelled the length and breadth of this country to hear my verse. The last thing I want is for them to be corralled into some undergraduate knavery project.'

'Don't be silly, Daddy – I'll be most discreet.'

'I'm just not sure.' Darwin plucked a piece of sausage from a back molar. 'I have my image to think of. I'm hoping this tour might shine a spotlight on my delivery.'

'I'm sure it will,' said Dusty. 'And we can always tell someone about your hairy Blondie.'

'Thanks.'

'Honestly, Daddy, it will be A-okay. You're just over-worrying like the time you had that growth on your—'

'Fine!' Darwin held up his hand. 'As long as you sell as many programmes as yesterday I'll be happy.'

'And what about the *signed* programmes?' Felicity enquired.

'Am I still to charge an extra pound for those?'

'I thought we agreed five pounds?'

'We did but I only sold one – and that was to a man from Croatia. Remember, he was trying to get rid of sterling before he flew home?'

'One round of toast,' said Aubrey, handing a plate to Logan. 'So are you going to crack the Da Vinci code today? Bring home the Holy Grail?'

'Well, time is against us,' said Dusty. 'I do hope we can find our Hamish today.'

'We're really pinning our hopes on Hammy MacPhedran,' Kat added. 'If his nephew – was it Alastair? – can give us a number or other contact, we might be able to speak to him today.'

'I wish you luck,' said Aubrey. 'Gregor and I will be waiting here to greet you with a traditional Sunday roast and all the trimmings this evening.'

'Or?' said Kat.

'Or something that's not been shot on a moor,' Aubrey winked.

'Thank you. Although, I can just eat the vegetables.'

'Not at all!' Aubrey protested as he piled plates on to a tray. 'It is well within Gregor's gift to rustle up a gourmet delight for you.'

'Cool,' said Kat. 'And *our* plan?'

'Right, well, you guys were at the games yesterday – what's the layout?' Logan asked the Flockharts, topping up his coffee.

Darwin moved the salt and pepper grinders to the middle of the table. 'You drive up to Culag Park and can leave the car in here.' He pointed to behind the saltcellar. 'There is a roped-off arena in the centre of the field where all the games take place.' A side plate was placed on the table.

'Except for the fishing,' Felicity interrupted. 'There's some type of fishing competition down by the shore of the loch.'

'Aye,' Darwin nodded. He moved the butter dish. 'These are the public toilets.'

'Nice,' Kat commented.

'Along this side there are all the stalls and demonstration areas – arts and crafts,' said Darwin, placing an unused spoon next to the plate. 'On the other side of the centre is where the crowd sits. Most people bring their own chairs but some like shelter in the grandstand.' He pushed his empty mug beside the spoon. 'This is the bar and food area.'

'You *must* visit my favourite French eatery,' said Felicity. 'It's next to the blind dog folk but they do the most fabulous crêpes, if you like that sort of thing?'

'That reminds me!' said Logan, leaving the table in a hurry.

'So where is your pop-up theatre, Darwin?' Kat asked.

'Oh, er, about here, I'd say,' Darwin replied, pointing to the butter dish.

Kat sighed. 'Right, well I suppose we'd better get ready. I think we'll just try to approach as many people as possible.'

'But I'm going with you, aren't I?' Dusty said anxiously. 'I don't think I could talk to strangers on my own.'

'You seemed to do alright with what's-his-face over there.' Kat nodded to the door.

'Logan?' Felicity offered.

Kat rose from the table. 'I'm going to get my coat. See you back here in five minutes?'

'Rightio,' Dusty smiled. 'I have a good feeling about today.'

'Me too,' said Felicity. 'I hope I'm your lucky charm.'

Chapter 30

Kat had the engine running when Logan jogged out to the car and jumped into the back.

'Better?' Kat asked.

'Sorry about that. Where are the others?'

'They were quick off the mark,' Dusty said, speaking over her shoulder. 'Darwin was keen to get everything all set up for today.'

Kat negotiated the few winding miles along the coastal road until she spotted the line of cars turning into Culag Park. 'It's going to be busy.'

'I guess that's good?' Logan ventured. 'Surely a bigger crowd is likely to generate more leads?'

'Or make it harder to find Hammy's nephew.'

Logan shook his head. 'You know what these wee places are like, Kat – everyone knows everyone. I'm sure we'll track him down quite easily.'

The traffic queue crept forward until Kat bumped the car across a field and was directed into a space by a teenager in an oversized high-vis waistcoat. Kat and Dusty stood by the side of the car as Logan retrieved his notebook from his rucksack. He swept his hair back behind his ears, surveying the crowded park, which had a carnival atmosphere. Off-colour tents, stalls and patched marquees were pitched round a roped-off grassy oval. The previous day's events had taken their toll on the central zone, which was mashed into boggy strips. Streams of families were arriving with folding chairs, cool bags and picnic hampers. Children darted in and around their parents, and dogs barked a warning as they marked their territory. A samba band had set up next to the entrance and was blasting out a Caribbean version of 'Flower of Scotland'. Logan felt a shove from behind as an elderly man on a mobility scooter revved forward. 'Sorry, son, I don't know where the brake is on this damn thing,' he complained, veering off towards a hay bale.

'This is just like the Loopallu Festival,' said Logan, stepping aside.

'Uh-oh! Something's burning,' Dusty remarked, sniffing the air.

'I think it's that,' said Kat, pointing to a pizza trailer that had black smoke spiralling from a bent chimney.

'So,' said Logan. 'I'll head to the far end and work my way back. Do you want to start here? Text me if you find this Alastair bloke. I better write down his name.'

'It's Alastair Aitken,' said Kat, reading from her notes. 'And he lives at Suilven Lodge near Baddidarach.'

'I've no idea if I've spelt that right. Shall we meet up at lunchtime? Compare notes?' Logan suggested.

'Or buy you a sandwich?'

Logan frowned as he marched off, pushing his way through a clump of youths who were kicking a battered football to one another.

'That was a bit unfair,' Dusty said mildly. 'He *has* been helping us in his own time.'

Kat zipped up her jacket. 'Hmm. Come on, let's get started.'

They approached the first stall, which was selling COFFEE AND DONUTS. 'Fresh doughnut?' the woman asked.

'No, thanks, we've just had breakfast,' said Kat.

'Oh, I'd love one!' Dusty smiled. 'They smell wonderful.'

'Freshly baked. Fifty pence each or three for a pound.'

'I only want the one.'

The doughnut was wrapped in a napkin and exchanged for the coin. 'I don't suppose you know someone from around here called Alastair Aitken?' Kat asked.

'I couldn't tell you, hen. I'm just making a bit of extra cash. Next?'

Dusty took a large bite, covering her face in sugar. 'I haven't had a doughnut in years,' she said, licking her lips.

Kat shook her head. 'Let's try the next place.'

An open tent housed a range of carved wooden animals – mostly squirrels and hedgehogs, some adorned with red ribbons and plastic flowers.

'Make ever so lovely ornaments for your garden,' the vendor said as he reclined in a folding chair. 'Them owls are the most popular – must have sold at least twenty yesterday. Still not enough to retire on,' he chortled, pouring coffee from a Thermos flask.

'I like this one,' Dusty said, stroking a wooden rabbit sitting on a log.

'I'm not lugging a squinting rabbit around all day,' Kat protested.

'It's not squinting – it's cute.'

'It has actually got a bit of a squint,' the man agreed. 'Old Jimmy that carves them has a dodgy eye himself. Can't seem to see beyond that look.'

'Thank you but we're actually trying to track down a man called Alastair Aitken. He apparently lives at Suilven Lodge.'

'Where?'

'It's near Baddidarach.'

'Nope, you've lost me there.' The man scratched his head. 'I've been coming to these games for years but I can't say I've heard of him. What does he look like?'

'We don't know.'

'Then how will you know when you've found him?'

'I'll ask if he's Alastair Aitken.'

'So you're going to ask every man here if that's his name? Let me help you out then, doll. It's not me! I don't know what goes on in youngsters' heads these days.'

'Did I hear you say Alastair Aitken?'

Dusty and Kat swung round to see a short woman in her sixties, wearing a wax coat fastened tightly with a knotted belt. Her grey hair was cut boyishly short and her smile creased her brown face like a crushed paper bag. She was holding a pot of jam in one hand and a frying pan in the other.

'Er …' Kat faltered. 'That's right.'

'There you go, then,' the sitting man announced. 'Someone who's actually heard of your bloke. Is it a blind date or something?'

Kat ignored him as she looked expectantly at the woman. 'We're looking for Alastair Aitken. Do you know him?'

'He's a right rascal!' she cried, waving the pan above her head. 'Is he avoiding you? What's he been up to?'

'Nothing, I mean … it's a bit of a long story,' Kat sighed.

'Tell me, then. I'm not in a hurry—'

'Now I know who *she* is,' the man interrupted. 'That's old Nancy Cooper but everyone calls her Nance.'

'Hey – less of the *old*! And you can call me Nance too.'

'Well, Nance,' said Kat. 'We're trying to find Alastair so we can ask him how to get in touch with a Mr Hammy MacPhedran.'

'Bloody hell! I remember Hammy.' Nance gripped the jam with knotty fingers. 'I was only a kid at the time but he was such a royal show-off. Up and down the main street he paraded with bikes and sports cars. Of course, every girl fancied the pants off him. Even *me*! But I'd have died if he'd even looked my way.' She grinned, revealing a handful of stained teeth.

'He sounds a right character,' said Dusty.

'You better believe it,' Nance nodded emphatically. 'He was the best thing to happen to the place in years. When he got packed off to France the whole village went into mourning. Except for Cecil Bryden, of course. There wasn't a day went past when there wasn't some commotion or other to do with Hammy. And *looks*! We should have had a cardiac surgeon on call for all the broken hearts he left behind.'

'Do you know if he was ever engaged to a Jessica or Jess?' Kat asked, her pen poised.

Nance screwed up her face in concentration. 'I can't say I knew all of the girls in high school – they were ten years older than me.'

'He might even have met her somewhere other than Lochinver.'

'No doubt. He was a wild child. Used to zoom down to Glasgow in his swanky wheels so who knows what he got up to?'

'Well, perhaps his nephew might know something about it? Maybe his mum might have told him more?'

'I doubt it,' Nance shook her head. 'She and Hammy weren't particularly close. I think she spent all her time trying to be the model daughter to make up for his shenanigans. And that can take its toll. She died of cancer when Alastair was quite young. *My* theory is—'

'Oh, here we go.' Rabbit-man rolled his eyes.

'That wee Alastair was quite devoted to his mum and has never yet come across anyone that can nearly measure up to her.'

'You're quite the Oprah Winfrey, Nance.'

She shrugged. 'I'm not the only one that thinks that.'

'So do you know where we can find him?' Kat asked. 'Apparently he's here today.'

'Oh aye, he'll be here alright. They need all the young men they can find – especially for the tug-of-war. Our Lochinver Lads try to win it every year, and every year they get thrashed by the Assynt Anchors. Of course, half of *them* are rugby players.'

'How will we find him?' Kat persisted.

'Here, Robbie, take these,' said Nance, handing him the jam and frying pan. 'I'll help these ladies track down their man. I'll be back soon.'

'Fair enough. And can I interest you in any of our wee friends?'

'Och, you know fine well my garden's full of that crap!'

Nance exited the tent and surveyed the landscape. 'Right, let's start with the shooting gallery.'

Her little legs pumped as she forged through the crowd and Dusty and Kat hurried to keep up with her. Passing a Highland Gin stall, Nance came to an abrupt halt. Swarms of hands grabbed at plastic thimbles of gin as fast as the vendor could pour them. He held the bottle at shoulder height and circled the tray of plastic. 'Hey, Mack!' Nance shouted. 'Chuck one over here.' Mack didn't miss a beat as, with his left hand, he passed a glass high over the heads. Nance knocked it back, licking her lips. 'Not bad. You want one?' Kat and Dusty shook their heads.

Nance moved on to the next stall, which displayed a selection of Scottish cheeses. Less frenetic than the gin stall, a woman in an apron was chopping cheese into miniature cubes on a plastic plate.

'How's tricks?' Nance asked, popping a piece into her mouth.

'No' too bad,' the woman nodded. 'Sold aboot a quarter of ma stock yesterday so I'll be looking to offload the rest today.'

'Aye, well, it's quite a crowd for a Sunday. Have you seen Alastair Aitken at all?'

'Nuh! Should I have? You wanting some of ma Mull cheddar?' She looked beyond Nance to Kat.

'No, thanks,' said Kat.

'Try a bit.' The woman stabbed a cube and held it out. Kat reluctantly nibbled on it. Dusty held up her hands. 'I've just had a doughnut.'

'Oh, they're rare! I once ate a whole bag on the way home. I can't say it did my diabetes much good.' She leant forward and whispered. 'I told the nurse that I just had the one so as not to offend her. Anyway, what do you want Alastair for? Have the moths come back? I keep telling him to get Tommy in to sort them but he won't pay the money. Where are you two from?'

'Oh,' said Kat, taken aback. 'Edinburgh.'

'Really? What are you doing up here? Taking your grandma on a wee trip?'

'She's not my—'

'I miss my granny, God rest her soul.'

'By the way, do you think Big Eck will be tossing the caber?' Nance asked.

'I doubt it. I heard he's had a bit of a dodgy back this last month. Went to see Dr Farquhar about it. He got given painkillers and told to have a break from the forestry stuff.'

'How do you know all that?' Nance asked, helping herself to another cube.

'Sheila in the Spar told me. Her sister answers the phones.'

'Right, let's go,' Nance said, waving Kat and Dusty on.

'*Oh!*' the woman suddenly shouted. 'Now that I think about it, I did hear that Alastair was maybe going to be playing the pipes today.'

'Well, why didn't you *say* so?' Nance tutted. 'This way.' She pushed past a couple leading a pair of matching huskies with red bandanas tied round their fluffy necks.

Chapter 31

Kat and Dusty could hear the band before they could see it; the drone of bagpipes warming up carried over the noise of the mob. In a nearby field a handful of fully clad tartan pipers were pumping the pipes with crooked arms and lithe fingers. A lone drummer at the far end of the field was wielding a couple of mallets in the air. She gave an elaborate twirl above her head before smacking the drum hard. One piper appeared to be rehearsing 'The Skye Boat Song' while the others were belting out 'Amazing Grace'.

Dusty stuck her fingers in her ears. 'Oh my.'

'Ach, you learn to live with it,' Nance commented. 'Although, I have heard strangled cats in less pain. Donald! *Donald!* Have you seen Alastair aboot here?'

One of the pipers stopped playing and sauntered over. 'Which one?'

'Aitken.'

Donald shook his head. 'Last I saw he was trying to get the dogs out of the loch. They chased a rabbit all the way along the beach.'

'Hoo's yer ma?'

'So-so. The doctor says she shouldn't have been taking those tablets at the same time as using the cream. It's so confusing now.'

'Did she get the box I left at yer back door?'

'The spider catcher?' Donald asked. 'Yeah, she says it's great.'

'I'm not even joking you, Donald, but last winter I caught one so big it wouldn't even fit. I felt a bit bad that I'd broken its legs in half.'

Donald gave a shudder. 'Not at all. I hate the wee bastards!'

'This was the size of my hand,' Nance complained. 'I sometimes question God's logic. Please forgive me.' She looked up at the sky. 'So where's Alastair now?'

'No idea. Everyone was meant to be here by eleven but, as you can see, half the band's slept in. You can try the Scots Pine Bar.'

Nance turned to Kat and Dusty. 'Right, let's go.'

Kat's hand tightened on the cow in her pocket as she followed Nance and Dusty across the field.

Logan held his notebook open, biro at the ready. He found a lengthy queue outside a tent and approached the last person – an old man with a straggly white beard, dressed in a worn tweed suit with leather elbow patches.

'Morning,' said Logan. 'Can I ask if you know somebody called Alastair Aitken?'

'You the polis?' He screwed up his face. 'I'm no grass. Whatever the lad did I'm sure he never meant it. Unless he's been knocking around young girls – I've no time for that. I was always brought up to respect the fairer sex. And as far as I'm concerned, respect doesn't include knocking seven bells out of them. I mean, what's fair aboot that? Eh, Norrie?' He stabbed the bloke in front with a bony finger.

'What?' Norrie turned round with a glare.

'I'm just telling this young polisman that I don't agree with wife-beating.'

'What's that got to do with me? What are you accusing *me* of?' His hands curled into fists. 'Have you heard something aboot my Margaret—'

'Look!' Logan interrupted the pair. 'I'm not the police – I'm just looking for Alastair Aitken.'

'And I'm asking what's he done?'

'He hasn't *done* anything – I just need to ask him a few questions.'

'That's what they all say. Norrie, don't speak a word! I've already told him I'm not a grass.'

Logan shook his head and moved further along the queue. He stopped at a young lad dressed in tracksuit and beanie.

'Hey, no pushing in!' the old man at the back protested.

Logan ignored the shouting. 'Excuse me, but do you know Alastair Aitken?'

'Might do.' The lad sniffed. 'What's it to you?'

'I just want to speak to him.'

'Oh aye? Well, maybe he doesn't want to speak to *you*.'

'He doesn't even know I'm looking for him.'

'Ah!' The lad grinned. 'Trying to catch him by surprise? Did he nick your girlfriend? What are you writing down? Don't tell him I said that!'

Logan groaned. He kept moving forward.

'I told you to stop pushing in!' the man in tweed yelled from the back.

A solid hairy arm shot out and Logan was stopped mid-chest.

'Say, wee man, have you never seen a queue before?'

Logan looked up into the face of a hulking red-bearded Viking, whose eyebrows knitted together in a worrying block. The whisky fumes might have powered a substation for a small town. Logan gave an apologetic smile. 'Honestly, I'm just looking for Alastair Aitken.'

'So … you're either the polis or the taxman. Either way, my

advice is to take a hike.' He jerked a sausage-sized thumb over his shoulder.

'I'm just a student,' said Logan, waving his notebook in the air. 'I've got a wee project I'm trying to do. I really only want to get a phone number from Mr Aitken. Surely he won't object to that?'

'What's your project?' The Viking folded his arms and stood his ground. 'See if it's about getting a Lidl in the village then you'll have all of us to answer to.'

The man in front of him – wild-haired and wearing an oversized rugby top – turned round. 'Jesus! Don't tell me they've sent a bloody student to do their dirty work.' He grabbed Logan by his jacket and lifted him off the ground so they were eye to eye. Logan made a quick assumption that the rugby-playing hooker enjoyed a garlic-based diet.

He threw Logan over to the Viking, who caught him by the shoulders. 'See, if we wanted a German marketplace on the main street, we'd be celebrating with our currywurst and sauerkraut. But that's my sister that works in Spar – *and* my auntie. What are you going to tell them when they're laid off, eh?'

'I'm really n-not …' Logan stammered, trying to free his arms.

'Not what? Not giving a shite?'

'Not from wherever it is that you think I'm from.'

'I've no idea where scum like you creeps out of.' He gave Logan a shake as though he were a freshly laundered jersey.

'Chuck him in the ring,' the old man bellowed from the back.

The Viking held Logan up to his face. 'I don't know how you sleep at night,' he growled.

'But I think you've got the wrong end of the stick. I'm studying forensic psychology at the University of Edinburgh.'

'And that makes it better? It certainly explains your mental ideas about what you think we Highlanders need up here. How about speeding up our broadband for a start?'

'I'm just trying to track down a man called Hammy MacPhedran.'

The Viking roared, 'How *dare* you utter that bastard's name in my company! Do you *know* what he did to my ma?'

'Well, how would I? I mean I ...'

The Viking carried Logan to the front of the queue, ducked into the tent and dropped him next to a table where an arm-wrestling competition was being fought out.

'You have my permission to break both his arms,' he snarled, exiting the tent.

Logan clambered to his feet, brushing the grass off his jeans. The arm-wrestlers had stopped, their hands clasped as they stared at him. Logan read a handwritten sign:

Anyone that beats Buster wins twenty quid.

Distracted momentarily, a lanky man wearing ill-fitting fatigues had his arm bent back with a *snap*! He muttered something unintelligible as he sloped away from the table.

'Looks like you're up next, son,' said Buster, who made the Viking look as though he shopped from the *Petite* range. His torso was encased in a stretched black vest, his ripped jeans revealing bulging quads. Every inch of his skin was tattooed with a different motto; a snake curled round his neck and up over one eye. His arm rested on the table, his meaty hand poised for action. Logan wondered whether now was an appropriate time to suggest that hand sanitiser ought to be made compulsory.

Buster scratched his armpit. 'Come on, then, I haven't got all bloody day.'

'I'm, er, not actually here for the arm-wrestling.'

'Then you've come to the wrong tent, sonny. Looking for some home-made jam or a nice woollen scarf?'

'I'm trying to find Alastair Aitken,' said Logan, straightening his jacket.

'And do you see him in here?' Buster barked, surveying the empty tent. 'Away and piss off before I use your arms to clean out my ears.'

'Of course.' Logan reversed out of the tent at speed. He picked up his dropped pen and pad, doing the walk of shame past the queue. When he reached the old man at the back he asked, 'Are you really hoping to beat that monster?'

The man shrugged. 'He cannae keep going all day – he's bound to tire at some point.'

Logan sighed, moving on to the next stall, which boasted a display of household items made entirely of locally foraged shells. He glanced at the ashtrays, photo frames and lop-sided lamps. A young girl, barely able to see above the trestle table, greeted him with a toothy grin. 'I made them all myself.'

'Nice,' said Logan, wondering whether there was much demand for shell-based teapot stands. 'I don't suppose you know an Alastair Aitken?'

'Who?'

'Never mind.'

Chapter 32

Dell cracked an egg into the frying pan and watched with a satisfied smile as the white bubbled and turned opaque in the hot fat. 'Two minutes!' she shouted. She heard thundering overhead and Ron appeared in the kitchen in his James Bond pyjamas. 'Smells fab.'

'Go and fill the *cafetière*, would you?'

'Sure. Nice outfit, by the way. Think you could get away with that look down at Tesco?'

Dell giggled as she held out her arms. Her flimsy nightie was hidden beneath a cotton apron. She lifted plates out of the oven and served sausages, bacon, tomato and black pudding, placing the fried eggs on top of the potato scones. Ron gave the ketchup a vigorous shake and squirted with a flourish. 'This is the life!'

'Well, a wife must keep up her man's stamina.'

'I didn't see you complaining last night!'

'Cheeky. Bottoms up!' said Dell, raising her mug.

'How's your ankle, by the way?'

'Oh, it seems to be much better. They do say that doing you-know-what releases endorphins, or whatever they're called. You know? They relieve pain?'

'I think that was just some randy scientist making up an excuse to have it away with his missus.'

'Oh Ron, what are you like?'

Ron winked and sipped his coffee. 'I wonder how our Kat's

getting on. Did you tell her about Arthur last night?'

'Of course not! Anyway, we don't actually know what we saw.'

'I saw enough,' Ron muttered. 'All that sneaking about at night, meeting strange men in dark alleys.'

'It's Cherie I feel sorry for,' Dell added. 'She's laid up after surgery and he's gallivanting around like some kind of gigolo! Do you reckon that's why he's been sorting through Dusty's ballgowns?'

'I've no idea.' Ron shook his head as he scooped beans on to his fork. 'Maybe he's having some kind of mid-life crisis?'

Dell pursed her lips. 'Then why doesn't he just buy a Harley-Davidson and be done with it? Why does he need to drag his poor wife down with him?' She stabbed a mushroom and dipped it into the egg yolk. 'I just wish— *Eeek!*'

'What?' Ron asked.

Dell let her fork drop with a clatter. Her hand shot to her mouth. 'It's a ...'

'A what? Too hot?'

'*There!*' Dell screamed, jumping up. She climbed on to her chair, pointing to the corner of the kitchen.

'Have you gone mad?'

'It's a *mouse!*' Dell screeched. 'Get it, Ron! Quickly!'

Ron took his time rising to his feet, peering at the corner. 'I can't see anything. Are you sure it wasn't just a—'

'A what? What else could possibly be running around the floor at this time of the morning?'

'I don't know. But there's nothing there now.'

'Then it must be under the cooker. Check under the cooker!'

Ron reluctantly got on to his hands and knees and bent his head. 'It's too dark to see anything.'

'Then get a torch!'

Ron gazed at his abandoned breakfast. 'Knew it was too bloody good to be true. Can't it wait?'

'*Ron!*' Dell began hyperventilating. 'You know I won't stay in this house a minute longer unless you get it out.'

Ron began half-heartedly opening and closing drawers.

'What are you doing *now*?'

'I need a torch, don't I? And I expect it'll need batteries and we never have any spare.'

'As God is my witness, if you don't get a move on I'll never cook you another meal again.'

'Promises, promises,' Ron muttered.

'*Ron!* How could you? Can't you see I'm in a state of distress.'

'State of *undress*, more like,' said Ron, nodding at her exposed thighs.

Dell began to cry. 'This is the worst day ever. My lovely home invaded by vermin. It'll never feel the same again. I mean – how can I go to bed each night thinking a horrible sleekit wee beastie may run across my face?' She gave a huge shudder.

'Aha,' said Ron, waving the torch. He bent down again and shone the light under the cooker. 'If it was ever there, it's well gone now.'

'But, what do you mean? Where's it gone?'

Ron scratched his head. 'It could have disappeared down a crack or anything. You know how tiny they are. Now, may I please finish my breakfast?'

Dell picked up the bottle of ketchup and threw it at her husband. 'Of course you can't! How can you possibly think about food at a time like this?'

'At a time like what? Breakfast time?'

'Don't be sarcastic.' Dell remained standing on her chair as she scoured the floor fearfully.

'It won't pop up like Whac-A-Mole.' Ron took a tentative step towards his plate, already furious that he was going to have to microwave his meal and that no good ever came of microwaving a fried egg.

Then the doorbell rang.

'Who's that?' Dell asked, gathering her nightie round her legs.

'How would I know? Last time I checked I didn't have X-ray vision.'

The bell sounded again, more insistently.

'It'll be one of those charity people,' Ron said. 'Ignore it.'

'Like we're ignoring the pest-control scenario we've got in here? *Wah!*' Dell cried.

A face with a ginger moustache appeared at the kitchen window. Arthur, hands cupped round his eyes, gaped through the pane.

'It's only Arthur,' said Ron mildly. 'Wonder what he wants at this hour?'

Arthur tapped on the back door.

'Don't open it!' Dell hissed.

'But he's already seen us.'

'You can't open the door. If you do, the mouse might escape.'

'I thought you *wanted* it out of the house?' said Ron, exasperated.

'But how will we know? We need to catch it and make sure it's absolutely right out of the house. I can't risk it nipping out when we're not looking.'

Ron sighed. 'So, you're asking me to escort it off the premises? Would you like me to stamp its visa while I'm at it?'

Arthur knocked again. 'What if I let him in the front door?' Ron suggested, moving towards the hall.

'You can't do that!' Dell shrieked. 'The wee bugger might run up the stairs!'

'This is ridiculous,' said Ron, opening the back door a crack. 'We have a bit of a situation here,' he explained to Arthur. 'I'm going to open the door for a couple of seconds but you must hurry inside.'

'Fine,' Arthur agreed, squeezing through the gap. He glanced at Dell then, spotting her podgy thighs, averted his gaze.

'So, how can we help you?' Ron asked.

'Have I come at a bad time?' said Arthur, fixing his eyes on the floor.

'Well, it depends ...' Ron answered. 'Are you any good at catching mice?'

'Ah, so that's what's going on.' Arthur smoothed his bushy moustache with his finger and thumb.

'What did you think?' Dell sobbed. 'Do you really think I'm in the habit of standing on a chair in my nightie? This is a crisis!'

'I'm quite sure I've no idea,' Arthur replied.

'Here,' said Ron, handing Arthur a plastic box. 'Perhaps you can take that corner.' Ron selected an empty cereal packet out of the recycling box. He crouched near the cooker. Without warning he slapped the laminate. A brown shape darted across the floor.

'*There!*' Dell screamed. 'Oh, I think I'm going to be sick.'

Arthur stamped his foot but too late. The creature disappeared behind the bin. Ron put his finger to his lips. He indicated for Arthur to stay low. The two men crept forward until they were huddled either side of the bin. Dell held her breath, hardly daring to look. Ron thumped the bin with a violent slap. The mouse shot out straight into Arthur's box. 'Aha!' Arthur said in triumph. 'Got you, you little pest!' He held his hand over the box as Ron flicked open the back door.

'Don't just throw it in the garden,' Dell warned. 'Can you take it to the end of the road? It'll only come back in again.'

Arthur gave a backwards glare as he retraced his steps down their path.

'Right, are you quite satisfied?' said Ron, offering Dell his hand. 'Maybe you better put something else on?'

'I think I need a wee lie-down,' said Dell, wafting her flushed face with a tea towel.

Arthur returned with the empty container. 'I chucked it into Mr Hendry's garden. He's always complaining when I park next to his drive.'

'Would you like a coffee?' Ron asked, lifting the *cafetière*.

'No, ta. Nice pyjamas, by the way. I didn't realise double-oh-seven was in the pest-control business.'

Ron slipped his plate into the microwave. It felt awkward having Arthur standing in his kitchen after spying on him the night before. He was most definitely not James Bond material. 'Sleep well?'

'What do you mean?' Arthur asked, leaning against the work surface.

'Er... I ... er ... I just meant I assume you stayed over at Dusty's house?'

'Where else?'

Ron turned crimson. 'Bacon sandwich?'

'Look, I'm not here for chit-chat. I've just come over because I had the photographer in yesterday to take photos of the house. It's featuring in the Property Press tomorrow and the estate agent is going to be showing people round.'

'I see. Heavens, so it's really happening. How does Dusty feel about that?'

Arthur shrugged. 'I'm not sure she's really able to make that kind of decision any more. You've seen how she is.'

'Kat seems to think she's doing fine this weekend.'

'Why?' Arthur said sharply. 'What has she said?'

'Just that she's not sure what all the fuss is about Dusty's memory. Kat thinks she knows exactly what's going on.'

Arthur twitched. 'It's all well and good when she's got round-the-clock supervision, but that's very different from maintaining a house on her own.'

'S'pose.'

'Anyway, what I came to say is that the estate agent feels that the photos of the garden are marred by your overhanging trees and you ought to do something about them.'

'Oh, really?' Ron said, chewing on a solid block of black pudding.

'Yes. So we would be most grateful if you could see to it before the viewing starts next week.'

Ron puffed out his cheeks. 'That's not likely. I mean I work all day and we've got a show on every evening this week. *The Sound of Music*, remember?'

'Indeed. Well, I've asked you politely but if the work isn't completed and it affects my house sale, then I may be forced to seek compensation.'

'*Your* house sale?' Ron echoed. 'Seems to me like you've sent poor old Dusty up north and stuck the house up for sale in her absence.'

'Don't be ridiculous!' Arthur snapped as he headed for the door. 'I need to get the train back to Dalgety Bay now. I had hoped to be sharing some good news with Cherie about your cooperation but I can see you're being unnecessarily obstinate. I hope there's a whole bloody mouse nest under your cooker.' He slammed the door and stormed down their path.

'Happy Sunday,' Ron said, pushing his plate to one side.

Chapter 33

'Programme?' Felicity asked the customer brightly.

'No, thanks.'

'I don't suppose your name's Hamish, is it?'

'No, why?'

'No reason.'

'I thought this was meant to be an homage to the Bard? Christ, I hope it's not one of those bloody psychic shows.'

'Not at all,' Felicity twittered. 'I'm just using this opportunity to gather some additional data.'

'Like a census, you mean?' The man frowned into the tent. 'You're going to take all day if your approach is to guess each person's name individually. Let me save you the trouble – I'm Bill.' He pushed past her and took a seat in the back row.

Felicity turned her attention to the next customer. 'Programme?'

'Yes, please,' the woman replied, fishing out her purse from a shoulder bag.

'Would you like a signed copy?'

'Depends. Signed by who?'

'By Daddy, of course! Darwin Flockhart.'

'*Who?*' The woman put on a pair of glasses and inspected the photo on the programme. 'I thought his name was Simon Callow or something?'

'Simon Cowell?' the young girl behind her said with incredulity. '*He's* not here, Granny. He lives in London in a big house. *And* he's famous.'

'On second thoughts, I won't bother with a programme.'

Felicity guarded the entrance to the tent. 'Darwin Flockhart in his one-man show!' she shouted to the passing crowd. 'Quote, "It's the most captivating performance to date," unquote, *The London Post*. The next performance is starting in five minutes.' She popped her head into the tent, where four people were dispersed around the plastic seats. She overheard the man in the front row on his phone, trying to switch his energy supplier. Two acne-infested teenagers, dressed in sports hoodies and skinny jeans, wandered past. One jutted his elbow, knocking the programmes out of Felicity's hand. They sniggered as she grappled to pick them up from the grass. A Labrador padded over them with muddy paws.

'*Really!*' she tutted.

'May I purchase a ticket to the next performance?'

Felicity looked up into the earnest face of an older gentleman. He wore a dark suit and lilac tie, his grey hair swept back from his creased forehead. The teenagers hovered as they lit cigarettes, throwing the matches on to the ground.

'Of course you can.' Felicity beamed as she straightened up. 'How many would you like?'

'Just the one, please.'

'I don't suppose *your* name is Hamish, is it?'

'Do I look like a Hamish?' he smiled good-naturedly.

Felicity sighed. 'We're looking for a Hamish but we've no chance, really.'

'Who's "we"?'

'Oh, my new friends at the guesthouse. One of them is doing

a forensic project. I wouldn't be surprised if it's made into a docu-drama. *Oh!* Maybe Daddy could feature as himself?'

'Why do you need to find Hamish?'

'Well!' Felicity gushed. 'My chums have come across a fabulous engagement ring that they believe belongs to a Hamish. And now they're trying to track him down.'

'I'm sorry I can't help you there. I'm a Tristan.'

'All they know is that he's probably about seventy years old and may have come from this area.'

'Then I must be wearing well,' said Tristan, smoothing down his hair. 'I'm eighty-three next year.'

'*Never!*' said Felicity. 'Programme?'

'Go on then – flattery gets you everywhere.'

'Would you like a signed programme? They're five pounds each.'

'I don't mind accepting a compliment but I'm not wanton!'

'Hear that?' one of the teenagers muttered to his pal. 'Sounds like she's looking for a Hamish.' He winked as they skulked off behind the tent.

Darwin gazed out into the middle distance, one hand gripping a pewter goblet, announcing,

'*That ends this strange eventful history*
Is second childishness and mere oblivion,
Sans teeth, sans eyes, sans taste, sans everything.

I thank you.'

He bowed deeply, the wig almost slipping from his sweaty dome.

Felicity clapped with an enthusiastic, 'Whoop!' The audience of five joined in with some hesitation.

'Is that it finished?' the girl asked her granny.

The mobile phone of the man in the front row burst into AC/

DC's 'You Shook Me All Night Long'. 'Hello? he answered. 'Yes, I still want to switch – that's what I've been trying to tell you.'

'Thank you for coming.' Felicity expressed her gratitude to each member of the audience as they left. 'Tell all your friends.'

'Tell them what?' the young girl queried.

'That's the best nap I've had in years,' her granny muttered.

Darwin cricked his head from side to side and rotated his shoulders in a circle. '*Wow!*' he grinned. 'I really felt a connection with the audience today. What do you think?'

'I think you were *wonderful*, Daddy.'

'Yes, yes. I could absolutely sense them hanging on to each and every syllable.' Darwin paced across the flattened grass. 'I'm really going to have to dig deep to recreate the same level of energy for my next performance.'

'I'm sure you'll be just as inspirational.'

'I hope so.' He glugged water from a plastic bottle. 'Thank God I practise mindfulness – it's the only way I'm able to draw on my inner resources. My mentor is always telling me to seek nourishment from my vigour.'

'And talking of nourishment, do you want me to fetch you a pie?'

'Yes, please – a mince round, if they have it.'

Hamish dozed in front of the dust-covered TV. A mug of tea grew cold on the stained table by his side. It irked him that he'd no money for the bookies. Tall Dave had given him a solid tip for the eleven o'clock at Doncaster last Saturday. *Electric Fence is a sure thing*, he'd been told. *And* it was seventeen to one. A tenner would have made him a hundred and seventy pounds. But no – he was stuck at home with that annoying fly buzzing around his sitting room. He rested his feet on a worn footstool, kicking off his holey slippers. His stomach rumbled, reminding him that he hadn't eaten since heating up a tin of tomato soup the evening before.

The front door crashed open.

'Only me!' Billy shouted. He burst into the fusty room. 'Oh, man, it stinks in here, Hamish.'

'That'll be ma feet.'

'When was the last time you got into the shower?'

'It's not my fault the water's freezing.'

'How not? You need to pay your bill.'

Hamish shrugged. 'Go and make me a cup of tea, son.'

'No time for that.' Billy shoved Hamish's legs off the footstool. 'Get your shoes on – we're going for a stroll.'

'Get lost, you wee shite. I'm not going anywhere. The racing's on.'

'And I know you haven't put on a bet since last week so all you're doing is watching a bunch of horses scooting past your eyes.'

'What's got the wind up you, anyhow?'

'Listen, Hamish – we've got a chance to make a quick buck so get your shoes on and stop asking stupid questions.'

Hamish spat into the half mug of tea. 'I'm not going anywhere until you tell me what this is all about.'

'Fine,' Billy snapped. 'There's some posh bird down at the games is looking for a Hamish.'

'Eh? It wisne me! I've done nothing to any posh bird.' Hamish stuck his hands in the pockets of his grubby jeans.

'Listen, old man. I just need you to come with me and say nothing. Bring your pension book or something that says you're Hamish.'

'What's in it for me?'

'This wifie says she's got a big ring and she's looking for a Hamish to give it back to. All I need you to do is to turn up and say, "Aye, that's my ring," and we're both going to make a wee profit. Tam from the dock has already told me he can get rid of anything and pays out cash.'

'I don't know anything about a ring.'

'*Hamish!*' Billy gripped the pensioner by his stubbly chin. 'I'm telling you – all you need to do is come with me. Now even *you* can't fuck that up.'

'Cheeky sod,' Hamish grumbled. 'So I'm not getting a cup of tea?'

'*No,*' Billy snarled. 'You're getting nothing unless you help me out. And – if you play nice – you'll score twenty quid. So that's two bottles of voddy you can enjoy at your leisure.'

'I prefer the Scotch.'

'You can spend it on bloody cocoa for all I care but you need to get a move on.'

Hamish grunted as he stood with some reluctance, searching the room for his shoes. 'Think I left my shoes by the door.'

'Come on, then.' Billy gave him a push from behind. He waited impatiently as Hamish fumbled with the broken laces.

'Is it raining oot?'

'No, but you'd better put a coat over that filthy jumper – looks like you've got a three-course meal down the front.'

'Well, I don't see you offering to do ma laundry. How are we getting doon to the games, anyway?' Billy shook a car key in front of Hamish's face. 'Willie's lent me his banger but I need to get it back any minute as he's taking what's-her-face from the garage to pick up a mattress off of her pal for her new flat.'

'Christ! I didn't ask for your life story.' Hamish pulled the front door behind him.

'Aren't you going to lock it?'

'There's nowt worth nicking from in there.'

Billy sped along the road, coming to a screeching halt as he arrived at the back of the lengthy queue to the car park. The same teenager in the high-vis waistcoat was directing cars with an apathetic sweep of his arm. Billy smacked his hand off the steering wheel. 'We'll be here all bloody day at this rate!'

'Aye, no doubt.'

The car inched forward. Billy wound down his window. He leant out shouting, '*Hey!* Lucas! Get over here!' The lad looked startled. He trotted across, fear in his eyes. 'Oh, hi, Billy – what's up?'

'Hamish here is having some kind of funny turn – I need to get him along to the first-aid tent.' Lucas bent down to inspect Hamish, who was picking his nose. 'What's wrong with him?'

The car behind blared its horn. Billy grabbed Lucas by the waistcoat. 'Just get us in, you wee nyaff.'

Lucas pulled himself backwards, waving Billy to the front of the queue.

'*Oi!*' the man in the car behind objected. Billy stuck his middle finger in the air as he overtook the cars and swung across the field to an empty space. He loped round the back of the car, heaving Hamish out of the passenger seat. 'Right, remember what I said?'

'I think it's *you* that's having the funny turn, Billy.'

'Aye, well, you'll thank me when you're pissed this evening.'

Billy used Hamish as a buffer to propel his way through the crowd until he reached Darwin's pop-up. The tent was closed. 'What now?' Hamish asked, his legs sagging. Billy cursed as he scoured the passing faces. He could hear voices coming from within. 'Knock knock!' he said. The voices stopped. Billy swatted the tent canvas. 'Anyone at home?'

The tent door unzipped and Felicity's head appeared. She

inspected the two visitors with distaste. 'The next show starts in an hour.'

'We're not here for that,' said Billy, tugging at Hamish's coat. 'This is the Hamish you're looking for.'

Felicity hesitated for a second before she beamed. 'Really? Hamish?'

'That's right,' said Hamish.

'And are you local?'

'Aye. Lived here all ma life.'

'But – hang on a moment – this is so exciting! Oh, I'm all of a tizzy! I must get in touch with my friends. Come in, come in.' She held the door open. Darwin was resting on a plastic chair, still dressed as Jacques in his white tights, purple velvet plus-fours and lacy shirt. He held a mince pie halfway to his mouth.

'Daddy, this is Hamish!'

'*The* Hamish?' Darwin asked, putting down his lunch. 'Why, that's *marvellous*! I knew you'd be the one to crack the case.'

Hamish sank on to a chair. 'I don't suppose there's any chance of a cup of tea?'

'Tea? We should be celebrating with something stronger than tea! Felicity, where did I leave my hip flask?'

'Now you're talking,' Hamish said, licking his dry lips.

'But first I must get in touch with Logan and Kat,' said Felicity, barely able to control her excitement. Her fingers fumbled with her phone. 'Logan, it's me – Felicity. You'll never guess; I've found your Hamish!'

Chapter 34

Nance plunged through the throng of men with their plastic pints of lager in hand, marking the entrance to the Scots Pine Bar. A shared joke resulted in one of the beefier lads erupting in laughter, stepping back and almost knocking Nance to the ground. Kat and Dusty bolstered her small frame as she grabbed at the back of the drinker.

'Hey, Kenny – watch yourself!' a man warned as Nance's head popped up.

'Sorry, Nance,' Kenny apologised.

'I should think so too!' said Nance. 'You nearly took me out.'

'Not my fault. Rab here was just telling us how Craig treated his girlfriend to a trip out in his poxy dinghy and she threw up all over it.'

'Aw, now,' said Nance. 'You know better than to laugh at Craig's expense.'

'You're kidding me?' said Kenny. 'That wee tosser dropped me right in it with the wife.'

'Kenny, your mother would turn in her grave if she knew you were blaming poor Craig for your indiscretion with Theresa.'

Kenny stared into his flat pint. 'Fair enough.' He looked heavenwards. 'Sorry, Mum.'

'That's more like it. Now, have you seen Alastair Aitken?'

'Aye, he was here a minute ago. Hey, guys, did any of you see which way Alastair went?'

'I heard he was headed for the pipe band.'

'We've just come from there,' said Nance, shaking her head.

One of Kenny's giant pals stood on his tiptoes. 'That's him over there – standing talking to Dr Farquhar.'

'Grand!' Nance smiled. 'Come on, ladies – follow me.'

Logan had just ventured into the Portakabin and was unzipping his flies when his phone burst into song. His neighbour at the urinal snorted. 'It gets me every time. Usually my mother.'

Logan retrieved his mobile and climbed down the steps.

'Hey, Felicity, how's it going? What? No way. *No way!* That's brilliant! You're a star. Where are you? Is that anywhere near the honey place? Oh, I know where you are. Give me two minutes.'

Logan forgot he ever needed the toilet and sprinted through the rabble. He tried to text Kat as he hurried along.

Kat's phone pinged. 'It's from Logan,' she informed Dusty and Nance. 'Oh! It looks like Felicity may have found our Hamish!'

'Honestly?' Dusty asked, clapping her hands. 'What's happened?'

'It's a text from Logan. He says, *Flic hs find hamisg. Cme to pop-up.*'

'Eh?'

'I think he's trying to tell us that Felicity has found Hamish.'

'Hamish?' Nance puzzled. 'I thought you were looking for Alastair Aitken?'

'We are. We were,' said Kat, turning and heading back in the direction they'd just come.

'But, this is the wrong way,' Nance protested. Her compact legs tried to keep up with Kat's eager pace.

Dusty attempted to explain as they weaved through the

ambling families. 'We have a ring that we think belongs to a Hamish or a Jess – or actually both.'

'You've lost me.'

'Kat – show her the ring.'

Kat flapped her hand in the air as she marched towards the pop-up.

'Ooh, nice ring. Congratulations!'

'It's not hers,' Dusty panted. 'My husband found it here in Loch Assynt while we were on our honeymoon. Now we're trying to return it to its rightful owner.'

'I don't mean to be cheeky but I'm guessing your honeymoon wasn't last week?'

'You'd be right. Anyway, I just found this ring a few weeks ago and we believe it belongs to a local Hamish. We – or should I say *Agnes* – thought the most likely candidate was Hammy MacPhedran.'

'Ah, what with him being a prize philanderer and all. But what makes you think it belonged to a Hamish then?'

Dusty stopped momentarily. 'Need to get my breath back.'

'It's probably none of my business,' said Nance.

Kat raised her eyebrows.

'I know it seems like I know everyone else's business,' said Nance. 'But that's what it's like up here – we need to keep ourselves entertained. Not everyone has Netflix, you know.'

'There's an inscription on the ring,' Kat replied. 'But I'm saying nothing until we check out whether this Hamish is the real deal.'

'Quite right,' Nance nodded. 'I wouldn't trust half this field as far as I could throw them. And I'm most definitely not a caber champion. So, if it's not Hammy MacPhedran you're after, then you've no use for Alastair Aitken?'

'Correct,' Kat said, taking a sharp left.

'Well, now, I wonder which Hamish is declaring ownership of this ring?'

'No idea,' Kat replied. 'All I know is that Felicity seems to think she's found the rightful claimant.'

'Fair play.'

The three arrived at the pop-up with its flagging banner advertising JUST ME, OR NOT JUST ME at the same time as a red-faced Logan.

'Bloody hell,' he panted, doubled over to get his breath back. 'This isn't good for me.'

'Too much fresh air?' Kat asked.

Felicity whipped open the tent with a delighted grin. 'Oh my goodness, you're all here.'

They ducked through the door, followed by the young girl who had abandoned her granny after the last show. The lass's curiosity had been aroused by the loathsome Billy, who lived over the road and was always swearing at her and her pals when they played in the street. She opted for a front-row seat and began chewing on a bar of nougat.

Billy glared at the new arrivals, and hopped from foot to foot with agitation.

'Hamish Tinker!' Nance pronounced. 'Now, this I must see.' She settled herself next to the young girl.

'Well, then,' Logan mused, taking charge. 'I believe we may have finally come to the end of a rather lengthy journey. And I mean that both literally and metaphorically.'

Kat and Dusty fixed their eyes on Hamish, who had the panicked ogle of a large salmon recently hooked from the river by an expert angler. His dry mouth gaped open.

'So you're the famous Hamish, then?' Logan enquired, pacing up and down the tent as though it were an interrogation room. Billy gave the old man a prod in the back.

'I am,' Hamish rasped. 'I expect you'll want to see some proof?'

'He will,' said Felicity, mooning over Logan. 'Logan is going to be absolutely rigorous in this investigation.'

'Good lad!' Darwin nodded.

Hamish raked around in his tatty jacket pocket and retrieved a worn wallet. 'Bank card do, son?'

He fiddled with dirty fingers, holding the cracked card out. Logan, Kat and Felicity crowded round the grimy plastic. Dusty put on her glasses and peered at the ID.

'Aye, that's Hamish alright,' Nance confirmed from the front row.

'Ha!' Billy crowed. 'Now where's the flashy ring that belongs to this poor old soul?'

Kat held up her left hand. Billy whistled. 'Whoa! That is a beauty. I bet Hamish will be very grateful to you for returning it. Won't you, Hamish?'

'Uh-huh. I thought we were getting a wee whisky?'

'All in good time,' Logan replied.

'I think we've been patient enough,' Billy snapped. 'Now hand over the ring.'

Kat lowered her hand. 'So you've confirmed that your name is Hamish but perhaps you could tell us a bit about the ring? We've been searching for weeks now. I'd love to know where you bought it and who it was for?'

Hamish's head swivelled as he searched for backup. Billy made a grab for Kat's hand, gripping her wrist. 'Right, we're not going to answer any more of these stupid questions. Can't you see the old man has had enough? Give him back his ring.'

Kat twisted her wrist. 'But we don't know it belongs to him. There's something about this ring that makes it particularly special.'

'Aye, like the diamonds that you're hanging on to.' Billy tugged again but Kat stood firm.

'Now, let's all just calm down,' said Logan, stepping between the two. 'Billy, please let go of Kat. When she's ready to pass over the ring, she will.'

Billy ignored the warning, his eyes narrowing. 'Give me the fucking ring, or you'll regret it.'

'Oh dear!' Dusty cried. 'This isn't how I imagined it would turn out. Edwin would be most upset.'

'I'm calling the police,' said Logan, pulling out his mobile.

'I thought you *were* the police?' said Nance, leaping to her feet. 'There's no one *here* going to come to your rescue.'

'What a bloody carry-on,' Hamish complained. 'I only wanted a wee dram.'

'This is theft!' Billy hissed. 'I mean it, you better hand it over or else I'll—'

'You'll what?' Logan said, convinced a punch to the face was coming his way.

'Let go of me!' Kat demanded. She jerked her arm back. In response Billy gave an almighty heave. Kat lurched forward into Billy who fell back on to Felicity. Felicity was knocked to the ground, her arm buckled beneath her. '*My arm!*' she screamed. 'Help me, Daddy!' Tears sprang to her eyes as Darwin crouched at her side. 'Oh, my darling girl – are you alright?' He tried to scoop her up.

'Ow – *ow!*' Felicity protested. Darwin helped her to her feet as her arm dangled at an awkward angle. 'I think it's broken,' she sobbed. 'It's just like when I fell off Dreamboat.'

'My poor love,' Darwin gushed. 'Someone get help!'

Billy still clung to Kat's wrist. He made an attempt to pull the ring off her finger but Kat wrestled her hand free.

'And *you*!' Darwin roared. Like a pouncing lion he launched himself at Billy. They crashed through two rows of seats, scuffling on to the grass. The wig skittered off under a chair. Darwin gripped Billy's throat with his fleshy hands.

'Help!' Billy squawked, turning crimson.

'Shame on you!' said Nance, rising from her seat. 'It's scum like you that give the citizens of our lovely community a bad name. And Hamish Tinker – you should know better than to go along with one of Billy's hare-brained schemes.'

'What did *I* do?' Hamish complained. He slumped on to a chair.

Kat had called 999 – only to be informed that a single police officer had been drafted in from Lairg and was holed up in his police vehicle at the main entrance. The station officer eagerly passed on the call to PC Drummond, who was just enjoying his second doughnut of the day.

Darwin and Logan hauled Billy to his feet. 'Come on, you little shit,' Darwin growled. 'We're taking you for a wee walk.' They bundled Billy out of the tent.

'But, Daddy,' Felicity wailed. 'What about me?'

Dusty moved over to Felicity, putting an arm round her shoulder. 'Don't fret, love – we'll get you assistance straight away.'

'There's a first-aid tent near the entrance too,' said Kat. 'Let's get you along there.'

'Oh, I don't think I can move.'

'I should have asked about an ambulance at the same time.' Kat said, re-dialling the emergency services. She apologised for bothering the operator again, ending with, '... thank you so much – that's great. Bye.'

'Is someone coming?' Felicity cried. 'I think I might faint with the pain. Last time this happened they gave me gas to knock me out.'

'Aye, well, a wee dram might do us all a bit of good,' Hamish grumbled. 'Anyway, how am I to get home now?'

'You men only ever think of yourselves,' Nance tutted. 'Away and piss off before the polis come looking for you too.'

'Eh? But I was promised cash and a ride home?'

Nance stood eye to eye with the seated Hamish. 'You'll get a bunch of fives off me soon if you don't clear out of here.'

Hamish cursed under his breath and staggered out through the tent door. As soon as the flap closed, it was opened by a male and female paramedic team kitted out in emerald jumpsuits. The bearded technician carried a weighty bag of equipment.

'Gosh, that was quick!' said Dusty.

'Och, we were just sitting watching the caber. Got a call for a patient with a broken arm?'

'That's me,' Felicity sobbed, her mascara running in black streaks down her cheeks. 'I think I'm going to ...' She slumped sideways on to Dusty.

'Steady there,' said the male. 'Carrie, you got the oxygen?'

'Yep.'

'Reckon this is a stretcher job. Give me a minute.' He ducked back out of the tent, where a sizeable crowd had gathered. 'Whit's goin' on, mister?' a lad shouted.

Carrie hooked an oxygen mask over Felicity's face while she

took her blood pressure. 'What happened here, then?'

'It's rather a long story,' said Dusty with sadness. 'It all started with me finding a ring in my attic and I had really hoped we'd found an answer to who it belonged to. But instead we—'

'Came across a greedy little thug,' said Kat.

'Billy Ormiston,' Nance added.

'Ah!' Carrie nodded. 'I can't say this is the first call-out we've had in relation to that young man.'

'Has he got previous?' Dusty asked.

Carrie laughed. 'You could say that.'

'I watch all the cop shows,' Dusty confided. 'My favourite is *Shetland*. I love the scenery.'

'Me too!'

The partner paramedic returned with the folded stretcher. He kicked a lever and the equipment sprang up like an ironing board. 'How are we doing?' he asked.

'Yeah, it looks like she might have a fracture dislocation of the left elbow. BP: one hundred and seventeen over seventy-eight. Pulse seventy-five. Nil else of note.'

'Analgesia?'

'Yep – she's had morphine.'

'Right, let's get her on to the stretcher.'

'You might want to stop off on your way out?' Kat suggested. 'Her father will definitely want to accompany her. He's taken the perpetrator to have a word with PC Drummond.'

'Sure.'

'Where are you taking her?' Dusty asked.

'Well, the nearest orthopaedic unit is at Raigmore,' said Carrie.

'Inverness?'

'I'm afraid so. We could take her to Golspie or Dingwall but she might need surgery. If we take her straight to Raigmore, she's more likely to see an orthopaedic surgeon.'

Carrie and her colleague assisted Felicity on to the mobile bed and manoeuvred it over the grass. Kat held the canvas door open as the crew wheeled her past the crowd. 'Coming through!' Carrie shouted. Kat let the flap close. The young girl in the front row stood and clapped wildly. 'That was just the *best* show ever! Will you be doing it again? I'll get my friend Tara to come down.'

Chapter 35

Kat sighed as though the world were on her shoulders. 'I need food.' Nance sidled up to her. 'This may not be the best time to ask, but I take it the search for Alastair Aitken is back on?'

Kat groaned loudly. '*Food!*' she repeated, gripping the wad of wool in her pocket. Nance took her by the hand. 'Come along, love. Let's get you some lunch.' Dusty followed.

'But what about the next show?' the girl repeated.

'Cancelled due to unforeseen circumstances!' Nance proclaimed as she led Kat towards the refreshments tent.

'Oh dear, is that rain I can feel?' Dusty held out her hand as the first plop of water splashed into her open palm.

'Come on, let's get a move on. The last thing we need is to get soaked.'

'Oh my!' Dusty declared as the heavens opened and rain cascaded down in buckets. 'I do hope Logan hasn't got too caught up with that hoodlum.'

Kat sent him a text: *In the tea tent*

'I suppose we might as well get a bite to eat while we're here,' Dusty suggested.

'The haggis pies are magic,' Nance recommended. 'It's my neighbour Iain that makes them.'

'Do they make vegetarian ones?' Kat asked.

'*Whit?*'

'I'll come with you. Dusty, do you want to keep the table?'

'Aye aye!'

Kat sent Logan a text: `Haggis pie?` to which she received the reply: `Always!`

As Kat wove her way through the crowd back to their table, Logan appeared. He shook off his wet coat. 'Please tell me that's my coffee?'

'It is,' said Kat, sliding the polystyrene cup across the plastic table.

'Man! What a morning.' Logan gobbled half the pie in one mouthful.

'They're grand, aren't they?' Nance asked, munching away.

'I've never had haggis in a pie before,' said Dusty.

'Ach, they're easy to get into a pie once you've chopped their legs off,' said Nance, winking at Kat.

'Mind you, I've never seen *macaroni cheese* in a pie before, either,' said Dusty, inspecting Kat's lunch.

'So what happened to the delightful Billy, then?' Kat asked.

Logan shook his head. 'What a tosser he was. It took three men to wrestle him into the back of the patrol car. I've no idea where he thought he was going to disappear to. It seems the whole of Lochinver knows him.'

'That they do,' Nance agreed. 'He set fire to his primary school at the age of ten and has never looked back. Got sent away to Glasgow for most of his teens and came back worse. My ma used to say that no one was ever born bad – but she didn't always get it right.'

'And did the ambulance folk come for Darwin?'

'Yeah. Darwin headed off with Felicity. He asked me to write a sign for the pop-up, saying *Next performance Sunday evening*.'

'That's not likely!' said Kat. 'Does he know how far it is to Inverness?'

'Shit! Is that where they're headed? I think he was under the impression they were dropping into some local minor injuries unit.'

'Aye, did you not notice the Emergency Department next to Spar?' Nance asked. 'It's about a three-hour drive down to Raigmore. By the time he gets back tomorrow these games will be all packed up and gone.'

'I don't expect we'll see Felicity again,' said Dusty sadly. 'Pity, really, she was such a charming girl.'

Kat stared into her tea. 'And now we're back to square one with Hamish.'

'Don't you worry about that,' said Nance, wiping her mouth. 'If the worst comes to it Alastair Aitken never misses the tug-of-war. We'll surround him and not let him out of our sight until he tells you what you need to know.'

'What time is it on?'

'It's normally towards the end of the afternoon but if the weather turns they might get it started early. Or else it'll be a mud bath.'

Logan huffed. 'I think it's too late already. When I came past the hammer throw, men were skidding around the field like an ice rink. One of the guys slipped and just about took out the crêperie.'

'Felicity would have been most upset,' said Dusty.

'Give me two minutes and I'll find out what's happening,' said Nance. She burrowed her way through the crowd until reaching a bearded man in full Highland dress. Returning with a grin on her face, she announced, 'Tug-of-war starts in fifteen minutes. Let's guard the entrance to the ring and we're sure to catch Alastair as he comes in or out.'

'Good plan,' Logan agreed.

The group of four huddled at the exit to the refreshment tent, reluctant to expose themselves to the constant drumming of Scottish rain. A few brave souls popped up golf umbrellas and darted for the grandstand. Kids were frolicking in the waterlogged grass as though on a Mediterranean beach. 'Poor sod,' said Logan, pointing to a confused-looking Leonberger that stood mutely as water coursed through its thick fur. Nance drew her hood over her head like an autumnal Yoda. She strode purposefully to where the roped-off area allowed the participants to enter the ring.

'Would anyone be offended if I stayed here?' Dusty enquired. 'I would hate to pick up another pesky chest infection?'

'I think that's probably quite sensible,' Kat agreed. 'This has to be the definition of madness. A bunch of grown men pulling a rope back and forth across a sea of mud.'

'And more fool us for watching,' Logan added, his hands thrust deep into his jacket pockets.

They loitered next to the poncho-covered stewards as the PA system crackled above their heads. '*Next up, please give a warm welcome to the Assynt Anchors!*' Eight titans stormed into the ring to the sound of jeering from the crowd. Two fingers were stuck in the air, triggering choice expletives. The Anchors made a show of stretching, bending and beating their chests as though about to do battle with the New Zealand Kiwis.

'Ach, they're all show,' Nance said to Kat. 'Wait till you see our boys.'

'*And now,*' the PA suggested, '*give it up for our legendary Lochinver Lads!*' The crowd let out a fierce roar. Or it might have been a rumble of thunder. Eight bodies ambled out from under a sagging gazebo. The last man out – a pensioner wearing a raincoat and plastic trousers – gave the crowd a thumbs up.

'Ah, that's Old Jimmy,' Nance announced. 'He tries to join in every year. Mind you, I'm surprised he's here today after last year's ruptured tendon.'

'Which one's Alastair?' Kat asked.

'Hey, Alastair!' Nance shouted.

A stocky red-haired man in Scotland's football strip turned his head.

'Over here!' said Nance, waving him over.

'What is it?' he asked, wiping the rain from his face. 'Do I still owe raffle money for the Guild?'

'Aye, but that's not what this is about. These folks here are trying to get in touch with your Uncle Hammy.'

'Hammy? What for?' Alastair gave Kat and Logan the once-over. 'Are they from the courts?'

'Don't be daft! They're from Edinburgh.'

'Oh aye? Must be serious.'

'So will you talk to them?'

'Not now! We've got a fight on our hands. In fact … here's the deal. If you join our side, I'll see what I can do.'

'*Me?*' asked Kat.

'Not you – *him!*' Alastair nodded at Logan. 'I'm guessing you're not all southern flab.'

'*Me?*' Logan echoed. 'I'm not really cut out for—'

'Take it or leave it,' said Alastair, walking away. 'I don't even think I know a Hammy.'

'Wait,' Logan sighed. 'Where do you need me?'

'That's the spirit,' Alastair grinned. 'What's your name?'

'Logan.'

'Right, Logan. Get Bruce behind you. Have you got a pair of gloves?'

He shook his head.

'Craig, you got a spare pair?'

'Nuh. How come?'

'Has anyone brought a spare pair of gloves?' Alastair asked his team.

'Here, have mine,' a cheery teenager offered. 'I can pull my sleeves down far enough.'

'Right – take the gloves and stand in front of Bruce. He's the one in the kilt. Dig your heels in, lean back and *don't* try to move your hands along the rope. It's the backward steps that give us leverage.'

'But I'm—' Logan protested.

'Useless?' asked Alastair. 'I get that but you're still a better option than Jimmy. Just *don't* let go of the rope. Jimmy, you're our captain. We're under your orders.'

'Aye, sir.'

The Lochinver Lads shuffled into an untidy line as the cold rain hammered down. The grass and mud were churned underfoot like a vegan trifle. Alastair took his place in front of Logan. 'Now get a good grip,' he called over his shoulder. 'Let's see what you English are made of.'

'I'm not English!' Logan grumbled. 'Nance told you, we're from Edinburgh.'

'Same thing. *Get ready, men!*'

A mascot dressed as a Highland cow shook a bell and scarpered out of the field.

'*Heave!*' Old Jimmy ordered. He positioned himself at the back of the line so he could mark out their progress. Logan leant back against Bruce and could already feel his hands slipping. He gripped with all his might. The rope drew him in as he resisted taking a step forward. His boots skidded on the mud and he almost went down. 'Steady,' Bruce warned. 'You go down, we all go down.'

'Heave!' Jimmy shouted. 'Come on, guys, you've lost a foot! Pull back.'

'Pull back!' Alastair commanded.

Logan sensed the team struggling to regain their ground. He felt Alastair take the strain and managed to inch backwards.

'You're doing it,' announced Jimmy. 'Let's show these northern bastards how we do it on the coast. *Heave!*'

Logan's entire body ached, every muscle protesting. He felt as though he were wrestling with a bucking cobra. His calves knotted as he fought against the drag from the Assynt Anchors. The opposing team smelt victory and began chanting, '*We win, we win, we win!*' They started to gather momentum. Logan's boots edged forward.

'Lads – come on!' Jimmy urged. 'Don't let the clowns run the show. *Heave!*'

'*Heave!*' Alastair repeated, blocking the move. 'Lean into it.' His team gave a ferocious draw and Logan gained a step backwards. The rain was stinging his eyes and running into his open mouth. '*Come on!*' he yelled in pain. *Please, God, let this be over,* he thought. His fingers were locked in agony. He couldn't bear to be the first to let go or bite the dirt. The cheering and booing from the crowd rang in his ears. Out of the corner of his eye he spotted Kat jumping up and down, punching the air. Nance was shaking her fists in triumph. And then, without warning, the rope spun through his hands and he felt himself plummeting backwards into Bruce. Alastair landed heavily on top, their heads clashing with a painful crack. Logan tasted the tang of iron as warm blood poured from his nose.

He lay on the ground staring up at the slate sky. A face loomed over him. 'Sorry about that,' said Alastair miserably. 'Must have caught you with the back of my head.' He held out a muddy hand. Logan wished he could sleep for a week. He felt the water from the ground seep through his jeans as his body began to shudder with cold.

'Come on, man. You need to get up,' Alastair insisted. Logan could barely focus on the concerned face. 'Do I get to ask, then?' he mumbled.

'Ask what?'

'Whether your Uncle Hammy was in love with Jess?'

Kat and Nance's faces appeared against the clouds. 'Are you okay? Oh my God, you're bleeding. Is he okay?' Kat asked Alastair.

'He seems to be a bit delirious. He's muttering something about Hammy and a Jess?'

Kat smiled, shaking her head. 'He's not delirious. We're trying to find out if your Uncle Hammy was ever engaged to a Jessica or Jess? Would you know?'

'Not that I'm aware of. But I can ring and ask him.'

'Would you?' Kat said. 'We'd be so grateful.'

'I told you we'd track him down,' said Nance. 'What are we going to do about *him*, then?'

Alastair and Kat stooped to pull Logan to his feet. His clothes were caked in mud. Blood ran down his face into his stubble.

'What a state you're in, young man,' Nance chided, as though it were of his own doing. 'You need to get home and have a bath.'

'Hnnn,' Logan mumbled, pinching his nose.

'*And* you stink!' Kat protested. In her pocket she felt her fingers pinch the cow's horns.

'Oh, that might be the ponies,' Alastair explained. 'The kids do a bit of a show after lunch.'

Kat and Dusty made their way towards the car park.

'Right – drinks in the bar!' Alastair slapped Bruce on the back. 'I guess that's us shagged for another year!'

'But what about our deal?' Logan complained.

Alastair half turned. 'Come down to the Lobster Pot this evening and I'll tell you if I've found anything useful.'

'Woo-hoo!' Bruce yelled to the grandstand. 'Lochinver Lads go down in a blaze of glory!' They were cheered off the field. Logan stumbled back to the car.

'Oh dear,' said Dusty, holding a tissue over her face. 'You smell awful.'

'I can't smell anything,' Logan muttered.

'Lucky you,' said Kat. 'My dad will kill me if you ruin his car. I'll have to see if he's got anything in the boot to cover the seats.'

Dusty hopped into the passenger seat as Logan waited forlornly like a disgraced pupil. Kat retrieved a plastic groundsheet from the boot. 'Here, sit on this.'

'Yes, Mum.'

By the time they arrived back at the guesthouse, the sky had darkened and Mill House welcomed them with glowing windows. Logan shuffled out of the car, heading for his tent.

'Don't be ridiculous,' Kat protested. 'You can't possibly get cleaned up in there. I suppose you could use my shower?'

'Or even better, I've got a bath,' Dusty offered. 'Why don't you have a lovely hot soak?'

Logan held up his dirty hands. 'That sounds like heaven but I couldn't impose, Dusty.'

'Nonsense! I'm going to have a wee lie-down before dinner. You won't be disturbing me in the slightest. And you can help yourself to as many of my smellies as you like.'

'That's amazing – thank you.'

'Oh, by the way, Kat,' said Dusty. 'I had a bit of a panic this afternoon. I couldn't remember if I'd ordered more of my blood pressure tablets. I don't suppose you could ask your mum whether she minds popping over to check my bedside table? I keep all my tablets there and I just can't remember whether I've got enough to last another week.'

'Sure – I'll send a message,' said Kat. 'Will she know what they're called?'

'Oh, I wouldn't know that … but they're the little white ones.'

'No problem.'

Chapter 36

Dell stirred the beef cubes as they began to brown. She was *starving*. After the whole fiasco with the 'thing' at breakfast-time she hadn't felt like eating all day. She had returned to the kitchen with trepidation, stopping in her tracks every few minutes to check for squeaking or – worse –signs of scurrying. Ron had assured her the 'thing' was a one-off. The lone creature probably snuck into the kitchen from the garden, with no intention other than to search for crumbs. She stamped her feet on the floor for good measure, hoping to send out seismic shockwaves to the rodent community. The radio was playing 'I Gotta Feeling' and she couldn't help but sing along. She'd dug out a recipe for beef bourguignon and the aroma coming from the frying pan was making her mouth water. The recipe suggested a bottle of Pinot Noir but she helped herself to a tumbler before emptying the remainder into the casserole dish.

Dell liked to treat herself on a Sunday evening to compensate for Monday morning looming on the horizon. Not that she minded work. She really quite enjoyed her administrative role at the community centre. At least she *had* done for the last four years until her new line manager – Karen (and that was Karen with the twins not Karen with the awful flatulence) – had announced that Dell needed to cover the reception desk every time that Tracy needed a break. And how many bloody breaks in a day did Tracy need? Dell gave the onions a violent prod. Tracy apparently had a medical condition that warranted a coffee break every two hours. When Dell had challenged this requirement Karen had peered over the top of her glasses with pity. 'Dell … you should be thankful that *you* don't have to cope with what Tracy has. It's ruined her life.' And what *did* Tracy have exactly? Apart from terminal laziness and a caffeine dependency that would generate an annual income for any small to medium Colombian business. Dell sighed. She better open another bottle of red – she was sure that Ron would want a glass with his dinner. They could recreate the magic of their silver wedding anniversary when Ron had surprised her (as he surprised himself!) with a weekend in Nice via Ryanair. She gulped back a mouthful. And before they knew it Christmas would be upon them. And that was another saga, what with Ron's sister and all. Her mobile clanged. Oh – a WhatsApp message from Kat:

Dusty says can you check she has enough blood pressure tabs for this week? They're next to her bed.

She'd go round after dinner and look. Better still, she'd get Ron to run over. She lobbed the casserole dish into the oven and reached for the remote control. It really impressed her that the TV remembered where she'd left off; series two, episode four. Perhaps just one more glass, then.

'Well, Dell, my love, you really have outshone yourself,' said Ron, wiping his mouth with satisfaction. 'That was fabulous. If I close my eyes I could be in Burgundy!'

'Oh, stop, you!' Dell blushed. 'I have to say, though, that was one of my best.'

'And dare I hope for a little something in the dessert department?' Ron burped loudly.

'*Ron!*' Dell tutted. 'Aren't you stuffed? That recipe was meant to be for four people.'

'Was it? Anyway, there's always room for pud.'

'You know I think I have a box of Mr Kipling apple pies in the cupboard. I could stick a couple in the microwave?'

'And don't tell me you've squirrelled away some Ambrosia custard?'

'Maybe.'

'Ha! Good girl!' Ron cleared away the plates. 'Shall I make a start on the washing-up while you see to those pies?'

'Actually, before I forget,' said Dell. 'Dusty wants to know whether she's got any more blood pressure tablets. She might need to call the doctor first thing in the morning for a repeat prescription. Would you mind going next door?'

'Me? Wouldn't you be better – you know what you're looking for.' Ron frowned.

Dell gave a shudder. 'I sometimes get the creeps over there. You know she still keeps Edwin on the mantelpiece?'

'Does she? I'm surprised he doesn't fall off.'

Dell gave Ron a friendly punch on the arm. 'Ron!'

'Look, I'll have a bash at this casserole dish while you nip over. This is going to take some effort, by the looks of it.'

Dell sighed. 'Oh, alright, then. But you better watch out that I don't disturb his spirit and he comes flying over here.'

Ron shook his head as he squirted washing-up liquid into the sink. 'The sooner you get going, the sooner I'll get my pudding.'

'Fine.' Dell reached for her coat and hurried out the back door, letting in a blast of autumn chill. Ron turned up the radio, singing along as he scrubbed at the crusted ceramic. He bobbed his knees up and down to the beat, aware of an intermittent buzzing. His eyes flitted over the kitchen floor, dreading a further appearance of that blasted beastie. That would put an end to any chance of him getting apple pie. When he spotted his mobile vibrating on the worktop he wrestled out of the Marigolds. It was Dell.

'What now?' he asked. 'And why are you calling from Dusty's? Are you in conversation with Edwin?' he chuckled. 'Dell, I can't hear you – why are you whispering? *A what?* Don't be ridiculous – the house isn't haunted! Okay, okay – I'm on my way.'

Ron grabbed his fleece and pulled the door behind him. 'A ghost,' he muttered to himself. The shared path to the back of Dusty's house was in darkness. He stumbled over the uneven surface and pushed open the door to find Dell cowering in a corner. 'What are you doing down there?' Ron demanded.

'Shhh!' Dell hissed, her eyes wide with fear. She grabbed Ron's jacket and dragged him down to the floor.

'What the …!' Ron protested. 'Mind my knees!'

'Shhh,' Dell repeated, flapping her hands. 'Listen. I think it's Edwin.'

'Don't be ludicrous,' Ron said.

'Listen!' Dell pointed a finger to the ceiling.

'I can't hear anything. How much wine have you had? I think you must be a bit tiddly. This is crazy, I'm getting—' A noise from upstairs stopped him in his tracks.

'What the …?'

'See?' Dell whispered. 'It sounds like a groaning noise. Dusty used to tell me that she'd have conversations with Edwin and could feel him in the room.'

'Really?' said Ron, less certain of himself. 'And that's definitely him on the mantelpiece, is it?'

Dell frowned. 'Of course! Edwin did actually die and most

certainly got cremated, if that's what you mean? We were all at the funeral.'

'I wasn't suggesting it might be Edwin upstairs, I'm just wondering what she meant by *feeling him in the room*.'

'And now you know why I get the heebie-jeebies.'

'Well, it can't be Arthur,' said Ron. 'I saw him leave this morning after giving me an earful.'

'Why would it be Arthur creeping around upstairs? He can come and go any time he pleases. Hey, I've just had a thought!' said Dell. 'What if it's Arthur's lover? The man from last night? What if he's letting him stay here while Dusty's away for the weekend? Maybe Arthur's been having sordid sex with him out of Cherie's sight? The *bastard*!'

'Then why all the sneaking about last night at the back of the station?'

'Maybe he kidnapped him?' Dell suggested. 'What if there's a man trussed upstairs on the bed and Arthur's holding him hostage, demanding sex whenever he feels the urge?'

'Right, enough of this nonsense!' said Ron, struggling to his feet. 'This isn't an episode of Fifty Bloody Shades of Red.'

'Grey.'

'Whatever!' Ron snorted. 'I'm going up to investigate.'

'Oh, Ron, do you think that's wise? Perhaps we ought to call the police.'

'And tell them our neighbour's house is haunted? They're not Ghostbusters, you know.'

Dell lifted a heavy frying pan from a hook. 'Here – take this.'

'In case Edwin fancies an omelette?'

Dell nudged Ron in the back. 'I'm right behind you.'

'With the cheese?'

Dell opened a drawer and selected a wooden rolling pin. The couple crept into the hall but heard nothing. 'It must be your imagination,' Ron said in a quiet voice.

'But you heard it too!'

'I heard your heavy breathing.'

Dell gave Ron a prod in the back, whispering, 'Dusty's tablets are on her bedside cabinet. We need to go upstairs and check. I think the moaning has stopped.'

'Not from me, it hasn't,' Ron grumbled. He tried the first step, which creaked in protest. With one hand on the banister and the other gripping the frying pan, he inched forward. Dell followed, one step at a time. They paused on the landing. 'In which room did you say Dusty could feel Edwin?'

'The bedroom, of course,' Dell whispered. 'I can't imagine why she'd have conversations with him in the bathroom. Or the spare room, for that matter. I think she mostly does her ironing in there.'

They heard the sound of a drawer opening and closing. Then the wardrobe doors banged open. Dell gripped Ron's arm so tightly he let out a strangled cry. The movement ceased. 'I think someone's in there,' Ron whispered into Dell's ear.

'A burglar!' Dell squeaked. 'What if he's armed?'

Ron indicated for Dell to stay put. He tiptoed into the spare room, returning with an iron. Dell made a face. Dusty's bedroom and the spare room were adjacent, their door handles only a few inches apart. Ron wrapped the iron's cable tightly round both handles, finishing with a reef knot. He made a sign for them to return downstairs. By the time they reached the kitchen Dell was trembling. 'Call the police,' Ron ordered. 'We need to try and keep the burglar in there until they arrive but I can't say how long the cable will hold.' With that, an almighty roar sounded from upstairs. '*Wah!*' Dell jumped. Her fingers fumbled with her phone. 'Yes – police, please. Yes, it's an emergency! We've apprehended a burglar in our neighbour's house. Please *hurry*! I don't know whether he has a weapon! Right, right. Will do.'

Dell gave the address and hung up. They heard thumping against Dusty's bedroom door. Followed by shouting and swearing.

'Oh, Ron, we'd better go and leave it to the police. He sounds very angry.'

'*I'm* angry,' Ron asserted. 'In fact I'm *furious*! Don't these scumbags realise the effect something like this can have on an old person? Poor Dusty will be devastated if she thinks the happy memories of living here with Edwin have been tarnished. She's lived here for what – over fifty years?'

'Must be.'

'And she raised a family here. Now some thug is going through her precious things and helping himself to whatever he wants.'

More banging from upstairs. It sounded like he was kicking at the door frame. Dell clutched Ron's hand. 'Come on, Ron – let's go before he gets out.'

'You know what – I'm not going to let him get away with this.' Ron rolled up his sleeves and picked up the frying pan again. 'I'm going to give him a piece of my mind.'

'Oh, Ron, I think the wine's gone to *your* head.'

'I can't let him get away with Dusty's valuables. For all we know he's been through her whole house and filled a case with her stuff. She'll be destroyed – the shock might kill her.'

'But what if he has a gun? Or a knife?'

'I'm not going to let him out. I just want him to think about the consequences of targeting a poor defenceless pensioner.'

'I don't think that's such a good idea – I can't imagine him wanting to engage in a discussion about the traumatic impact of violent crime. Oh – that's my phone!'

Dell listened to the caller and began walking to the front of the house. She opened the door to find two female police officers standing on the doorstep. 'Good evening, madam. My name is Police Constable Walker and this is my colleague PC McGill. We received a call about a possible intruder?'

'Yes, yes come in,' said Dell, moving to one side. 'That was quick!'

'Just happened to be in the area.'

'He's upstairs in Dusty's bedroom.'

The two officers wiped their feet and entered the house. 'Hope we weren't interrupting a cookery session?' PC McGill quipped.

'Ha ha,' said Ron, hiding the frying pan behind his back.

'I hope there was no intention of inflicting injury on another person?' PC Walker frowned.

'What? Oh no, officer,' said Ron. 'For protection only.'

'Yeah – I've heard that fried eggs can turn real nasty.' PC Walker smirked but stopped when more banging sounded from upstairs. The four heard a voice shout, 'Fuck! *Fuck!*'

The two officers exchanged a look. 'Think we need backup?'

'Let's try to assess the situation in the first instance. Sorry, what were your names again?'

'I'm Dell Carmichael – I'm the one who called you. And this is my husband, Ron Carmichael. We live next door to Dusty Harris, who lives here. But she's away this weekend, thank goodness. I don't know how she would have reacted if she'd come home to find a burglar in her house. She's eighty-two.'

'Thank you. Now, Mr and Mrs Carmichael, if you could please take a seat downstairs. You must remain down here while we take reconnaissance of the situation. Is that understood?'

'Over and out!' Ron joked.

'Of course, officer. Come on, Ron, let's wait in the living room.'

'With Edwin, you mean?'

The officers halted in their tracks. 'Is there someone else in the house? We must know the whereabouts of all personnel.'

'It's nobody,' said Dell, glaring at her husband. 'Please ignore him.'

PC McGill unclipped a truncheon from her belt and held it in front of her body.

'Want to borrow this?' Ron offered her the frying pan. 'This is much more substantial.'

'We're fine, thanks,' PC Walker replied, also reaching for her truncheon.

Dell and Ron hovered at the entrance to the living room, listening for what was happening upstairs. They heard one of the officers knocking on the bedroom door. 'This is Police Scotland, sir. My name is PC Walker and I have a second female police officer with me – PC McGill. Now, we're hoping we can resolve this situation in a calm and orderly fashion. Can you please let me know your name?'

The two officers noted with alarm that a pair of scissors was sawing frantically in the gap between the door and its frame. With each aggressive yank on the handle the cable frayed. They stood guard either side, truncheons at the ready. 'This is PC Walker,' she repeated in a firm voice. 'Let's all just stay nice and calm, shall we? I'm going to ask you again, whether you can let us know your name, sir? We're here to ask you a few questions. We just need to verify the facts, sir.'

'Verify *this*, pigs!' a voice growled from behind the door. With a final heave, the cable snapped and the door flew open. The intruder burst out of the room like a fighting bull. He charged at PC Walker, knocking her to one side. PC McGill took a baseball swipe with her truncheon, missing him and hitting the wall. He stormed down the stairs, taking them two at a time. Just as he was about to cross the hall, Ron stepped out from the living room, swinging the frying pan in a backhand that would have made Andy Murray proud. The collision sent a shudder up Ron's arm as the intruder was smacked in the face. He fell backwards, knocked out cold. The body lay on the carpet, arms and legs splayed. He was dressed in black, a woollen balaclava over his head. Heavy-duty boots protruded from canvas trousers.

PC McGill was the first to arrive. She kicked the perpetrator on to his front, pulling his arms behind his back and handcuffing them together. PC Walker jogged down the stairs, rubbing the back of her head. She smoothed down her hair and replaced her cap. 'Caught me off guard there. Well done, Lynn.'

PC McGill rolled the body over again, removing the balaclava. The man's face was already swelling; his lip was cut and blood was seeping from another lesion on his eyebrow. The blood trickled into his flattened ginger moustache.

Dell gasped. 'It *is* Arthur! Oh my God, Ron. You've killed Arthur!'

'*Arthur?*' Ron said in bemusement as he gazed down on the familiar face. 'But what was he doing in Dusty's bedroom? I don't understand.'

'You know the perpetrator?' asked PC Walker. She bent to check on Arthur's pulse. 'Don't worry, you haven't killed him, but better call an ambulance, Lynn.'

'On it.' PC McGill barked orders into her radio.

PC Walker hoisted the leather holdall that Arthur had dropped on impact. She tugged on one of the zips and peered inside. 'I think we can guess what he was doing in Mrs Harris's bedroom. Looks like there's a fair bit of jewellery in here, a ceramic vase, a set of crystal glasses, a decanter.'

'Edwin's decanter?' Ron asked.

'But why would he rob Dusty?' Dell asked. 'How despicable! Bad enough to be robbing anyone, but why would he steal from his own mother-in-law? What will Cherie say?'

Arthur groaned in pain as he regained consciousness. His eyes flicked around the four faces – the resigned expressions of the police officers and the disgusted frowns of Dell and Ron.

'How *could* you, Arthur?' Dell cried. 'Your own mother-in-law!'

'I can't believe this,' said Ron. 'You always make out how caring you are – and the whole time robbing her blind.'

A thought occurred to Dell. 'Don't tell me your suggestion to send Dusty away with our Kat was just a ruse to get her out of the house? You scheming—'

'I can explain!' Arthur mumbled through bruised lips.

'Yes, you'll have a fair bit of explaining to do down at the station. Come on.' The officers assisted Arthur to his feet. 'And what did I say about using that frying pan?' PC Walker turned on Ron.

'What, this?' Ron asked. 'I was just practising a few squash manoeuvres, wasn't I, love?'

Dell nodded. 'Yes, Ron's very good at squash.'

PC Walker frowned. 'I will be in touch tomorrow – I'll need a statement from you both. Do you have keys to the property? Can we leave you to secure the premises?'

Arthur continued to protest as he was led away. 'This is all some dreadful misunderstanding. I was just packing up my mother-in-law's belongings in preparation for the move! Please don't tell my wife!'

'More lies!' Ron said in disbelief. 'Get out of here.'

'You should be ashamed of yourself, Arthur Kerr,' Dell added. And indeed, Arthur did hang his head in shame.

Chapter 37

While the deep, freestanding bath filled with hot, frothy bubbles Logan posed at the bathroom mirror with a pair of nail scissors. He wiped a towel across the steamed-up pane and cocked his head. Tufts of blond hair dropped into the basin. He dabbed at the dried blood round his nostrils, a purple mark tender across the bridge of his nose. Goosebumps appeared on his arms as he slipped into the almost-scalding water. He closed his eyes and allowed his body to be buoyed by the creamy foam.

'Oh my!' Dusty effused. 'Now don't you look handsome?'

Logan blushed as he sidled into the dining room. He had retrieved the only clean outfit from the bottom of his rucksack – a crumpled linen shirt and pair of chinos. His golden hair was blow-dried, his face clean-shaven. He smelt like a cologne stand in duty-free. His hand reached for a can of Strongbow and he settled next to Dusty. 'Finished with the bathroom?' she asked.

'Yes – thank you so much,' Logan smiled, patting her knee. 'It was heaven.'

'And you found everything you needed?'

'I did. Perfect!'

'Right – I'll go and make myself decent. Although I don't think the transformation will be as impressive.' She winked.

Kat entered the room and poured herself a glass of mineral

water. She glanced quickly at the back of Logan's head. 'Oh, hi – have you just arrived?'

Logan stood up and turned in a circle. 'What do you reckon?'

Kat opened her mouth to say something.

'Ha! You're actually lost for words!'

'You smell clean,' was all Kat could come up with. She sat in one of the armchairs, unable to stop herself from staring. 'When was the last time you had a bath?'

'A *bath*?' Logan echoed, running a hand across his smooth chin. 'That would be at my parents' house about five years ago. I'm a shower-man, me.'

The kitchen door swung open and Aubrey appeared with a bottle of red in one hand and a glass in the other.

'Taken to carrying around a bottle with you now?' Logan asked.

'Oh, I was just, er, just ...'

Logan held up his hands. 'None of my business, mate. It's your gaff.'

'Gregor is in a right tizzy. He's prepared a sumptuous Somerset roast pork and apple delight and is so disappointed that the Flockharts aren't able to join us.'

'You heard, then?'

'Yes ... poor Felicity. I'm sure she would have taken great pleasure in sampling Gregor's *Pommes Anna*.'

'She'll be lucky if she gets so much as a cheese sandwich this evening,' Logan agreed.

'Or she could be fasting if she needs surgery,' Kat said, sipping her water.

Aubrey nodded towards the HAMISH and JESSICA chart. 'How's progress? Please share some good news ...'

Logan let out a deep sigh. 'What a day, man. We've followed more leads than a devoted Labrador.'

'And?'

'We – well, *Logan* – finally managed to have a conversation with Hammy MacPhedran's nephew,' said Kat. 'He says he's going to try to find out what he can for us. We've to meet him tonight in the Lobster Pot. Is it near here?'

'Oh yes, you can just pop over the fence at the foot of the garden. There's a dip at the fisherman gnome. The path takes you right down to the harbour. Is it just you young ones heading out or are you taking Grandma with you?'

'She's not—'

'It's just that she asked whether I could put on a DVD after dinner and I've got *West Side Story* all lined up,' said Aubrey, refilling his glass.

'Yeah, that's fine,' said Logan. 'Kat and I will be happy to lead the investigation.'

'Lovely. And while I'm here, may I just bring your attention to the latest house rule? We're asking all our guests to return the complimentary plastic toiletry bottles into a recycling bin we've placed on the landing. Mill House *will be* moving towards the avoidance of single-use plastic but unfortunately we have an entire garage of Wash & Go Gregor picked up online,' said Aubrey, backing towards the kitchen. 'Dinner will be served at seven.'

Logan busied himself with his Link Chart Investigation Board. He picked up a felt pen and drew a large question mark over HAMMY MACPHEDRAN. 'We're running out of options.'

'And time,' Kat added. 'We go home tomorrow.' She was desperate to retreat to her bedroom amongst the piles of cloth-covered volumes. In her pocket her fingers curled round the cow's horns. 'I hope this hasn't all been a big waste of time.'

'Well, it's certainly been a bit of an adventure,' Logan suggested. 'But it would be a shame if we came up empty. Let's hope Alastair can deliver.'

Chapter 38

It was nearly nine o'clock by the time Kat and Logan pulled on their coats and picked their way towards the bottom of Mill House garden. The only light came from the bright stars scattered across the inky sky. They stumbled along the dark path in silence, guided by the sound of the loch waves lapping against the gravel shore. 'You okay?' Logan called over his shoulder as he led the way.

'Fine,' said Kat.

'And how was your broad bean and aubergine bake?'

'Nice. The pork?'

Logan patted his stomach. 'I must confess, all this food is a treat I hadn't expected. I generally live off noodles while I'm festivalling.'

'Hardly getting your five-a-day.'

'Quite. Ah, I'm guessing that's the Lobster Pot.'

The hundred-year-old watering hole marked the tail end of the high street. Bay windows on two sides of the building lit up the shadowy corner of the harbour. Between empty plant-holders, a painted sign swung from an iron bracket. Both sides of the entrance were marked by stacks of disused lobster pots. 'A theme pub, I see,' Logan joked, holding the heavy wooden door open for Kat. The pub had most likely once housed a family, as individual rooms sprang off the main vestibule. The beige walls were adorned with faded photos of fishermen proudly standing on the harbour in front of their boats. Nets had been strung from the ceiling and a couple of distressed oars crossed above the bar. Logan carried out a quick hunt, finding a handful of locals huddled in corners. 'I can't see Alastair yet. Let's sit here, then we're sure to catch him,' said Logan, perching on a stool. Kat climbed up beside him. A beefy barman in plaid shirt and jeans wiped the counter with a grey cloth. 'You kids got ID?'

Logan and Kat fumbled to produce their driving licences.

'Cheers. Now what can I get you folks?'

'I'll have a pint, please,' said Logan.

'Tennent's?'

'That'll do. Any chance of a student discount?'

'Nice try, son, but no.'

'Kat, what would you like?'

'Hmm,' Kat mused. 'I don't really drink.'

'Yeah, I noticed that. Do you not drink at all?'

'It's not that I *don't* drink, I just …'

'Don't drink?'

Kat frowned, peering over the bar. 'Okay, well, maybe I could have a half of Thistly Cross?'

'Of course.'

'You pair up for the weekend, then?' the barman asked as he pulled the pint.

'Och, it's a long story,' said Logan, handing over a tenner.

'Yeah, so I heard. Also heard you had a bit of an encounter with Billy Ormiston.'

'The old boy?'

'No, the young lad you handed over to the polis.'

'Oh, him,' said Logan. 'He was one of the more colourful characters we've encountered since we arrived. Anyway, we're waiting for Alastair Aitken. He said he'd meet us in here this evening.'

'You sure about that? He never drinks in here. His local is the Fat Trout.'

'*Shit!* Do you think he was just trying to get rid of us?'

The server shrugged as he poured another pint and passed it to a grizzled man hugging an empty glass at the end of the bar. A thumb came up in appreciation. 'All I know is that Ali hasn't drunk in the Lobster Pot in the last two years I've worked behind the bar.'

'What do you think, Kat?' Logan asked, gulping down his pint. 'Should we wait here or go looking for him?'

'He definitely said he'd meet us here? Sure he didn't say the Fat Trout?'

'Kat, I do know the difference between a lobster and a trout!'

'So you say.'

'I think you'll find that a trout has a cartilage skeleton and a lobster has an exoskeleton.'

Kat giggled. 'Oh – hark at the professor. An "*exoskeleton*"?'

'Well, some of us paid attention in biology.'

The pub door opened and a rosy-cheeked woman encased in a shiny raincoat bustled towards the bar. 'Evening, Cath, what brings you in here?'

Kat turned round. 'Oh, hi, Cath. Logan – this is Cath from *Cath's Craft Cave.*'

'Pleased to meet you,' said Logan, shaking her hand. 'It's all in the name, huh?'

'*He's* nice,' Cath whispered in Kat's ear.

'Drink?' the barman asked.

'I'm just in here to speak to Kat. Ach, you know what? Give me a gin and tonic – better make it a double.'

'Coming up.'

Cath drew up a nearby barstool. 'I've got some information for you!' she said with excitement.

'Oh yes?' asked Kat, sipping her cider. 'Hang on a mo – I better take notes.' She reached into her bag and pulled out her notebook and pen. 'Carry on.'

'Agnes is as good as her word. She got right on to the other parishes and guess what?'

'What?'

'*Guess!*'

Kat shook her head. 'There's a Hamish living in Lochinver who's married to a Jessica?'

'Close.' Cath took a long draw through the straw.

'Well?'

Cath bumped her stool a few inches closer and dropped her voice. 'Seemingly there's a lovely lady called Jess Duns who lives in a wee hamlet just east of Assynt. She only moved there in the last year. Apparently she grew up in this area but got married to a chap from near Brora and moved away … but then wanted to retire back nearer family. She started going to St Mary's about six months ago.'

'And please tell me she's married to a Hamish?' asked Kat, not daring to hope.

Cath made a face. 'I knew you'd ask that.' She drained her glass. 'Another?'

'Aye, go on, then. Monday morning can wait.'

'Well?' Kat prompted.

'Honestly, I can't say.'

Kat groaned. 'We're never going to solve this.'

'But – and there *is* a but.'

'I like a but,' Logan said.

'Agnes can't pass on her details to you but she did try to get in touch with Jess. She got no reply when she called yesterday afternoon and this morning. However, she was doing her rounds of the old folk this afternoon and one of them was getting her hair done by Irene.'

'Irene?' Kat repeated.

'She's a mobile hairdresser. Anyway, she started telling her about this Jess and how she's having some trouble getting planning permission to build an extension on her house. I expect you're wondering what this extension is for?'

'Do tell,' Logan urged.

'Apparently Jess moved back to the area and bought this beautiful cottage with wonderful views overlooking Loch Assynt. Which is great, except that her husband is disabled and needs a downstairs bathroom. So he has been living in the Ben More nursing home while she tries to get this blasted extension built for him.'

'And is he called Hamish?' Kat asked on tenterhooks.

Cath sighed. 'He *might* be. Irene was recounting this story then, when it got to the crucial part, she drew a blank. She said that the whole reason she started the story was because Agnes asked about a Hamish. But then she suddenly couldn't remember.'

'So – let me get this right – Agnes has found a local Jess who may or may not be married to a Hamish?'

'Yes. Sorry.'

'Well, I guess that's more than we've got at the moment,' Kat nodded.

'Thank you,' said Logan. 'Another pint, please. Kat?'

'Might as well. So how can we get in touch with this Jess?'

'Good question! So, Agnes said she will try again tomorrow and I can let you know if I hear anything. The other option is to go along to the nursing home and see if you can meet her yourself. Apparently she visits her husband every morning.'

'What's it called again?'

'The Ben More nursing home in Assynt. It's only about ten miles from here – you follow the road round the loch.'

'Okay – maybe we can call in on the way home?'

'We're definitely running out of options,' Logan agreed.

Cath pushed her empty glass across the bar. 'By the way, Alastair is on his way. I saw him picking up a Chinese. Then he needs to sort out his boiler service with Johnny. Should be here soon. Right, I'm off. Good luck, you pair.' Cath hugged them both before striding towards the door. She stopped, turned and shouted to the old soul at the end of the bar. 'Hey, Jim! Don't forget you've got an appointment with Dr Farquhar at ten tomorrow morning.' The thumb came up again.

Kat read through her hastily scribbled notes. 'This is sounding promising.'

'It's a bit tenuous,' Logan argued. 'Someone who cuts someone's hair might know someone else who might be called Hamish? Bloody hell, Kat, it feels like we're chasing a leaf down a windy road.'

'I know but we can't pin our hopes on Alastair. If he comes up with nothing, then we really have reached the end of the line. I've told Dusty we're heading back down the road after breakfast.'

'Oh! That soon?' Logan said with disappointment.

'There's not much point staying if we've exhausted all leads.'

'S'pose.'

'And I expect you'll be wanting to get to the Loop-the-Loop festival or whatever?'

'Absolutely.'

'We've really taken up too much of your time.'

'It's no problem. I— Here he is!'

Alastair strolled up to the bar, showered and in clean clothes, a Chinese carry-out in one hand. 'Fancy meeting you here. Logan, isn't it? How's the nose?'

Logan dabbed at his face. 'I'm sure I'll survive.'

'I don't expect your girlfriend appreciated me rearranging your features.'

'I'm not—' Kat began.

'Ah ... my mistake, I see. I meant your *fiancée*. Congratulations, by the way.'

'What?' Kat stammered.

'That's quite a rock.' Alastair nodded to the engagement ring. He nudged Logan in the ribs. 'You old romantic. I take back what I said about your southern flab.'

Kat blushed as she hid her hand behind her back. 'This isn't ... we're not ... I'm Kat.'

'Whoa – sorry!' Alastair laughed loudly. 'I didn't mean to cause offence. It's none of my business if you're having a final fling before the big day. Good for you, girl! You can be married the rest of your life!'

'But—'

'I'm Alastair.' He shook Kat's hand.

'Can I get you a drink?' Logan asked.

Alastair leant on the bar. 'I'll get it. Pour us a dram, would you, Rob?'

'What are you after?'

'What's your malt of the month?'

'Old Pulteney.'

'I think I've got a whole bottle of the stuff at home. Never mind – make it a double.'

Alastair took his first sip. 'You like whisky?'

Logan groaned. 'Please don't bring that anywhere near me.'

'He liked whisky a bit too much last night,' said Kat.

'Ah, fair enough.' Alastair swilled the malt round the glass and breathed in deeply. 'That's Scotland in a glass. How about you, Kat?'

Kat shook her head furiously. 'Never tried it.'

'You don't know what you're missing. Anyway, mustn't dawdle.' He patted the plastic carrier. 'I've got a chicken chop suey and special fried rice with my name on it. So, you were asking about my Uncle Hammy?'

'That's right,' said Kat, producing her notebook again.

'I hope you're not going to use this as evidence against me,' Alastair joked.

Kat shook her head. 'It's just that we've been given so much information – it's hard to keep track.'

'What's this all about?'

Kat slipped the ring off her finger and laid it on the counter. The barman raised his eyebrows and whistled. 'Nice ring.'

'It is indeed,' said Alastair. He picked it up, turning it in the light to make the diamonds glint.

'Read the inscription,' Kat urged.

'*Marry me, Jess? Love Hamish,*' Alastair read out loud. 'That really is rather lovely.'

'You're not going to cry, are you?' the barman grunted. Alastair carefully replaced the ring on the bar.

'My neighbour, Dusty, found it in her late husband's belongings.

265

It was in an envelope – as good as new – seemingly fished out of Loch Assynt fifty years ago.'

'Right. Well, I can see why you might have thought it belonged to my family but I'm sorry to disappoint you. I rang Hammy before I came out this evening. Other than swearing a lot and asking why I was digging up ancient history, he told me that his parents packed him off abroad when he was twenty-one. He was sent to live with an older cousin who worked in a bank in Paris. He got taken on as a very junior clerk and left after about a year to work on an estate, where it suited him to lead an outdoor life. He married a local lass called Odette and they had two boys – both now grown up. Odette divorced him when the boys were still young, after he had a misjudged affair with the estate owner's wife. So he lost his family *and* his job.'

'Sorry to hear that,' said Kat.

Alastair shrugged. 'My mum used to say that Uncle Hammy had a bit of a self-destruct button. Just when things were going well he liked to shake it up a bit. After both their parents died my mum bought him out so he got his share of the property. I think he blew that too.'

'And so no Jessica?' Logan asked gloomily.

'Hammy said he had his fair share of lassies in Lochinver but doesn't remember going out with a Jessica and certainly was never engaged or proposed to a Jessica.'

'Damn!' said Kat. 'It felt like we were so close.'

Alastair picked up the ring once more and tapped it against the wooden counter. 'This will have its own story. I'm just sorry that I can't help you. What will you do with it?'

'I'll have it,' the barman offered, holding out his hand.

'Dusty says if we can't find its owner before we leave, she'll throw it back into Loch Assynt. At least, that way, it will be returned to where Edwin found it.'

'Sounds as good an idea as any,' Alastair agreed.

'That's a rubbish idea!' the barman protested. 'Why don't I take it, sell it on eBay and get myself a decent car? Surely if you let me sell it, you'll bring someone some pleasure?'

'You mean *you*?' Alastair laughed.

'Aye! Why no?'

Kat pursed her lips. 'We've got one more chance tomorrow. A possible Jess.'

Alastair clapped Logan on the back. 'Well, I hope you find a happy ending to your story. You seem like a nice couple – not that you are!' He winked at Logan.

'Thanks, man.'

'Thank you for your time,' said Kat with a smile. 'You've been very helpful.'

'Right, let's get this into the microwave. Night, folks.'

'Another round?' the barman enquired.

'Not for me,' said Kat, slipping off the barstool. 'Oopsy!'

Logan held her hand as she straightened up. 'Come on, let's get you home.'

'Enjoy the rest of your trip.' The barman saluted as he cleared away the glasses.

Chapter 39

Kat felt a rush of cool air against her flushed cheeks as she stepped out into the darkness. She zipped up her coat, thrusting her hands deep into her pockets and feeling the reassuring clump of wool. The loch glittered under the heavy white moon, the water rippling with a gentle swish over the pebbles.

Logan traced the shore until he found the path that led through the back gardens of the cottages. As she stumbled along Kat hadn't remembered the track being quite so uneven. She extended her arms, letting her fingers skim along the fences at either side.

'You okay?' Logan called over his shoulder.

'Fine,' Kat mumbled, wondering why her legs kept moving in opposite directions. The pair arrived at the back of Mill House and Logan unlatched the garden gate. His lone tent occupied a corner under a rowan tree, ripe with orange berries. 'I guess this is me.'

'Thanks for all your help,' said Kat.

'Any excuse for a couple of pints,' Logan grinned.

'Not just this evening, though. I can't see how Dusty and I would have got very far on our own.'

Logan shrugged. 'Just returning the favour. I wouldn't have got far on *my* own. I'd still be walking up the A9 if you hadn't stopped.'

'So we're quits?'

'Quits.' Logan held out his hand. 'Unless I can interest you in sneaking a final nightcap?'

'No chance! Night, Logan,' said Kat, shaking his hand with great solemnity.

Kat crept under the heavy linen bedding. When was the last time she had allowed herself a drink? To let down her guard? The evening had made her feel confused. Her thoughts were interrupted by a muffled clunk and she wondered whether Dusty had dropped something. There it was again – a noise coming from the hall. She slipped out of bed and listened – this time hearing a quiet knock on wood. Kat opened the door a fraction, to find Logan begging like a lost puppy. 'Have you space for one more?'

Kat hesitated, trying to make sense of what might happen. He waited patiently with hopeful eyes. She compared his two nights holed up in the tent with her own luxurious experience – the room's spacious double bed, lush carpet and pillows of bliss. With a nod she opened the door, wondering whether she would regret it before the end of the night.

Logan padded in, his tail wagging. Without a word she slid back into the warmth. Logan stripped off his clothes, leaving them in an untidy pile on the floor. He trotted round to the other side of the bed and lay down beside her. She was curled, her back to him. Logan paused before inching closer. Kat held her breath - her heart rate quickening. She tensed as he nestled against her slender frame. He gently kissed her cheek, then her neck. As his hand moved lightly over her skin she felt her body unfurl. 'I can stop if you want,' Logan whispered.

'No – I like it,' Kat said in a small voice. As he bent to kiss her lips she turned to face him. His soft hair brushed her face as he lay over her. She felt him respond to her touch as his weight pressed down on her. Logan moved in gentle rhythms until his yearning became more urgent. Kat felt her body burn with a stab of pain as he let out a relieved sigh.

Logan rolled on to his back, his arms spread wide. His hand grazed her arm as she coiled into a ball. The first tear felt hot and wet on her cheek. She couldn't stop the flow as her body shuddered. 'Hey,' Logan said with concern. He turned on to his side. 'Hey, Kat, what is it? Did I hurt you? Speak to me – what is it?' He tried to cradle her in his arms but she sat up in bed, her arms hugging her knees.

'Kat? Did I do something wrong? Please don't cry.'

Kat shook her head silently. She reached for a tissue and blew her nose.

'Come on now,' said Logan. 'Please tell me what's wrong.' He put a finger under her chin, trying to read something in her tear-stung face. 'Kat? Is that not what you wanted?'

'It's not you – it's me.'

'Ah! The *Let Down*,' Logan said with a wry smile. 'But I thought you didn't have a boyfriend?'

'I don't.'

'But you're not free to be with someone else?'

Kat sniffed, blowing her nose again. 'I *had* a boyfriend,' she mumbled. 'His name was Jack.'

'But you split up?'

'He died. Last year.'

'Oh, Kat, I'm so sorry. What happened? Was he ill?'

Kat shook her head. 'He died while we were in Magaluf on our high school leavers' trip. He was only eighteen. We both were. It was such a stupid accident …'

'Tell me.'

'We'd only been there for one day. His room was on the third floor. We'd been enjoying the pool and had come out to get changed. He hung his swimming stuff over the edge of the balcony to dry. He got showered and ready to go out. We were going to have a drink on our own before we met the others.'

Kat sniffed as Logan held out another tissue. 'Jack went back out on to the balcony to get his shorts and towel – didn't want to leave them there all night. Anyway, it had been really windy that day. Just as he reached out, his towel blew off the balcony. Without thinking, he made a grab for it, but fell right over the edge.'

'Oh, Kat,' said Logan, holding her tightly. 'How awful.'

She began to sob. 'It was just horrible – the whole thing. His parents flew out. They were so upset. Everyone was devastated. Jack was one of those people who was so full of life – was always bouncing around. I think about him every day. This was his.' She pointed to the miniature Highland cow sitting on the bedside cabinet. 'I bought him this key ring and he really liked it – always kept it in his pocket. It was in his pocket when he died,' Kat murmured. 'I miss him so much.'

'I'm sure you do.'

'I mean – what a stupid accident! He died trying to save a towel that probably cost about ten pounds in TK Maxx.'

'Life can be crazy.'

Kat shook her head. 'But the worst thing is that I'm such a shit girlfriend.'

'Now, I'm sure that can't be true!'

'It is,' Kat said quietly. She swept aside her fringe. 'You see, we agreed we would hold off – you know – until we were both eighteen. I wanted it to be special – and so did he. So then he was eighteen just after our exams, before we both left school. And I said why don't we wait until we're in Majorca – find an isolated beach, somewhere we could be alone. I suppose I had got a bit carried away with *Mamma Mia*.' Kat gave a small smile. 'He was lovely about it and agreed we should wait. And then … and then it was too late and he was gone. I can't believe I denied him that special time that we should have shared. And now I've done it with someone I've only known for three days!'

'It's not your fault.'

'But it is! I withheld sex like I had all the power, which wasn't fair. He was such a sweet guy – he didn't deserve me. He could have gone out with any other girl in our year.'

Logan shook his head. 'He chose you and I'm sure he wouldn't have changed a thing.'

'And now I feel so guilty. I have to live every day of my life knowing that I'm here enjoying life and he's not.'

'I'm not being funny, Kat, but it strikes me that you're *not* enjoying life – far from it.'

'What do you mean?'

Logan shrugged. 'I knew something was wrong but didn't like to say anything. It's none of my business. But you walk around under a cloud. I've hardly seen you smile once since we met. Not even when Darwin tried to pull off his Debbie Harry stunt.'

'So I look like totally miserable?'

'I could see you weren't happy. Of course, I knew nothing about your life – had no idea what might be going on at home.'

'Logan, nothing makes sense to me any more. I don't know what to do with myself – how to fill my days. When I'm walking along the road I look down. I can't look people in the eye. I'm scared people can see something in me that I don't want them to see.'

'You're hurting – that's normal. It's part of the grieving process.'

'Then I'll *move on*? Find another boyfriend?'
'Life does go on, Kat.'
'I know. But it's hard.'
'Yep. It is.'

A shaft of light crossed the bed, dividing the room in half. Kat turned and sensed the empty space next to her. Her head felt fuzzy as she checked her watch – it was still early. She turned over and allowed herself to doze.

Chapter 40

'So, let me get this right,' said PC Walker, sipping coffee from a stained mug. 'You entered the property of Mrs Harris through the back door at approximately seven p.m. You were about to go upstairs to check for her medication when you heard a sound. You believed this sound to be a ghost so you called your husband on your mobile?'

'That's right,' Dell nodded. 'We'd just been saying how Dusty keeps her husband's ashes on the mantelpiece, which gives me the creeps. Plus, Dusty tells me she has conversations with her Edwin and she feels his presence.'

'So it didn't cross your mind that there might have been an intruder on the premises?'

'Not really. I'd had quite a bit of red wine and was planning to rustle up a hot pudding for Ron. I can't say I was thinking anything very much.'

'So you didn't call your husband – Mr Carmichael – with the intention of challenging this possible intruder?'

'Oh no! I was trying to prove a point about the ghost.'

'That the house was haunted?'

'Exactly.'

'So then your husband joined you at the property, where you tried to convince him you could hear your deceased neighbour moving around upstairs?'

'That's right.'

'And did he believe you?'

'At first he couldn't hear anything. But that's not really surprising. Sometimes I can be standing in the kitchen and shouting at him for his tea and I'll be like *bawling* and he won't hear a thing. Then I'll have to go upstairs and get him and he still won't have a clue.'

'But then – when he *did* hear a noise – what did he think it was?'

'Well, then he saw me in the bedroom with my apron on and knew it was teatime.'

'I meant,' said PC Walker, trying to be patient, 'last night, next door?'

'Oh, well I could tell he didn't actually think it was a ghost. He doesn't really believe in stuff like that. I think he's scared of anything that he's never seen up close. He doesn't even believe in UFOs or aliens, which is ridiculous! I mean – how do you explain *ET*? Is he calling Steven Spielberg a liar—'

'Mrs Carmichael,' PC Walker interrupted, checking her watch. 'What *did* he think the noise was?'

'We both wondered whether it was the man Arthur met from the night before, and that he might be keeping him hostage for sex.'

'Sorry, what? You've lost me.'

They heard a brisk knock and PC McGill stuck her head round the door. 'That's me finished with Mr Carmichael. Are you nearly done here?'

'I've no idea.'

Dell said, 'If that's you finished with Ron – just tell him he can head back without me. I can get a bus into work. Only perhaps you can ask him – since he has my car – whether he minds picking up some Persil on the way home. Tell him to get the large size –

the purple one. That'll save me carrying it on the bus. Oh, and we need more toilet rolls – better get a sixteen-roll pack. The ones with a koala on the side, not the plain ones – the quilted ones. They're much nicer,, don't you think?'

'Er … I'll try to remember all that.' PC McGill quickly closed the door.

'Now, where were we?' Dell asked.

PC Walker read back her notes. 'Something about Arthur having a sex slave?'

'Oh yes! Well, on Saturday I was in the garden hanging out the washing – it was such a lovely autumnal day – when I overheard Arthur saying that he was going to meet his lover that night. So Ron and I finished our dress rehearsal for *The Sound of Music* – I was just standing in for Daft Donna who had fallen off a scooter – then we belted down to the back of Waverley and found him in a tryst with another man. Poor Cherie – she'll be in ruins.'

'But why were you following him? Is that usual behaviour, spying on your neighbour like that?'

'It was for Cherie's benefit, not ours! You see she's laid up on crutches after surgery and it seemed very unfair that Arthur was cheating on her while she was incapacitated. It's all so sleazy!'

'And what made you think he was holding someone against their will?'

'We just put two and two together and got five.'

'So you proceeded upstairs to find out what was going on? Why didn't you just call out? Say hello?'

'Because the house was in complete darkness – not a single light was on. It was all very suspicious. We could hear movement in Dusty's bedroom, so that was when Ron decided to take action. He can be very masterful at times. Like when we were celebrating our anniversary in—'

'I'm just wondering, though – since we now know it was Mr Kerr in the house and technically *he* was on his own property, unlike you – why didn't you check who was in the room?'

'Because he might have attacked us with a Samurai sword or something! You read about these things in the paper. Well, I say *paper*, it's all online now, isn't it?'

'And what made you think it was *unlikely* to be Mr Kerr in the house?'

'He'd been round at ours earlier, asking us to trim back our trees. Even though they're hardly even overhanging the fence. We had just seen a … a mouse in our kitchen and once Arthur had helped catch it, he threw it in our neighbour's garden.'

'So he helped you out?'

'Well, we were both in our pyjamas and I was in no state to do anything. I had to have a lie-down for the rest of the day. Then Arthur stormed off saying he was going back home to Fife.'

'So you guessed it wasn't Mr Kerr but you proceeded to apprehend the individual?'

'We did.'

'Might I suggest that – rather than defuse the situation – you actually inflamed the circumstances? Some might say that you incited a violent response?'

'Some can say what they like! All I know is that Dusty has been a good neighbour to us for many years and Ron wasn't going to let some thieving scum help himself to all her valuables.'

'And what if Mr Kerr was telling the truth? What if he really was just gathering up valuables to take to her new home?'

'In a balaclava?'

'I'm just playing devil's advocate. Mr Kerr could very well

lodge a grievance against *you*.' PC Walker counted off points on her fingers. 'You listen in to his phone calls, you stalk him on a Saturday evening, you force him into pest-control duties, you enter *his* property while he is there on legitimate business, you imprison him in a room, then you smash him in the face with a frying pan. You can see how it looks?'

'But it wasn't like that at all!' Dell protested. 'We were just trying to find out why Arthur has been wearing Dusty's ballgown!'

'I'm not even going to ask what that's all about. You know what? Thank you for coming down to the station this morning and for providing a statement. I think I have all the information I require at this point.'

'But don't you want to know about the weird things he's been doing with her clothes?'

'We'll get a statement from Mr Kerr in the first instance. I can always ask more questions at a later date.'

'Really, though, I don't mind waiting until you've spoken to him. I mean – if I can help in any way. I won't even mind if this takes all day.' Dell leant back in her chair and crossed her arms. *Let's see how Karen likes covering Tracy's coffee breaks*, she thought.

Chapter 41

When Kat realised she had woken up later than intended, she sprang out of bed and quickly showered, brushing through her wet hair. She hurled her clothes into a bag, grabbed her boots and picked up her mobile. Hurrying down the stairs, she had almost reached the dining room when her phone slipped out of her hand. She bent to pick it up, aware of Dusty and Logan in mid-conversation.

'I think we agreed a hundred pounds?' said Dusty.

'That's very kind of you,' Kat heard Logan reply. She pushed the door open to find Logan folding twenty-pound notes into his back pocket.

'What's going on?' Kat asked.

'Nothing,' said Logan, blushing crimson.

'It can't be nothing. Why is Dusty giving you money? You shouldn't be taking money from her – she's a pensioner.'

'Leave it, Kat,' said Dusty in a quiet voice.

Kat felt anger rising. 'Why is Dusty giving you money?' she repeated.

'I just wanted him to have some money for taking you out,' said Dusty. 'You've been so down in the dumps since Jack died, I thought you deserved someone to give you some attention, that's all.'

'So you paid *Logan*?' Kat cried. 'You *paid* him to take me out?' She turned to Logan in fury. 'And you? You took her money? Did she pay you to sleep with me too?' Tears pricked her eyes.

'Come on now, Kat – you know it wasn't like that,' said Logan, taking a step towards her with open arms.

'Wasn't it? How was it, then? Did you get value for your money?'

Logan tried to give her a hug. She pushed him away. '*You!* You can just stay the hell away from me. You took money for last night? So Dusty's your pimp now, is she?'

'Kat, you're being ridiculous,' Logan said. He ran a hand through his hair.

'Get out!' Kat snapped. 'Get out of my sight. I never want to see you again.'

'I'm not leaving like this.'

'No? Well, I am.' Kat strode out of the front door, slamming it behind her. She ran across to the Volvo, collapsing on to the bonnet in tears. Her fingers gripped the Highland cow so tightly the horns pierced her palm. She heard footsteps on the gravel behind her.

'Come back inside, Kat – let's talk about this,' said Logan. He leant on the bonnet.

'I'm not talking to you. I mean it. Leave me alone.'

'Okay, well you don't need to talk. Just listen. Don't go being mad at Dusty – she just had your best interests at heart. She sees your pain and wants to help. I know how this looks but this is no reflection on you whatsoever. *I'm* the one who took the money so it says a whole lot more about me than it does about you.' Logan sighed. 'If it makes you feel any better – you were really lovely. And I *didn't* do it for the money – obviously. You're gorgeous and maybe you haven't let anyone tell you that for a while. And … well, it's been a long time since I had anyone hold me like that. It was nice.'

Kat stayed silent, her face buried in her folded arms.

'Okay, so I'm going to head off now. Take care of yourself, Kat.' He stroked her hair. 'Just do me one favour – go out and grab a bit of life. If there is one thing I've learnt – life is like that osprey up there. It'll swoop down from the sky, maybe even do a little hover in front of your eyes. Then before you can reach for your camera, it'll be gone. Bye, Kat.' Logan hoisted his rucksack on to his back and walked up to the main road.

'Oh, has he gone?' Dusty asked as she came out of Mill House. She put her arms round Kat. 'Don't cry, dear. I'm sorry things turned out like this – it wasn't how it was meant to happen.'

Kat wiped her eyes with her jumper. 'You mean I wasn't supposed to see you paying off Logan? How *could* you, Dusty? Do you know how humiliating this is for me?'

'I just wanted to do something nice for you – a thank-you for driving me around and coming on this mad adventure with me.'

'But paying Logan to *sleep* with me?'

'We didn't discuss that. I just suggested that he take you out and make your last night special. I guess he takes his work very seriously.'

'Dusty!'

'Look,' said Dusty gently. 'Logan mentioned about this guilt you've been carrying around with you.'

'Oh, so *more* humiliation, then!'

'Kat – you denied Jack nothing. Most people's first experience of sex is an awkward fumble in a teenager's bedroom when neither of you know one end of a condom from the other.'

'Please stop talking.'

'I'm just saying this, then I'll shut up. You'll always remember your first time as being in a magical place – yes? With someone who actually cares about you? Which he does. Logan was smitten with you from the moment we picked him up. Anyone could see that. And, apart from anything, I bet he knew what he was doing?'

Dusty patted Kat on the back. 'Now – we'll say no more about this. Agreed?'

Kat sniffed.

'I'll take that as a yes. So how about a bit of breakfast before we set off?'

Chapter 42

Kat nibbled on a slice of toast in silence, downed a cup of tea and carried her bag out to the car. She sat in the driver's seat and started the engine. Aubrey lifted Dusty's case and placed it in the boot. 'Well, thank you both so much for choosing to stay at Mill House – did you get a chance to write something in our visitors' book? We do like to reflect on our guests with affection.'

'Yes, I put in a wee note,' said Dusty. 'And what's the latest on dear Felicity?'

Aubrey scrunched up his face. 'Seems she has a rather nasty broken elbow that requires an operation. She may be a few days in hospital, I'm afraid.'

'Oh, poor love.'

'Darwin rang to say he's getting a bus back here today so he can pick up his car. He has no idea what has happened to his pop-up theatre. He's hoping that an unscrupulous local hasn't scarpered with it … but I wouldn't be surprised if they find it in someone's back garden!'

'I'm sure he'll get it back,' said Dusty, sitting in the passenger seat.

'So where are you headed now? Are you going back to Edinburgh?'

'We've got one final detour,' Dusty replied. 'Our last chance to speak to a Jess. Bye, then, Aubrey – and please say cheerio to Gregor.'

'Will do. Good luck!' Aubrey stood and waved a tea towel in farewell as Kat pulled out of the driveway.

'Do we know how to get there?' Dusty asked mildly.

'Well, *I* do!' Kat replied, keeping her eyes on the road.

'Can I help at all?'

'Haven't you done enough for me?'

'Oh, so is this how it's going to be for the whole day?' said Dusty. 'How many times do I need to say I'm sorry? I'm sorry, *I'm sorry.*' She gazed out of the window at the passing hedgerows. The hills were ablaze with trees of copper, red and brown.

They both spotted Logan's figure in the distance as he sauntered along the road. Kat's hands gripped the steering wheel as they passed, a little too closely. He gave their car a friendly wave but Kat put her foot down and sped away. She handed Dusty a piece of paper torn from her notebook. 'The directions.'

'Hang on.' Dusty reached into her handbag and put on her glasses. 'Leaving the Mill House, turn right and head for the main road. Take the A eight three seven following the loch for nine-point-eight miles. Pass the Highland View Hotel and you'll come to a viewing point with a small car park by the loch. You will see a long row of houses. Ben More Nursing Home is the last of the big houses. If you get to Ardvreck Castle, you've gone too far. Oh! I've been to Ardvreck Castle. If I remember rightly we got lovely views but it's a bit of a ruin. No coffee shop.'

'Thanks,' Kat muttered.

Dusty suddenly clapped a hand to her mouth. 'Oh, Kat!' she cried.

'What? Don't give me a fright like that. What is it?'

Dusty pointed to Kat's bare left hand. 'Where's the ring? The ring's gone!'

Kat shook her head. 'I took it off.'

'Why? It really suited you.'

Kat shrugged. 'It wasn't mine.'

'At least it's not lost. Thank goodness for that. Could you imagine coming all this way here and then losing the ring?'

'I thought you were going to throw it into the loch anyway?'

'I suppose. But at least I'd know where it was. I'd hate to think the story ends with some random like that awful Billy chap picking it up off the ground, or the ring falling down a ladies toilet.'

'Thanks – glad you trusted me with it.'

'I didn't mean ... oh, there's the Highland View Hotel. It can't be far now. There – Ben More Nursing Home!'

'I see it.'

Kat turned into the private parking area. 'Wow! What a view the residents must have,' said Dusty. The traditional stone mansion stood on a slope overlooking the tree-lined loch. To their left they could just about make out the shape of the ruined castle.

Kat pushed open the glass front door into a warm reception area that had been painted a neutral cream colour. Large potted ferns gave it the feel of a conservatory. The smell of coffee wafted from an open door marked LOUNGE on a sign that included a picture of a chair. A stronger smell of bleach emanated from another door with a notice depicting a toilet. A young girl with a blonde ponytail and navy suit was sitting in front of a PC, tapping away at the keyboard. She carried on with intensity, focused on the screen as her hands flitted in front of her. Her ponytail bobbed as she read over her digital document.

Kat and Dusty approached a welcome desk, where a brass bell had been placed next to a sign-in book, a biro attached by a chain. They waited patiently while the girl worked away. An oversized clock on the wall ticked. Twenty-five minutes past ten.

'Shall I?' Dusty suggested.

'Go ahead.'

Dusty tapped the bell with a firm '*Ding!*' The girl leapt up from her chair, removing earbuds at the same time. 'Sorry!' she blurted. 'I never heard you come in.' A sudden look of panic swept across her face. 'You're not here for the inspection, are you? I thought that was tomorrow. Oh my God, we're not ready! I mean ... not that we'd be doing anything different!' She gave a nervous laugh.

'No, we're not here to carry out an inspection,' said Dusty with a smile.

'Are you hoping for a look round? Is it for yourself, madam? Only my boss, Mrs McDonald, is out at the moment. She knows all the costs and everything. I just do reception and sometimes, if the staff are busy I help with teas and things. Of course, you're welcome to look round yourselves – although not in the bedrooms. *Obvs*. That wouldn't be right at all, would it—'

'Actually,' Kat interrupted. 'We were hoping we could have a word with a lady called Jess Duns?'

'Who's that, then?'

'We think she might be visiting a relative? That her husband might be here?

'And what's his name?'

'We're guessing it might be Mr Duns?'

'Oh! Now we *do* have a Mr Duns. He was only meant to have been with us about six months while his extension was being built but it's been nearly a year. He's lovely. Is he your granddad?'

'No,' said Kat, 'but that sounds like the right person we're looking for. We heard that Jess Duns comes to visit every morning.'

'She does. She's in with Mr Duns at the moment.'

Dusty clapped her hands in excitement. 'Do you think we could have a wee word with her?'

'Do you have an appointment?'

'No, we're just visiting on the off-chance,' said Kat. 'We're heading back to Edinburgh today and really hoped we could just quickly ask Mrs Duns something.'

'Mrs McDonald says we're supposed to make appointments for all visitors. Acts as a deterrent for bogus callers, you see.'

Kat retrieved her driving licence. 'I have ID.'

The girl frowned. 'I suppose I could go and ask her.'

'Would you? That would be fabulous,' said Dusty.

'Who will I say you are?'

'If you can let them know we might have something that belongs to them,' said Kat.

'Like what?' She peered over their shoulders as though expecting to see a box or package.

'Something valuable.'

'Fine.' She sniffed.

The receptionist opened a door and appeared at their side. 'Wait here,' she commanded, heading off down a corridor marked BEDROOMS, the sign accompanied by a picture of a bed. She returned a few moments later. 'Mrs Duns is not aware that she's lost anything but she doesn't mind you having a word.'

'Great!'

'Wait! You need to sign the register first. If Mrs McDonald thinks I've let in random strangers I'll get the chop. Jamie once let in a man in a uniform who said he'd come to fix the telly. Next thing you know he's got it in the back of his car and is off with it.' She appeared round the other side of the desk. First Kat, then Dusty signed the book.

'What about *your* ID?' she asked Dusty.

'Er, well. Let's see. I have my bus pass.'

She handed it to the receptionist, who scrutinised it. 'Off you go, then. Oh – and the room is no smoking. If you want to have a cigarette you'll need to go out the back. Mrs McDonald doesn't like people hanging around the front garden with all that smoke. Even those vapour things.'

'Thank you,' said Kat. 'You've been most thorough.'

'Room number twelve!' she shouted at their backs.

Chapter 43

The door stood open, revealing a light spacious room boasting a bay window overlooking the still, grey loch. Against one wall was a single bed with a plain duvet cover and, in the corner, an oak wardrobe. An elderly couple sat side by side – Mr Duns in a wheelchair, his wife sitting in a low wing chair. They were drinking coffee from a pot on a shared occasional table.

'Thank you so much for agreeing to see us,' Dusty began as she hovered at the entrance. 'My name is Dusty Harris and this is my young neighbour, Kat. We've come all the way from Edinburgh to find you.'

'Really? Do come in,' said Mrs Duns with a smile. She had a petite frame and was smartly dressed in matching wool jacket and skirt. Her hair was like white candyfloss, her face browned from a summer working in the garden. 'I'm Jess Duns and this is my husband, Hamish.'

Kat and Dusty exchanged a look of amazement and relief. '*Hamish?*' Dusty repeated to be sure.

'That's right.' Hamish, also slightly built but with broad hands resting in his lap, had dark eyes and a neatly trimmed beard, his silver hair parted to one side. He wore a pressed shirt and slacks, his shoes a shiny chestnut.

'Please – have a seat.' Jess indicated a two-seater bench in front of the window. Kat and Dusty settled themselves in anticipation.

'So, how can we be of assistance?' asked Jess. 'Pam mentioned something about lost property?'

'Well, it's a very long story,' said Dusty.

'Would you like some coffee?'

'No – we won't take up any more of your time than necessary.'

Dusty recounted how she had come to find the ring in her attic and provided a brief summary of the events leading them to this point. 'So we're really, *really* hoping that we've found the right Jess and Hamish!' She waved two sets of crossed fingers.

Kat unzipped her jacket pocket and produced the ring. Hamish held out his right hand, aged with liver spots. He grasped the ring between his index finger and thumb – holding it up to the light. Kat said a silent prayer. Hamish turned it first one way, then the other. He screwed up his eyes and examined the inscription. His eyes welled with tears as he shuffled forward in his seat. Without warning, he fell on to his knees with a crash.

'*Hamish!*' Jess cried. 'Are you alright?' She jumped up to assist him. 'Oh my goodness. Will I get help? You've never fallen out of your wheelchair before.'

Kat and Dusty looked on in shock. 'Shall I go for help?' Kat offered, rising.

'*Sit!*' Hamish instructed. 'All of you, sit down. *Please*. Jess … I'm fine.'

Jess hesitated before resuming her position. Hamish remained on his knees. He held the ring up for all to see. Brushing away his tears he said in a wavering voice, 'Jess Christie. Will you do me the honour of becoming my wife?'

'Oh, Hamish! Is this the ring?'

'Yes – *this is the ring*! It's been fifty years in the wilderness and finally it's come home to us.'

Jess held out her left hand, which bore a single gold band. Hamish slid the ring on to her finger. Jess laughed in delight. 'Yes, Hamish Duns, I *will* marry you. I *will* be your wife.'

'Hooray!' Dusty gave a rapturous round of applause. Much to her embarrassment, Kat began to cry.

'I wish we had some champagne to celebrate!' said Jess as she admired the engagement ring. 'You chose well, Hamish. This really is stunning.'

'Aye – and so it should be,' said Hamish. '*Now* you can help me up.' They all hurried to his assistance.

Jess shook her head, unable to take her eyes off the ring, which she held at arm's length to appreciate its splendour.

'So, you're saying you think your husband found it in the loch out there? Had it been there all these years? Surely not, it looks brand new.'

'I think he came across it when we were here on our honeymoon fifty years ago,' said Dusty. 'That's the only time we've been to this area. And, ever since I found it, I've been desperate to know its story.'

'Well, I can help you with that,' said Hamish with a wry smile. He settled back in his seat. 'I was a young mechanic apprentice when I first met Jess. She was so pretty. Still is.'

'And he fell in love with me!'

'Aye, I did that.' Hamish patted her arm. 'I didn't have much money but I bought a second-hand and rather worse-for-wear Classic Mini Cooper in racing green. In all my spare time – when we weren't winching – I was working on that car. Anyway, I got it to a grand condition and sold it to a keen lad who worked on the boats. I used all the money to buy the best ring I could afford for this very special lady.'

'Och, *Hamish!*' Jess blushed.

'Flashy, I know. And with no thought of saving for a wedding, either. It was my own bragging that was my downfall,' Hamish tutted. 'My pal Tommy and I were out fishing on the loch and I couldn't help but show off. I told him I was going to propose to Jess and held up the ring for him to gawp at. Only did he not go and land a mighty trout at the same time. He leapt to his feet, knocking the ring out my hand into the loch. We never saw it again. I could have strangled him there and then in that bloody boat. But it was my own doing,' Hamish sighed. 'And then, naturally, I had no ring to propose with.'

'I didn't mind,' said Jess.

'Of course you did! What young lass wants to get engaged without a ring?'

Jess shrugged. 'We still got married – it'll be fifty years next year.'

'But your parents never believed me,' said Hamish bitterly. 'I'm sure they thought I came up with some cock and bull story for being so cheap. Your dad thought I'd spent the money on myself.'

'Nonsense!'

Hamish held up his hands. 'And then my job went and we had to move home with my folks, who thought I'd lost my mind – swapping a car for a ring! Everywhere in Brora there's a brae. Because we had no car poor Jess had to walk everywhere.'

'Ach, it was good for me!'

'Yes, but I know your parents blamed me when we lost the first wee baby.'

'I had a miscarriage,' Jess told them.

'I'm sorry,' said Dusty.

'Her parents said that she wouldn't have lost the baby if she hadn't had to walk up and down all those hills.'

'Come on now, Hamish, that's all in the past,' said Jess. 'And we've been blessed with three wonderful daughters. Our youngest has recently moved to Inchnadamph so we wanted to be close to her.'

Hamish held his head in his hands. 'I never thought I'd see this day. It's really quite unbelievable that the ring has turned up after all these years. Incredible!'

Dusty beamed. 'I'm delighted we were able to return it to its rightful owner. Edwin will be so pleased when I tell him.'

Kat shook her head and stood up to leave. 'One thing I don't understand, though,' she said. 'I did a pretty thorough search and found no reference to an engagement or marriage between a Jessica and Hamish?'

'Ah ... that'll be my fault too,' Hamish said, nodding. 'My given name was John but as that was also my father's name, I was always known by my middle name – Hamish. The local paper would have put me down as John Duns.'

'Another mystery solved. Okay, well we better leave you two in peace. It's been nice to meet you.'

'I can never thank you ladies enough,' said Jess, admiring her hand again. 'It really is beautiful. Can we at least reimburse your expenses? Your petrol and accommodation? You've come an awfully long way to find us.'

'Not at all!' Dusty protested. 'It's been a pleasure. I haven't been away from the house since my Edwin died, so it's been brilliant. Hasn't it, Kat?'

Kat grunted, car keys in hand. 'We really best make a start. It's a long drive home.'

They closed the door to number twelve and made their way back to the foyer.

'Thank you!' Dusty called to the receptionist, who was engrossed in a spreadsheet.

Chapter 44

Kat and Dusty completed the journey home in six hours, with one brief lunch stop at Inverness. Kat kept the radio on while Dusty dozed. They arrived in Edinburgh in darkness, a steady drizzle keeping the wipers moving.

As Kat turned the Volvo into Murrayfield Close they both spotted the red FOR SALE sign at the same time. 'Oh!' said Dusty. 'I suppose Arthur has been making arrangements since I've been away.'

'So it seems.'

Kat parked the car in the drive. The front door flew open and Dell and Ron came bounding out. Dell hugged Kat tightly. 'Oh, I'm so glad you're home safe and sound. Good trip?'

'Fine,' Kat muttered.

'I expect you're exhausted after all that driving?' her dad asked. He patted the car. 'Still in one piece, eh? Good girl.' He opened the boot and unloaded their luggage.

'Oh, Kat, I bet you'll be hungry too … I've made your favourite fajitas! Perhaps Dusty would like to stay for dinner?'

'Thank you for your kind offer Dell but I wouldn't like to impose,' said Dusty, door key in hand. 'I think Kat has done enough for me this weekend.'

'It's no bother!' said Dell. 'I'd like to hear all about your adventure.'

'Why don't I pop over tomorrow, then?' Dusty suggested. 'I could do with an early night myself.'

'But I've got fajitas for everyone! Refried beans and all the extras!'

'Dell,' said Ron. 'They've had a busy weekend and are probably needing a bit of time out.'

'Have you got something to eat in the house, though?' Dell persisted. 'I can't imagine that Arthur has bought you anything in?'

'I'll be fine, honestly. I can whip something out the freezer.'

'Right, well, let me at least help you in with your bag,' Ron offered, hoping she wouldn't notice the missing valuables. He didn't think she looked fit for a lengthy explanation.

Kat picked at her food as Dell and Ron watched with concern. She finally pushed her plate away. 'Thanks, Mum, but I think I'll go upstairs now.'

'Sure? I've got profiteroles in specially – and Cornish clotted ice cream.'

'Leave it, Dell,' Ron murmured, shaking his head. 'Anyway, I better get a shifty on. Mo will wonder where I've got to. Wish me luck for opening night!'

'Good luck, Dad,' said Kat. 'What's it again?'

'*The Sound of Music!*'

'Oh yeah. The Dalek.'

Later that evening Dell passed Kat's room. The sound of sobbing came from within. She waited for a few minutes before tapping lightly on the door. After no response she pushed the door open. Kat was lying face down on her bed, crying into her pillow.

'Oh, love, whatever is the matter?' Dell asked, sitting on the bed beside her. She put her hand on Kat's back. 'Did something happen while you were away?'

'I miss Jack, Mum.'

'I know you do, darling. We all miss him.'

'But I've lost his key ring.' Kat sniffed loudly.

Dell handed her a tissue. 'The wee Highland cow?'

'Yes. I've had it with me every day since he died – I *always* have it in my pocket. And now it's gone!' she wailed. 'I must have lost it this morning. What will I do?'

Dell sighed. 'Well, maybe you can think of it as a sign.'

'What do you mean?' Kat sat up, her face blotchy.

Dell picked her words carefully. She put her arm round Kat's slight shoulders. 'Maybe it's Jack's way of saying that you don't need something to hang on to – something physical. The wee cow has probably trotted off to the great field in the sky.'

'But it reminded me of Jack.'

'Perhaps you don't need it any more, Kat. And you'll *always* remember Jack. He's part of you … in here.' She patted Kat's head. 'And in here.' Dell pointed to her heart.

'It's hard, Mum.'

'I know, love.' She held Kat tightly. 'But you need to make room in that big heart of yours for someone else.'

'What's Dusty been saying?'

'Nothing – why?'

'No reason.'

Chapter 45

It was late on Monday evening when Arthur put the key in his front door. He was met by a frantic Cherie, who came hobbling into the hall on her crutches. 'Oh my God, Arthur, what happened to your face? What's been going on? You just said you were staying an extra night at Mum's. Then I get a call from Morton and Callander. Arthur?'

'Can I at least get in the door?' Arthur snapped. He hustled past Cherie and headed for the lounge, where he poured himself a generous whisky. He heard Cherie's crutches pounding along the laminate behind him. She stumbled towards a high-backed chair, throwing the crutches to one side. 'Whisky? On a school night? Really, Arthur!'

'Shut up, woman, and give me five minutes!'

Cherie recoiled. 'There's no need for that attitude, Arthur. I've been worried sick. Mr Callander said something about breaking and entering, burglary, aggravated assault? Is that what happened to you?'

'It's all your fault,' Arthur snarled, reaching for the whisky bottle.

'*My* fault? What do you mean?'

'You know very well!' said Arthur. 'You and your dirty little habit. I'm out at work all day and you're sitting at that computer bloody gambling away more money than I can make in a year.'

Cherie's face drained of colour. 'But … but … how do you know about that?'

'We *agreed*, Cherie. *You* agreed to stop. But apparently your word counts for nothing. You just needed to keep on going and going.'

'But I had … an arrangement.'

'I know all about your little *arrangement* with Gordon.' Arthur emptied his glass.

'He said it would be absolutely confidential. He *promised*.'

'Just like you kept promising to pay him back? Don't be such a fool, Cherie. A man like Gordon knows you can't get your hands on that kind of money.'

Cherie looked down at her feet. 'I thought that eventually I'd inherit something from Mum and could pay him back.'

'*Eventually?* He's not bloody Mastercard! He was getting more impatient – threatened to tell my boss at work. Well, I couldn't have that, could I? So it was me who planted the seed in your daft mother's head about selling up now and moving in with us. I'm the one who's been getting her all in a muddle so she doesn't even know what day of the week it is. *It was the only way I could force her hand.*'

'Oh, but I thought you really liked the idea of Mum coming to live with us!'

Arthur pulled a face, then winced as his cracked lip began to bleed again. 'But then, even my assurance that the money was on its way wasn't enough for good old Gordon. He kept pushing and pushing for more cash. I found some bits and pieces I could sell on but – like your wee habit – more wants more. So I had no choice but to stage a burglary.'

'You broke into Mum's house?'

'You think she'd just hand over all her valuables? Do you think she'd agree to part with her precious stuff just so you can put it all on black?'

Cherie shook her head sadly. 'Oh, Arthur, what have I done?'

'What have you done indeed?'

'I've turned you into a criminal. I'm so sorry.' She began to snivel. 'What happens now?'

Arthur stood up. 'Well, *now* I'm going to bed. Let's hope that your mother's house sells before my day in court because – once that happens – it will be game over.'

'Oh, Arthur,' Cherie sobbed. 'It *is* all my fault.'

'Yes, it is.'

Chapter 46

Kat arrived at the library and was greeted by Janice and Morag with mugs of coffee in hand. 'Here she is!' Janice cried. 'The wanderer returns.' Kat hung up her coat and made herself a cup of lemon tea.

'Come on, then,' Morag said with a smile. 'Spill the beans – what happened?'

They jostled Kat on to a chair and formed a compact triangle. Kat puffed out her cheeks. 'Do you want the short or the long version?'

'The long version, of course!' said Janice. 'To hang with the shelving rota!'

Kat flicked through her scribbled notes as she described all the Jessicas and Hamishes they'd met along the way. Janice grimaced when Felicity's broken elbow was mentioned. 'That was like the time when I slipped coming out of Greggs,' she said.

'When was that?' Morag asked.

'Oh, it was before I worked here.'

'I fell on my whatchamacallit,' said Janice, flapping her hands.

'Your what? Your hip?'

'No, my Yum Yums. They were ruined.'

Kat concluded with her encounter with Jess and Hamish Duns, which was met with a round of applause and a 'Woo-hoo!' from Janice.

'Well done, Kat,' said Morag with a grin. 'I *knew* you'd do it. That's amazing you were able to find them after all these years.'

They were interrupted by the first visitor bang on ten o'clock. 'You open yet?' a man asked as he drifted into the Western section.

The following day Kat received a text from Cath.

check out yesterday's Northern Times — yor famous!

Kat crossed the library to the bank of PCs and pulled up a seat. Morag and Janice moseyed across and stood reading over her shoulder. Kat typed into the search field and scrolled down. The front page of the local paper declared, Fifty-Year-Old Ring Found For Fiancée. A re-enactment of Monday's excitement had been captured in a glossy photo. Hamish, dressed in his kilt, was on his knees as Jess posed beside him showing off her ring.

'Oh, how romantic!' Morag declared. 'What a fabulous story.'

Kat smiled to herself as she read,

Head Receptionist at Ben More Nursing Home, Miss Pamela Kirk, stated: 'It was really me that reunited all parties. I could see that these ladies from Edinburgh had travelled such a long way and so I was keen to do all I could to make the meeting happen. If I hadn't used my initiative, the once-in-a-lifetime opportunity might have been missed.'

Even Cath (*'Mrs Cath McLeod from* Cath's Craft Cave') had managed to get in a quote.

'We have our own form of the internet here in Lochinver. It's called talking to people.'

'Oh, look at you!' Janice laughed. Someone had produced a long-distance blurry photo of Kat and Dusty as they were being led through the crowds by the four-foot-eleven high Nance. The photo identified them as '*The Intrepid Investigators*'.

'Fame at last,' said Morag. 'You've made quite a splash.'

Kat printed off a copy and slipped it into her pocket.

Kat took a deep breath and rang the doorbell. Dusty appeared, a vegetable knife in one hand. 'Oh, hello!'

Kat kept her eye on the blade. 'Expecting trouble? Had enough of those charity pests?'

'What? Oh, this? I'm just making lentil soup.'

'Right, well, I'm here to apologise.'

'Nonsense! No need at all.'

'I do need to. I've been stuck in my own head,' said Kat, looking down at her boots.

'All water under the bridge. Are you coming in?'

She followed Dusty into the kitchen.

'Tea? I even have some mint tea, if you'd like? I tried it but it tasted like toothpaste. Still, maybe it's a good way to have tea and do your teeth at the same time!'

'Regular tea is fine,' said Kat. 'And I see you have your kettle in the right place.'

Dusty gave a sad smile. 'So I take it you've heard about that rascal Arthur and his wily tricks?'

Kat snorted. 'He sounds like he's been a complete monster! Screwing with your mind? Selling off your things?'

'Well, I can't be too harsh on him. Not now we'll be living under the same roof.' Dusty poured from the teapot and passed the milk jug over the table.

'But surely you don't need to move now? I thought you were only selling the house because you were worried that you weren't able to manage on your own any more? And obviously your brain is working fine.'

'That's true – and was the original reason for me taking up Cherie and Arthur's kind offer.'

'So?'

Dusty sighed. 'Well, I do so miss Edwin and really don't enjoy living on my own. I know Arthur can be a royal pain at times but it will mean I get to spend every day with Cherie, which will be lovely. I might even get to see more of my grandson.'

'I suppose.'

'And, according to Cherie, there's the offer of a local tap group called the *Dalgety Dancers*.'

'Well, there you go!'

'I mean I know Arthur is desperate to get his hands on my money but at least I can see them enjoying some of it. Cherie is even talking about us all going on a cruise next year. I haven't been on holiday since Edwin died. And I forgot how much I missed seeing the world.' Dusty patted Kat's hand. 'I've got you to thank for that.'

'Oh, that reminds me!' said Kat. She handed Dusty the printed front page of the *Northern Times*. 'Here's the happy ever after you wanted.'

'You mean you and—'

'No! Here – read this. Right, I better get back. Mum and I are going to see Dad's show this evening.'

By the end of the week the odyssey to Lochinver had been dropped from the conversation, replaced with speculation over the new *Strictly Come Dancing* line-up. Kat sat in the staff room finishing a veggie wrap when Janice bustled in. 'There's a polite young man asking for you,' she announced eagerly.

Kat groaned. 'Tell him to find his own books. Where's Morag?'

'She's with that blind lady from the complex. Anyway, he specifically asked for you.'

'Is it that geek from the coffee shop next door?'

'No, I don't recognise him. He looks like a surfing dude.'

'In Balgreen?'

Kat wiped her mouth and wandered out to the reception area, to find Logan standing sheepishly. 'Hi, Kat,' he said, giving a nervous wave.

'Logan! What are you doing here?' She blushed.

'Well,' he said, stepping closer. 'Some people have been blocking my calls.'

'Then take the hint,' Kat scowled. 'I told you to get lost.'

'Yeah, I remember that. You also know how pig-headed I am.'

'I thought you were going to that Loopy Loo festival.'

'Nah, I didn't feel like it in the end. It's taken me all week to get back home. I reckon I walked most of the A9.'

'Thought you were flush with cash?'

Logan shook his head. 'I never kept Dusty's money. I said I'd give it back to her but she refused. I stuck it in a Cats' Protection box. Some cat's going to dine like a king this evening.'

Kat couldn't help smiling. 'So what are you doing here? Doesn't Edinburgh Uni have its own library?'

'I just came to return this,' said Logan. He opened his hand to reveal a small, rather worn and matted Highland cow key ring.

'What! Where?' Kat said, tears welling in her eyes. She grasped it and closed her fist tightly, comforted by the familiar mascot.

'Well, I got to the end of the road when I realised I'd left my mobile phone on the dining-room table. I did leave in a bit of a hurry.' His pale grey eyes twinkled. 'I found it in the car park at Mill House.'

'Oh well, thank you so much for returning this.'

'I knew how much it meant to you. Anyway ... that's all I wanted to say. I hear from Dusty that she's moving out next week?'

'Yeah, they thought they might as well empty the house.'

'And if she finds any other relics in the attic, tell her just to keep them!'

'I will.'

Kat heard Janice behind the counter repeat in a loud whisper, 'She's just said, "I will". But I don't know *what* – I missed the last part.'

'Friend of yours?' Logan asked with a smile.

Kat made a face. 'Colleague.'

'Right, well, I'll be off, then.'

'Bye.'

'Unless ... that lady said you were on your lunch break. I don't suppose you've got ten minutes and fancy some fresh air?'

'Isn't it raining?' Kat said.

'Go – for God's sake, *go*!' Janice yelled. She unhooked Kat's jacket and threw it across the library.

'Ten minutes, then,' said Kat, slipping the key ring in her pocket.

Chapter 47

Dalgety Parish Church, 25th November

'It's not a *bad* production, as far as Broadway musicals are concerned,' said Ron, handing out tubs of vanilla ice cream along the row to Dell and Kat. 'I mean – it started off a bit ropey but I think it improved towards the end of the first half.'

'Except when that man fell off the stage,' Dell added.

'You know, we've never really put on a dancing musical,' Ron mused. 'I wonder whether Mo has ever considered it?'

'Shh! They're coming back on,' Kat said, finishing her ice cream.

The lights dazzled, the velvet curtain was wound back and a line of misshapen sequinned dancers tapped their way out from the wings. One dancer huddled over two walking sticks that had been covered with sparkly tape. Kat chuckled throughout the entire second half, finding more animation in Zach's wig than his wooden performance.

At last it came to the finale and the eight men – looking like a bus queue of pensioners – launched into,

'One singular sensation, every step that she takes,
One, thrilling combination, every move that she makes …'

When the ladies joined the men on stage, Kat couldn't take her eyes off Dusty, who had been relegated to the back row. Her timing was completely off and she bumped into her irritated dance partners on more than one occasion, but had the proudest smile on the stage. She gripped her cane in both hands as she tapped in a circle, her glittery jacket swinging over her shiny tights.

The finale came to a rousing climax, the chorus line tap-dancing in three ranks, each row entirely out of sync. As the curtain stuttered to a close, got stuck halfway across, and was rewound open again, the audience was on its feet.

Kat waved at Dusty, who peered out into the darkness. 'More!' shouted Kat, throwing a red rose on to the stage. '*More!*'